'Ah, what a **touching sight, the** dutiful wife remaining awake in order to welcome her lord and master to bed.'

Katherine started so violently that the hairbrush shot out of her hand to land on the wooden floor with a clatter. It was as much as she could do to stare in horrified silence as the smugly smiling Major Ross entered the room and calmly closed the door. Just how long he had been standing there in the doorway, watching her, she had no way of knowing, for she certainly hadn't detected the click of the latch, but she could not fail to hear the grating of the key now as it was turned in the lock.

'What on earth do you imagine you are doing, sir?' she demanded in a voice which had suddenly risen by an octave, making her sound more like a frightened child than the self-possessed young woman she had wished to appear.

'What the devil do you imagine I'm doing, madam wife?' he responded, sounding distinctly bored as he proceeded to slip the key into the pocket of his tight-fitting breeches. 'I am about to retire.'

Anne Ashley was born and educated in Leicester. She lived for a time in Scotland, but now lives in the West Country with two cats, her two sons and her husband, who has a wonderful and very necessary sense of humour. When not pounding away at the keys of her word processor, she likes to relax in her garden, which she has opened to the public on more than one occasion in aid of the village church funds.

Recent titles by the same author:

A NOBLE MAN*
THE RELUCTANT MARCHIONESS
LORD EXMOUTH'S INTENTIONS*
TAVERN WENCH

The Steepwood Scandal mini-series

BELOVED VIRAGO

Anne Ashley

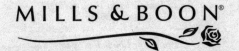

MILLS & BOON®

*First published in Great Britain 2003
Harlequin Mills & Boon Limited,
Eton House, 18-24 Paradise Road, Richmond, Surrey TW9 1SR*

© Anne Ashley 2003

ISBN 0 263 83518 9

*Set in Times Roman 10½ on 12 pt.
04-0803-86185*

*Printed and bound in Spain
by Litografía Rosés S.A., Barcelona*

BELOVED
VIRAGO

Chapter One

January 1815

Despite the vast improvements to many of the roads, the majority of those who could well afford to journey about the land remained unwilling to suffer the discomforts of winter travel unless the trip was totally unavoidable. Consequently Miss Katherine O'Malley had found no difficulty in attaining rooms for herself and her maid the previous afternoon, when a strengthening wind and the threat of snow had persuaded her to veer on the side of caution and seek refuge in a superior posting-house. Fortunately at some point during the night the wind, having changed direction, had eased considerably, and Katherine had woken to discover a landscape prettily laced with only the finest covering of snow and bathed in watery winter sunshine.

After glancing out of the window to view the highly encouraging sight of a carriage bowling along the road, Katherine returned her attention to her companion in time to see a freshly baked roll, liberally covered with jam, being consumed with relish, and succumbed to an imp of pure mischief.

'Most people might be forgiven for supposing that the substantial amount of strawberry preserve with which you manage to coat your bread would succeed in sweetening your disposition, Bridie. But I have known you far too long, and therefore do not hold out much hope.'

The instant she had swallowed the last mouthful, Bridie showed no reluctance in responding in kind. 'And to be sure 'tis a mystery to me how anyone with a tongue sharper than a barber's razor could have the brass-faced nerve to criticise an easygoing soul like myself.'

Reaching for her coffee cup, Katherine silently acknowledged the truth of what her lifelong companion and self-appointed protector had said. Ashamed though she was over this undeniable flaw in her character, the fact of the matter was that she had never been afraid to speak her mind, not even as a child.

Regardless of the fact that in recent years she had attempted to control her occasionally ungovernable temper, she was still sadly inclined on occasions to wound with a cutting barb, and remained impatient of folly. This did not mean, she sincerely hoped, that she had become so intolerant, so self-willed, that she wasn't prepared to listen to the views of others. At least, she amended silently, she would always try to take account of the feelings of that plump and loving female who had taken care of her with such touching devotion for a score of years and more.

'We should be with your aunt and uncle by early afternoon, providing we suffer no further mishap.' Bridie tutted. 'But I'll say it again, Miss Katherine, 'tis plain daft to be gadding about the country at this time of year.'

A tender smile went some way to dimming the teasing

gleam in Katherine's strikingly coloured blue-green eyes. 'You know full well why I was determined to make the trip.' She paused to sample the contents of her cup. 'You didn't truly expect me to forgo the pleasure of celebrating my cousin's engagement, and enjoying the company for a week or so of the only family I have left in the world, simply because of the few discomforts I must be prepared to suffer in travelling at this season of the year?'

'I know you well enough, Miss Kate, to be certain sure that when your mind is set on something there's no reasoning with you, and that you had every intention of attending the party. Though why in the world your cousin couldn't have arranged to become betrothed in the spring, like any sensible girl, when the weather is warmer and law-abiding souls can journey about the land without fear of becoming stranded, I'll never know!'

'It wasn't through choice, as you're very well aware,' Katherine reminded her. 'Caroline's future husband is a soldier. Captain Charlesworth wouldn't be able to obtain leave at the drop of a hat. He still has duties to perform, even though the war with France is now, hopefully, at an end.'

'To be sure, that's true enough,' Bridie acknowledged, before transferring her gaze to the clock in the corner of the private parlour, and rising to her feet. 'And I suppose we ought to be thinking of making a move, if you wish to arrive in plenty of time to have a wee rest before the party. The weather's fine at the moment, but there's no saying it'll remain so. I'll away now to check our overnight bags have been returned to the carriage, and arrange for the post-boys to have the vehicle waiting at the door.'

After nodding assent, Katherine remained for the time it took to put on her bonnet and collect her reticule and gloves from a side table, and then followed her Irish maid's example by going out into the coffee-room, where she discovered only the landlord lurking in the shadows.

Eager to recommence the journey, she wasted no time in settling her bill, and then made her way towards the front entrance, slipping her purse safely back inside her reticule as she did so. Consequently she didn't observe the tall gentleman, swathed in a voluminous grey cloak, entering the inn, and promptly collided with what felt like a solid wall of bone and muscle. Air left her lungs in a rush, and it was only the two long-fingered hands which immediately clasped her upper arms which saved her from reeling from the impact.

'I'm so very sorry, ma'am. I trust you are unhurt?'

The deep voice clearly betrayed concern, and Katherine didn't hesitate to assure him, the instant she had regained her breath, that she had suffered no real harm. 'And it was as much my fault as yours, sir,' she added, graciously accepting her share of the blame, 'for I wasn't attending where I was going.'

The continued clasp of strong hands was oddly reassuring, and strangely reminiscent of a certain someone's touch in the dim and distant past. Katherine raised her head, only to find the breath leaving her body in a faint gasp for a second time as she gazed at the swarthy, wholly masculine features looming above.

For a moment it was as much as she could do to stare into thickly lashed, dark eyes, as she tried ineffectually to capture an elusive memory. She saw them widen fractionally, clearly revealing a hint of appreciation in their warm brown depths, as they calmly began to scan every contour of her face. Although not precisely unaccustomed to receiving admiring glances from members of the opposite sex, she was forced silently to own that there was something both faintly disturbing and remarkably engaging about the directness of this tall gentleman's unwavering gaze.

He seemed reluctant to release her, but after a further unsettling moment he allowed his hands to fall to his sides. 'Are you certain you are all right, ma'am? Perhaps I should summon the landlady. You are a little pale, if I may say so.'

'I am perfectly well,' she assured him swiftly, if not quite truthfully. 'But I thank you for your concern, sir.'

Bemused by the peculiar sensations this enigmatic stranger had somehow managed to evoke, Katherine successfully slipped past him and out into the crisp morning air. Fortunately he made no attempt to detain her further, but she could almost feel those attractive, almond-shaped eyes boring into her back as she hurried across the forecourt to the waiting carriage.

'Why, you look as if you've seen a ghost!' Bridie remarked the instant her young mistress had scrambled into the post-chaise and had begun to make herself comfortable on the seat opposite.

'I feel as if I've just seen one,' she didn't hesitate to admit. 'Did you happen to notice that tall gentleman who entered the inn a few minutes ago?'

'Can't say as I noticed a soul, miss. Why, was it someone you know?'

Katherine frowned in an effort to remember, for there was something there still lurking in the dim recesses of her memory which she just could not capture. 'He seemed oddly familiar, yes. But for the life of me I cannot imagine where I've seen his face before—certainly not in Bath, I feel sure.'

'And was it a handsome one?' Bridie couldn't resist asking, thereby earning herself an impatient glance.

'I wouldn't have described it so, no. He was attractive, certainly, but not what I would call handsome.' Katherine paused to straighten the skirt of her dark blue carriage dress. 'Not that it would have made a ha'p'orth of difference to me if he had been a perfect Adonis.'

'No, I know it wouldn't!' Bridie retorted, with the speed of a striking snake. 'And we both know why, don't we?'

Katherine elected not to answer, and turned her head to stare resolutely out of the window, a clear indication that she considered the conversation at an end. Unfortunately the action didn't prevent her from thinking about her maid's prompt rejoinder.

She didn't suppose for a moment that Bridie had intended to be heartlessly cruel. It was not in the woman's nature. In fact, the opposite was true. Bridie, loving and unfailingly loyal, had always been there to offer comfort and encouragement. Which was possibly just as well, Katherine reflected, for she sometimes felt she would never have survived the many heartaches she had suffered in recent years without the constant support of that occasionally infuriating and frequently overprotective Irish woman.

It was from Bridie, who had been there to witness the event, that Katherine had learned that she had been born during what had been one of the worst storms to hit Ireland in living memory. While the high wind had been battering the country, leaving a trail of devastation in its wake, Charlotte O'Malley had been giving birth to a daughter, a protracted and agonising ordeal that had almost brought about her own death and had resulted in her not being able to have any more children.

Oh, yes, she had indeed been a scourge to those close to her since the day of her birth, Katherine reflected dismally. Although blissfully unaware of the fact during her idyllic childhood, she had been forced to accept in recent years, after the series of tragic events which had struck her life, that she did indeed bring ill fortune to those for whom she cared most deeply. Only one person seemed immune to the lethal Katherine O'Malley curse.

She couldn't prevent a tiny sigh escaping as she instinctively cast a glance at the plump, middle-aged female seated in the opposite corner of the carriage. It would be foolish to hope that any prospective husband might be similarly protected, and Katherine certainly had no intention of burdening her conscience further by encouraging the advances of some poor unsuspecting male. It was perhaps fortunate, therefore, that her silent resolve never to marry had not been tested thus far.

During the six years she had lived in Bath, she had been introduced to numerous very personable gentlemen, and yet not one had ever succeeded in arousing in her more than a faint interest. Not once had she ever experienced the pull of mutual attraction… At least, she silently amended, never until today.

She couldn't deny that she had felt oddly drawn to that tall gentleman back at the inn. His touch had been strangely reminiscent of her father's—gentle, yet wholly protective. It was perhaps just as well that their paths were unlikely ever to cross again, for she very much feared that the enigmatic stranger might be just the type of man who would test her resolve to remain a spinster to its limits.

*　*　*

By early afternoon, when the hired carriage had pulled up outside her aunt and uncle's charming house in Hampshire, Katherine had succeeded in thrusting the brief encounter with the disturbing stranger from her mind. After being admitted to the house by Meldrew, the very correct manservant, and discovering that both her aunt and cousin were at home, Katherine removed her outdoor garments and, leaving Bridie to take charge of the unpacking, went directly into the comfortable parlour where she discovered the two female members of the Wentworth family happily engaged in their favourite occupation.

Mrs Lavinia Wentworth, raising her head at the opening of the door, betrayed her delight by a warm smile. Setting aside her sewing, she was on her feet in an instant, her arms outstretched in welcome. 'How lovely to see you, my dear!' she announced, after placing a kiss on the face which so closely resembled her dear, departed sister's.

After returning the embrace with equal warmth, Katherine turned to the only other occupant of the room, who betrayed no less delight at her arrival. 'You look blooming, my dear Caro. Captain Charlesworth is a lucky man! I trust everything is in readiness for the party tonight?'

'Yes, indeed,' Caroline assured her. 'Mama and I have been busy all week finalising the arrangements. We are expecting around a hundred guests. And I'm so very glad that you are to be among them. When you failed to arrive yesterday, both Mama and I began to fear that you had changed your mind, and didn't choose to risk making the journey, after all.'

Eyes glinting with unholy amusement, Katherine sat beside her pretty cousin on the sofa. 'My, my! What a feeble creature you must think me! I might be almost three years your senior, Caroline, but I'm not in my dotage quite yet. No, it was merely that a threat of snow yesterday afternoon forced me to take shelter at a posting-house. That, and a desperate need to silence the dragon-lady's continual carping.'

Knowing precisely to whom her niece had referred, Mrs Wentworth could not forbear a smile. Although Katherine had grown into the image of her lovely mother, she had inherited her wonderful dark auburn hair and blue-green eyes, made more striking by dusky brows and lashes, from her Irish father. She certainly favoured her sire in temperament too, for she possessed a fine Irish temper and could be quite outspoken on occasions. 'Bridie has only your best interests at heart, Katherine,' she remarked. 'And I must confess that it has relieved my mind during these past years knowing that she has always been there to care for you.'

Katherine chose not to comment, for although she valued Bridie highly, there had been occasions, most especially in recent months, when she had found her loyal Irish maid's continual cosseting increasingly irritating. So, instead, she changed the subject by enquiring into the whereabouts of Caroline's elder brother. 'Is Peter not here at present?'

'No, he's back at university, although he did spend Christmas with the family,' Caroline enlightened her. 'To be frank, I believe he was relieved to be going. I do not think he quite relished the prospect of having to aid Papa in entertaining the dowagers this evening.'

Katherine cast a glance brimful of wicked amusement in her aunt's direction. 'And does my esteemed uncle look forward to such an onerous duty, I cannot help asking myself?' she remarked, knowing full well that Henry Wentworth, although a most agreeable, warm-hearted gentleman, was not disposed to socialising to any very great extent.

Reaching for the tambour frame once again, Mrs Wentworth could only admire her niece's perspicacity. 'I think it would be more truthful to say that he is resigned to the task expected of him, Katherine. Unless I much mistake the matter, when he rode out a little earlier it was for the sole purpose of calling on a neighbour of ours, Sir Giles Osborne, in order to enlist the baronet's aid.'

His wife's suspicions were uncannily accurate, for Henry Wentworth had set out for Osborne House, and was at that moment enjoying a glass of burgundy in the company of his friend.

'I have already assured you that I shall not fail to attend,' Sir Giles answered in response to the heartfelt request. 'My sister would never let me hear the end of it if we didn't put in an appearance. We shall arrive promptly at eight, and you may rely upon my unfailing support.'

'You're a good friend, Osborne.' Mr Wentworth tugged at his cravat, as though it had suddenly grown uncomfortably tight. 'Don't mind admitting that I'm not relishing the prospect of entertaining a pack of fiendish harridans.'

Sir Giles, a master at concealing both thoughts and emotions, permitted himself a thin smile. 'The Dowager Lady Charlesworth is certainly a formidable matron. It is something of an enigma how she and that apathetic late husband of hers ever managed to produce two such well-balanced, engaging sons. I know you and Lavinia must be delighted with the match. Richard is an agreeable young man and a credit to his regiment.'

Unlike his sister, who enjoyed nothing better than a comfortable coze, Sir Giles only ever indulged in small talk when it was to his benefit to do so. Today, however, he was prepared to exert himself a little more than usual in an attempt to prevent his amiable neighbour from brooding unnecessarily over the ordeal ahead of him.

'I have every faith in that charming wife of yours to be sure that everything will run smoothly this evening.' There was no response, though Mr Wentworth, looking moderately more relaxed, did lean back in the chair and stretch his feet out towards the blazing fire. 'I seem to remember my sister remarking that almost everyone who received an invitation has accepted. And the weather appears to be favouring you thus far.'

'Yes, thank the Lord! At least we haven't had snow, except…' The worried frown returned. 'My wife's niece didn't arrive yesterday as expected. Which makes me wonder whether the rest of the country is so fortunate, and bad weather might be heading our way.'

'Had she far to travel?' Sir Giles enquired, striving to maintain a polite show of concern, even though his interest in the unknown female was zero.

'From Bath. My daughter will be very disappointed if she doesn't arrive. Caroline simply adores her. My wife does too, come to that! Lavinia has been trying to persuade Katherine to make her home with us for the past twelve months, but without success. Still…' he shrugged '…the girl seems happy enough to remain in the house left to her by her great-aunt. And it isn't as if she's a chit straight out of the schoolroom. She'll attain the age of three-and-twenty later this year. And she doesn't reside alone. There's a companion living in the house, and an Irish maid who is devoted to her.'

'Evidently her parents are dead,' Sir Giles remarked, successfully stifling a yawn.

Henry Wentworth confirmed this with a solemn nod of his head. 'Yes, it was all very sad. It so happens that her father was approached by the government to take a cargo of horses out to Portugal in readiness for the arrival of the British expeditionary force in the summer of '08. There was no better man at breeding or handling horses than Liam O'Malley. The craft he was on met up, as previously arranged, with two other vessels that had left England, also carrying urgently needed supplies. They were attacked by the French just off the Bay of Biscay.'

His expression changed, and he suddenly appeared more angry than sad. 'Damn it! Where was the British Navy? Where was that promised protection, that's what I'd like to know? Some damned mix-up at the Admiralty was what we were told! Apparently they had received information stating that the cargo vessels wouldn't be setting sail for another ten days.'

Only for a moment did a speculative gleam flicker in the baronet's steely-grey eyes as he digested these disturbing facts. 'Yes, that does seem strange.'

'Deuced odd!' Mr Wentworth agreed. 'My wife's poor sister never recovered from the shock of losing her husband. She died a few weeks later after contracting a simple chill which went to her chest, and my father-in-law, Colonel Fairchild, went over to Ireland and brought Katherine back to live with him.' Again he shook his head. 'Poor little mite was just beginning to recover from her parents' deaths when the Colonel suffered a fatal heart attack.'

'Indeed, your niece is to be pitied,' Sir Giles acknowledged, whilst momentarily wondering why the name Fairchild should seem vaguely familiar.

'She was in Bath at the time. The old Colonel considered the girl was in dire need of a little polish, as you might say, and packed her off to live with his spinster sister so that she might attend a seminary. The house in Bath now belongs to Katherine, and she's comfortably circumstanced. I can vouch for that, as I'm one of her trustees. Although she cannot touch so much as a penny piece of the money she attained from the sale of her father's sizeable property in Ireland, and the money her grandfather left her in his will, until she attains the age of five-and-twenty, her great-aunt, Augusta Fairchild, ensured that she will live very agreeably until then.'

Once again Sir Giles found his interest in this unknown young woman swiftly waning, and experienced a modicum of relief when his butler unexpectedly entered to announce the arrival of another visitor. He was on his feet in a trice, surprising his neighbour somewhat by betraying a degree of delight when a tall gentleman, his muscular figure swathed in a voluminous grey cloak, came striding purposefully into the book-lined room.

'Ross, my dear boy! This is an unexpected pleasure!'

The new arrival betrayed no similar joy as he shook the baronet's proffered hand, although Mr Wentworth noticed a less hard set to Major Daniel Ross's well-shaped mouth when the visitor was introduced to him.

'Just a flying visit, Osborne,' the Major announced. 'I've a letter here from Cranford, which I undertook to deliver personally as I was making a trip to the capital in order to attend a reunion dinner with some fellow officers and spend some time with a particular friend, and therefore wouldn't be inconvenienced too greatly by the slight detour.'

'Thank you, my dear boy,' Sir Giles responded, as he relieved the Major of the sealed missive and consigned it to the safety of his jacket pocket.

'Cranford? Would that be the Honourable Charles Cranford, a member of Parliament?' Mr Wentworth asked, thereby regaining his neighbour's attention.

'Why, yes,' Sir Giles confirmed. 'Are you acquainted with him?'

'Not personally, no. But I dealt with my late father-in-law's estate after he died, and unless I much mistake the matter it was none other than Charles Cranford who purchased the Colonel's house in Dorset.'

'Ah, yes! You may possibly be right, Wentworth. And that is perhaps why the name Fairchild seemed vaguely familiar to me,' Sir Giles confessed, before casting an enquiring glance in the Major's direction. 'Young Daniel, here, should be able to enlighten us. Also he ought to be able to set your mind at rest over the state of the roads in the west.'

Although betraying mild surprise, the Major didn't hesitate to assure Mr Wentworth that, although there had indeed been a light covering of snow overnight, all the main routes were passable. 'I set out before dawn, and had no trouble whatsoever in reaching Andover, where I ate a late breakfast. And to answer your first query— yes, Charles Cranford did purchase the late Colonel Fairchild's property. My home is situated close by. I knew the Colonel very well.'

'Good Lord! It is a small world, indeed!' Mr Wentworth exclaimed. 'You must be acquainted with my wife Lavinia, the Colonel's younger daughter. Although,' he added, as he saw dark brows draw together above the Major's faintly aquiline nose, 'I expect you were a mere boy when we married and she moved away from the county.'

'I remember that the Colonel had two daughters, sir. But as you remarked, it is a long time since last I set eyes upon either of them.'

'Well, sir, I'm certain my wife would enjoy seeing you again. She retains fond memories of that part of the country. In fact,' he added, as a thought suddenly occurred to him, 'we're holding a party this evening. Why not come along? You'd be most welcome. I know Lavinia would enjoy nothing better than chatting over old times.'

'First, let us see if we cannot persuade him to remain long enough to enjoy a glass of wine,' Sir Giles intervened, sensing that Major Ross was on the point of declining Mr Wentworth's kind invitation.

Quickly finishing off the contents of his own glass, and refusing a second, Mr Wentworth cast a brief glance at the mantel-clock, which clearly informed him that it was time he was heading homewards. 'And I must be on my way. Hope to see you at the party tonight, Major.'

'He genuinely means it, Ross,' Sir Giles assured him, the instant his neighbour had departed. A ghost of a smile once again flickered about his thin lips. 'Not that I suppose for a moment that I could influence your decision one way or the other, but you're most welcome to put up here for the night. It would grant us the opportunity to reminisce pleasurably over old times.'

The Major's dark eyes were brightened by a decidedly cynical gleam, as he accepted the glass of burgundy, and lowered his tall frame into the chair recently vacated by his host's neighbour. 'You will forgive me for saying so, Osborne, but I cannot recall that our dealings were ever precisely enjoyable.'

'You are thinking of that delectable French filly, Justine Baron, I do not doubt.' Sir Giles settled himself in the chair on the opposite side of the hearth, and gazed meditatively down at his glass. 'Undeniably that must rate as my greatest failure. I came so close to catching *him* then.'

'Are you certain that she would have kept to her part of the bargain?' the Major asked, sounding decidedly sceptical, and after a moment the baronet nodded his head.

'I could of course have attained the information I wanted by—er—other means. But in Justine's case I chose to be merciful. She did not become a spy through choice, but because she was forced into it, although she was well paid by her country for her services. There was only one thing Justine loved above money…and that was her sister. We kept to our part of the bargain, and I'm certain in my own mind she would have kept to hers by revealing that British traitor's name, if the devil hadn't discovered where I'd hidden her. I knew even then it had to be one of two people. That belief has not changed. Nor my resolve to unmask the rogue.'

The look in the Major's eyes contained neither sympathy nor encouragement. 'The war is over.'

'It might be for you, Ross,' Sir Giles countered, reaching into his pocket for the letter his companion had kindly taken the trouble to deliver. 'But there are still a few of us remaining who are determined to see justice done.'

He took a moment to apprise himself of the contents of the missive before returning it to the safety of his pocket. 'Cranford writes to inform me that he is organising a party at his home at the beginning of April, and has, it seems, been successful in persuading several—

er—interesting people to attend. Will you be among the guests?'

'Possibly,' the Major answered, clearly unwilling to commit himself.

'By the by, I had heard that you'd sold your commission,' Sir Giles remarked with an abrupt change of subject. 'What will you find to do with yourself now your career in the army is at an end?'

'Look after the property I've neglected for far too long.'

'Ah! So those old, festering wounds have finally healed, have they? I'm glad to hear that you are ready to settle down.'

Daniel stared intently into the baronet's shrewd eyes. 'My God!' he muttered, experiencing a mixture of anger and grudging respect. 'Not much ever escapes you, does it, Osborne?'

Just a hint of smug satisfaction crept into Sir Giles's expression. 'I have endeavoured over the years to ensure that not much ever does. And since you are to attend a reunion dinner you must have brought suitable evening attire.'

'Only my dress uniform,' Daniel disclosed.

'Excellent! Then there's no reason why you shouldn't attend the party tonight.'

Chapter Two

'I think I shall wear the pearls, Bridie,' Katherine decided, after studying her overall appearance in the full-length mirror.

Although Bridie's apron had covered many duties over the years, including those of nursemaid, housekeeper and cook, she was also a very proficient lady's maid, and Katherine was delighted with the more elaborate arrangement of her auburn curls. She was satisfied too with her choice of gown for the special evening ahead. She had wished to look her best for the occasion, and considered the dark green velvet dress suited her very well, its soft folds emphasising the shapely slenderness of her figure, while its colour subtly enhanced the green in her eyes.

'I think we chose wisely when we selected this new gown,' she remarked, seating herself once again at the dressing table in order that Bridie, several inches shorter, might fasten the pearl necklace more easily, while she herself concentrated on securing the matching earrings to her small lobes. 'It makes me appear neither a chit just emerged from the schoolroom, nor yet a female at her last prayers.'

Bridie could not help smiling to herself at this candid admission. Her young mistress was so lacking in conceit that she could never be made to appreciate just how very lovely she was. Blessed with delicate, regular features, and a trim shapely figure, she had little difficulty in igniting a glint of admiration in the vast majority of masculine eyes, even in those not disposed to admire her particular colouring. 'You look lovely, Miss Katherine.'

This sentiment was echoed a few moments later when Mrs Wentworth entered the bedchamber to bear her niece company down to the large salon where the party was to be held. 'Every time I look at you, Katherine, I am struck by the resemblance you bear your dear mother,' she admitted, not reluctant to disclose the thoughts that had passed through her mind shortly after her niece's arrival earlier in the day.

Katherine, her eyes shadowed by a moment's bitter regret, cast a surreptitious glance up at her aunt through the dressing-table mirror. Undeniably her mother had been the far prettier sister. None the less, she might have wished that her mother had possessed some of her younger sibling's strength of character. Her dear aunt, Katherine felt sure, would not wither like an exotic bloom touched by the first frost if—God forbid!—anything should ever happen to her husband. Lavinia Wentworth would fight and survive for the sake of her children.

'And you resemble your maternal grandmother too, now I come to consider the matter,' Mrs Wentworth added. 'Little wonder dear Papa was so very fond of you!'

'And I was very fond of him,' Katherine was not slow to confess. 'My one bitter regret is that we were not given the opportunity to enjoy each other's company for a great deal longer.'

'Yes, I too feel that was a pity,' her aunt agreed softly. 'My father, I clearly remember, very much appreciated modesty in our sex. Surprisingly enough, though, he also admired intelligent women who were not afraid to voice their opinions. He would have found much pleasure in your company, my dear.'

Katherine couldn't prevent a wry smile at this, as she cast a brief glance in her maid's direction. 'You are the second person today who has remarked on the fact that I am not afraid to speak my mind,' she admitted, rising to her feet, and entwining her arm through her aunt's. 'However, I promise to be on my best behaviour this evening, and will endeavour to keep a firm hold on my occasionally ungovernable tongue.'

Katherine then accompanied her highly amused aunt downstairs to the large salon, there to discover both her cousin, looking bright-eyed and excited, and her uncle, noticeably less so, hovering near the door in readiness to receive their guests.

Captain Richard Charlesworth, accompanied by his family, and a large party of friends, was the first to arrive, and very soon afterwards Katherine, without quite knowing how it had come about, found herself seated beside Caroline's future mother-in-law.

Possibly because she had had experience of dealing with haughty, opinionated matrons, her great-aunt Augusta having possessed a somewhat vitriolic tongue, Katherine was disposed to be more amused than annoyed by the Dowager Lady Charlesworth's blunt manner and caustic remarks. Added to which, Katherine was determined not to do or say anything that might lessen her sweet-natured cousin's enjoyment of what, quite naturally for Caroline, was a very special occasion. Consequently she bore with great fortitude the dictatorial matron's company for a full twenty minutes, and was even gracious enough to agree to partner the Dowager in a rubber or two of whist later, before cunningly engineering her escape.

'Do not allow my mama to monopolise you, Miss O'Malley,' an amused voice whispered in her ear, and Katherine turned to discover the newly engaged couple standing directly behind her.

Caroline bestowed a look of mild disapproval upon her future husband. 'Now that we are officially betrothed, I think you might be a little less formal with my cousin, Richard.'

'I should be delighted to comply, providing Miss O'Malley has no objection, that is?'

Katherine was not slow to assure him that she had none, for she very much approved of her cousin's future husband, appreciating his gentlemanly and unaffected manners. 'I assume that you two have abandoned your positions by the door in order to lead the first set of country dances.'

'We have indeed,' Caroline confirmed. 'And I had better warn you now that you are unlikely to be sitting by the wall yourself for any length of time. All of Richard's army friends are intent on securing you for a partner.'

'And I dare swear I shall be too weak-willed to refuse,' Katherine responded with more tact than truth, for unlike the majority of her sex she had never been drawn to a gentleman merely because he happened to be sporting a scarlet coat. Nevertheless, she felt obliged to add, as she glanced about the room at the numerous dress uniforms on display that evening, 'I believe it is grossly unfair to permit officers to attend parties wearing regimentals. They look so very smart and dashing that they cast those in plain evening garb quite into the shade.'

'They do indeed,' Caroline agreed, before catching sight of a new arrival wearing a very striking dark green uniform of almost exactly the same shade as her cousin's lovely dress. 'Who is that, Richard? Surely not a cavalry officer?'

'No, indeed, m'dear. That is the uniform worn by riflemen. Can't say I recognise the fellow, though.' He appeared genuinely intrigued. 'There's a few minutes wanting before we need take the floor. If you will both excuse me, I'll go over and discover who he is.'

'Mama appears very well pleased to see him, at any rate,' Caroline was not slow to observe, after Richard had departed. 'He's with Sir Giles Osborne's party. I wonder who he is? I've certainly never seen him before.'

Katherine cast the merest glance over the distinguished, grey-haired baronet and the middle-aged lady clad in a rather startling orange gown, before focusing her attention on the well-muscled gentleman sporting the smart green regimentals. 'Great heavens!' she muttered as he turned at Richard's approach, and she saw his features clearly for the first time. 'It cannot be…'

Caroline regarded her cousin with slightly raised brows. 'Are you acquainted with him, Katherine?'

'Yes…no…well, I'm not sure. But I do believe he's none other than the gentleman I bumped into earlier today when I put up at that posting-house. What a coincidence!'

Once again Katherine found herself teased by that elusive memory annoyingly playing hide-and-seek in the recesses of her brain, while at the same time experiencing a rather startling surge of pleasure at seeing him again so unexpectedly. She watched his approach with keen interest, admiring the fluid way he moved, the way he seemed to stand out from the other gentlemen present. Then, for the second time that day, she found herself gazing up into those attractive dark eyes, which clearly betrayed recognition.

'It would seem, ma'am, Fate has decreed our paths should cross again.' The deep voice was no less pleasing than the warmth of the smile which instantly softened the harsh contours of a wholly masculine countenance.

Katherine discovered herself automatically placing her fingers in the hand reaching out to her, just as Richard said, 'Miss Katherine O'Malley, may I present Major Daniel Ross, an officer whose courage is admired throughout the British Army.'

With the name pounding against her temples like so many torturous hammer blows, Katherine withdrew her hand so abruptly from the Major's gentle clasp that anyone observing the action might have been forgiven for supposing that her fingers had just been burned. That she had been so stupid as not to recognise at once a man whom she had secretly despised for years added to her swiftly mounting rage, and it was only the vow she had made to behave with the utmost propriety throughout the evening that prevented her from releasing the tumult of emotions warring inside in a blistering tirade.

With praiseworthy self-control, Katherine quietly excused herself, and sought immediate refuge in the room allocated for the female guests' private use. Having discovered it blessedly empty, she slumped down on one of the chairs, her thoughts racing back over the years to those few short months when she had lived in her grandfather's charming house in Dorsetshire, and had struck up a close friendship with the daughter of one of his nearest neighbours, Helen Rushton.

Looking back, she now realised that their similar sufferings had been the bond which had drawn them together, swiftly turning friendship into a deep sisterly affection, for Helen's father, serving in his Majesty's Navy, had also perished at sea.

Helen had confided in Katherine from the first. Always eager to share her most private thoughts, she had revealed her rapidly deepening attachment to a young gentleman who, after living abroad for several years, had returned to the area, and who had recently acquired a commission in the army. Every time Captain Daniel Ross had paid a visit to Helen's house, Katherine had been regaled with a detailed account of what he had said and how long he had remained.

Undoubtedly Helen had been totally besotted, and then utterly devastated when she had discovered that Captain Ross, rakishly free with his favours, had been paying numerous visits to a dashing young widow living in the locale. Having to face the fact that she had not been the sole object of the Captain's desire had been a grievous blow from which poor Helen had never been granted the opportunity to recover.

The door quietly opening put an end to these sombre reflections, and Katherine was not unduly surprised to see her cousin slip quietly into the room.

'Are you not feeling quite the thing? Do you wish me to summon Mama, or Bridie?'

The prospect of having her lifelong bodyguard fussing about her like some demented hen was all it took to restore Katherine's equilibrium. 'Whatever for? I'm in no danger of fainting, I assure you. I have merely received a most unpleasant shock, that is all.'

'But what on earth overset you?' Caroline was utterly bewildered and it clearly showed. 'One moment you were looking so radiantly happy to be making the acquaintance of Major Ross, and yet in the next—'

'Kindly do not remind me of my shortcomings!' Katherine interrupted, acutely annoyed with herself, if the truth were known, for betraying such unbecoming delight.

Rising to her feet, she began to pace the floor, a sure sign to those who knew her well that she was doing her utmost to maintain a firm control over herself. She had no desire to cause any unpleasantness during the evening by making her intense dislike of the Major generally known. Nor did she wish to run the risk of joining the ranks of those contemptible gossipmongers who did not scruple to ruin reputations. Yet, at the same time, she felt that Caroline deserved some explanation for her odd behaviour towards the Major.

Raising her eyes, she discovered her cousin regarding her intently, and decided to settle on a compromise. 'You are possibly not aware of it, Caroline, but Major Ross was well acquainted with our grandfather. Whilst I resided in Dorsetshire, he paid several visits to Grandpapa's house—' her smile was twisted '—as well as visiting several others in the area. I discovered that his reputation where our sex is concerned is not precisely stainless. Not to put too fine a point on it, he is nothing more than a callous philanderer who isn't above breaking the odd heart or two,' she finished, anger momentarily overriding her resolve not to slander the Major.

'Good heavens!' Caroline muttered faintly, while taking advantage of the chair conveniently positioned directly behind her. 'Are you certain about that? I do not mean to doubt you,' she hurriedly added, swiftly recognising the telltale glint of annoyance in her cousin's blue-green eyes. 'But you were quite young when you lived with Grandfather. Might you have misunderstood the rumours about him?'

'Yes, I might,' Katherine was forced to concede, though it almost choked her to do so. 'Now is not the time to be discussing this, however. Come, let us return to the party, otherwise that handsome fiancé of yours will justifiably blame me for depriving him of the pleasure of leading you out on to the floor.'

As they re-entered the salon, Katherine was not unduly surprised to discover Captain Charlesworth still bearing the Major company. For her cousin's sake she was prepared to be polite and rejoin the gentlemen for a short while, and then slip quietly away in order to mingle with the other guests, thereby neatly avoiding comment.

Unfortunately, this ideal scheme was foiled at the outset, for no sooner had they arrived back at the gentlemen's sides than the musicians struck up a chord, announcing the commencement of dancing, and Katherine found herself, much to her chagrin, quite alone with the person whom she had stigmatised as the biggest beast in nature for almost six years.

'I trust you are feeling a little better now, ma'am?' he remarked, breaking the short silence that had ensued after the engaged couple's departure. 'If I were a fanciful man I might imagine that it was my sudden appearance which had the power to overset you.'

Suppressing the strong desire to walk away without uttering a word, Katherine forced herself to meet a gaze that she might have supposed contained a deal of genuine concern had she not known better. Heartless philanderers did not worry themselves unduly over the feelings of others, she reminded herself, resolved to be polite but no more.

'Disabuse yourself of that notion, sir. I am not so easily overset.'

Much to her surprise, Katherine saw the Major's eyes narrow fractionally at her cool tone. She might dislike the man intensely, but she was obliged to acknowledge that he was no fool. Unless she much mistook the matter, he sensed the antagonism raging within her and was more than slightly puzzled by it.

It was quite evident that he hadn't recognised her, not even her name. This in itself did not strike her as in any way odd. After all, she mused, transferring her gaze to those taking part in the dance, she had only ever spoken to him once in her life before today.

Her grandfather, Katherine recalled, had retained some rather antiquated views, and even though she had attained the age of sixteen he had considered her a mere child. Consequently she had never been invited to join her grandfather when he had been entertaining guests. None the less, Katherine clearly remembered coming face to face with Captain Ross, as he had been then, just once, when she had happened to be in the stable-yard when he had arrived at the house. It was unlikely, however, that he would remember such an insignificant occasion, when he had taken the trouble to pass the time of day with someone whom he also had undoubtedly considered a mere child.

'Miss Wentworth and Captain Charlesworth make a charming couple, do they not?' he remarked, once again breaking the lengthening silence.

'They do indeed, sir,' she agreed, momentarily forgetting her animosity, as she continued to follow the engaged couple's progress down the floor, noticing in particular the way Caroline smiled lovingly up at her handsome fiancé whenever they came together in the set. 'They are well matched, and very much in love.'

She expected him to say something further, if only to maintain the conversation. When he made no attempt to do so, curiosity got the better of her. She turned back to look at him, and was slightly disconcerted to discover him staring at her intently, before his expression was softened by the winning smile of a practised seducer.

No, she must never lose sight of what he was, she reminded herself. Even so, she was forced silently to concede that, had he truly been a complete stranger, he would have been the very last person she would have stigmatised as a hardened rake. He seemed so earnest, so reliable, the kind of person to whom one instinctively turned in time of trouble. Which just went to show that one should never judge by appearances!

'Do you hail from this part of the country, Miss O'Malley?' he asked, while his eyes flickered momentarily over the arrangement of her curls.

'No, Major. I lived for many years in Ireland. However, I now reside in Bath.'

Having decided that she had now conformed to the rules governing polite behaviour, and could leave Major Ross to his own devices with a clear conscience, Katherine was on the point of excusing herself when the dance came to an end and he forestalled her by requesting her to partner him in the next set.

Those good intentions deserting her completely, Katherine weakened to an imp of pure mischief. With a smile of artificial sweetness curling her lips, she looked him over from head to toe. 'Believe me, Major Daniel Ross, nothing in this world would ever induce me to stand up with you. I have made it a rule only ever to take the floor with those gentlemen sporting scarlet coats.'

Beneath their half-hooded lids, brown eyes began to sparkle with a distinctly menacing gleam. 'That decision, if you'll forgive my saying so, ma'am, betrays a shocking lack of judgement for one with your particular shade of hair.'

Only partially successful in suppressing a squeal of indignation, Katherine could quite cheerfully have boxed his ears, and swung away before the temptation to do so became too great.

Daniel, following her almost flouncing progress across the room with narrowed, assessing eyes, found himself experiencing both annoyance and puzzlement in equal measures. How anyone could be radiant and smiling one moment, then offhand and disdainful the next, treating a fellow as though he were a pariah, he would never know. But there again women, he reminded himself, were a law unto themselves, unpredictable and totally illogical!

He continued to watch her as she headed towards the room set out for cards, certain in his own mind that she would have left him far sooner had the opportunity arisen, and might not have conversed with him at all if she could possibly have avoided doing so. But why? Why had she taken him in such swift dislike?

He shook his head, at a loss to understand the workings of the female mind. When Captain Charlesworth had first brought him over, Miss O'Malley had betrayed clear signs of delight at coming face to face with him again so unexpectedly. He had found that initial reaction so very refreshing. She had made not the least attempt to dissemble, to pretend their paths had never crossed before. Then, quite suddenly, she had grown pale, and a look akin to loathing had flickered momentarily in those striking turquoise eyes before she had slipped quietly away.

Undeniably, Charlesworth and his delightful fiancée had been as mystified as he had himself at such odd behaviour. Yet when Miss Wentworth had returned, her face had worn a decidedly thoughtful expression, as though she were not quite certain about something. But what could she possibly have learned to his discredit during that brief absence? He had never met either young lady until today…or had he?

'Something appears to be troubling you, Major,' a smooth voice remarked, and Daniel discovered Sir Giles hovering at his elbow, looking remarkably well pleased about something.

He was instantly suspicious, for he knew well enough that the man beside him was not quite what he seemed. He had the utmost respect for Sir Giles's acute intellect. None the less, if their association during the past years had taught Daniel anything, then it was not to trust the well-mannered, silver-tongued baronet an inch.

'I swear, Osborne, that you were a cat in some former life. Like the pampered feline who lazes in the most comfortable spot in a room, you appear sublimely content. Yet, it would come as no great surprise to me to discover that you sleep with one eye permanently open.'

Sir Giles's shoulders shook in silent, appreciative laughter. 'Ah yes! Cats—remarkable creatures, are they not? I hold them in the highest regard. Lying quietly in wait to strike when least expected, they do their utmost to rid this world of ours of loathsome vermin.'

Extracting his silver snuffbox, Sir Giles made use of its contents before returning the elegant trinket to his pocket, while all the time his eyes stared through the open doorway leading to the card-room. 'Lavinia Went-worth's niece is a strikingly lovely young woman, do you not agree, Major Ross?'

Daniel followed the direction of the older man's gaze in time to see his former companion taking a seat at the table occupied by a forbidding matron sporting an ugly turban of puce satin. 'I did not realise that Miss O'Malley was related to our hostess,' he admitted, eyes narrowing. 'Then her maternal grandfather was none other than…'

'Colonel Fairchild,' Sir Giles finished for him, when the Major's voice faded. 'I understand that she lived with him for a short time. I thought perhaps you knew her.'

How very interesting! Daniel mused, his mind racing back over the years. Then it was just possible that he had met Miss O'Malley in the dim and distant past, though she must have been little more than a child at the time, for Colonel Fairchild had been dead for a number of years.

'Such glorious hair, do you not agree?' Sir Giles remarked, successfully recapturing his companion's attention. 'I myself have always had a particular weakness for auburn-haired fillies.'

'Oh, you have, have you?' Daniel did not believe a word of it, and wasn't reticent about making his own views clear. 'Well, I certainly have not! The few I've come across during my lifetime have all been devious little firebrands—totally unpredictable and not to be trusted. And Miss O'Malley has certainly not induced me to alter my opinion!'

It had taken Katherine a minute or two only to become aware that those of her fellow guests who were drifting into the card-room were keeping well clear of the table

where she and the Dowager Lady Charlesworth now sat.
Several wicked possibilities occurred to her for this de-
liberate avoidance, all of which were most definitely to
the formidable Dowager's discredit. She was just beginning to come to the conclusion that it was unlikely that
there was anyone among the guests brave enough to
challenge Lady Charlesworth, when a shadow fell across
the table, and she found herself meeting the steely gaze
of the distinguished-looking gentleman who had arrived
with the disreputable Major.

'Ah, Osborne!' There was a distinct note of approval
in the Dowager's booming voice, which gave Katherine
every reason to suppose that the baronet would prove to
be a worthy opponent. 'Come to challenge me and my
young partner, have you? Well, sit down! Sit down,
man! Have you met Miss O'Malley?'

'I understand that you are Mrs Wentworth's niece,'
he remarked, after Lady Charlesworth had made the in-
troductions so loudly that Katherine was fairly certain
that, had anyone else in the room been ignorant of her
identity before, such was no longer the case.

Katherine nodded. 'My mother was her elder sister,
sir.'

'I also understand that you reside in Bath.'

'Yes, sir. I have lived there for a number of years.'

'But not alone, I trust,' the Dowager put in, looking
faintly disapproving.

It would have afforded Katherine the utmost pleasure
to inform the dictatorial lady seated opposite that her
domestic arrangements were entirely her own concern,
but having given way once to her occasionally volatile
temperament, she had no intention of doing so again. It
would have afforded her even greater pleasure to be able

to say that she did live quite alone. Unfortunately she could not do so.

'No, ma'am,' she admitted. 'My late aunt's former companion still resides with me.'

'Very proper,' the Dowager approved, before turning her attention to Sir Giles and demanding to know if he had secured himself a partner.

'My sister will be joining us, ma'am… Ah! And here she is, ready to do battle.'

It would have been hard to find a less formidable-looking opponent, Katherine decided, as she watched the middle-aged lady, dressed in the startling orange-coloured gown, nervously twisting the strings of her reticule round her fingers as she seated herself at the table.

The baronet's spinster sister put Katherine in mind of the companion whom she had unfortunately inherited from her late aunt. Poor Miss Mountjoy, always eager to please, whilst bracing herself for the inevitable cutting remarks, had always displayed the same degree of nervous tension, whenever in her late employer's presence, as Miss Mary Osborne was betraying now.

Katherine well expected the Dowager, undoubtedly fashioned in the same mould as the late Miss Augusta Fairchild, to utter some blistering remark. Yet, surprisingly enough, apart from sniffing rather pointedly as she cast disapproving eyes over the dazzling orange creation, which clashed alarmingly with her own puce gown, she refrained from comment. Which gave Katherine every reason to suppose that the mouse-like Miss Osborne, though lamentably lacking an eye for fashion, had somehow managed to earn the formidable Dowager's approval.

This certainly proved to be the case, for Miss Osborne was undoubtedly a very skilful card player, and her partner no less so. They easily won the first game, and Katherine found herself having to concentrate very hard, which was no easy matter when she was having to contend with her partner's hard-eyed scrutiny, and the frequent, penetrating steely-grey-eyed glances she found herself receiving from the baronet. None the less, her nerve, though sorely tested, held firm, and she and her partner won the second game, and took the first rubber convincingly with the final game.

'I knew I chose wisely when I selected you for my partner, Miss O'Malley,' Lady Charlesworth boomed approvingly. 'A female who can hold her nerve, eh, Osborne?'

'It would certainly appear so, ma'am,' he answered softly, his eyes once again firmly turned in Katherine's direction. 'Miss O'Malley appears to possess all the necessary requirements... Yes, she might prove to be an excellent choice.'

Chapter Three

'I've been giving some thought to what you disclosed on the evening of my engagement party.'

The surprising admission succeeded in capturing Katherine's attention, and she transferred her gaze from the spot beyond the parlour window, where the morning's continuous rain had succeeded in creating a huge puddle on the terrace, to her cousin, who had been industriously plying her needle for the past half-hour. 'About what?' she prompted.

'About Major Ross.'

The immediate response did not precisely please Katherine. Although his name had never once been mentioned within her hearing since the night of the party, she had been irritated by the number of times he had managed to encroach into her thoughts.

'Before he returned to London Richard happened to mention,' Caroline continued, 'that Wellington himself thought very highly of the Major, and used him on many important missions.'

'His bravery is not in question,' Katherine pointed out, striving not to sound waspish. 'I merely maintain that he is a heartless wretch who cares naught for the feelings of others.'

'I'm not so certain you're right about that,' Caroline argued. Highly complaisant and sweet-natured though she was, she wasn't afraid to voice an opinion if she held strong views on a subject. 'I found myself in his company on more than one occasion during the evening of the party. I have to own, I rather liked him, even though I found his conversation a little—how shall I put it?—forthright. But Richard assured me that seasoned campaigners do tend to be plain-spoken and a little abrupt. And the Major was kind enough to fetch me a cup of fruit punch.'

'Oh, well, that just goes to prove I misjudged him entirely, doesn't it?' Katherine rolled her eyes ceiling-wards. 'Any gentleman who would fetch a lady refreshments must surely be a paragon of all the virtues!'

'Furthermore,' Caroline continued, smiling faintly at this blatant sarcasm, 'Richard did furnish me with one tale about the Major that he'd heard from a fellow officer. Seemingly, appalling atrocities took place after our troops were successful in storming Badajoz. Major Ross, by all accounts, offered his protection to the wife of some French officer. I do not know all the details, you understand, because Richard didn't consider it a suitable topic to discuss in my company. Nevertheless, what he did disclose was sufficient to convince me that any gentleman who would put his life at risk to protect a lady's virtue must be a very honourable man. Which makes me wonder whether what you were told about him years ago was completely true.'

'We do not know for certain that the story of his heroism at Badajoz is true either,' Katherine pointed out.

'You know how these tales are much embellished in the retelling.'

'Mama was talking with him a good deal at the party. We could always ask her if she knows anything about his exploits,' Caroline suggested, just as the door opened, and Mrs Wentworth herself entered the parlour.

Although Katherine had no wish to engage in a discussion about someone whom for years she had been happy to stigmatise as a heartless lecher, her cousin, evidently, was not of a similar mind, for Caroline hardly waited for her mother to settle herself comfortably in a chair, before she asked outright whether she was well acquainted with the gallant Major.

'I wouldn't go so far as to say that, dear,' Mrs Wentworth responded, reaching for her embroidery. 'When I left Dorsetshire to marry your father, Daniel was merely a boy, no more than six or seven, though I do remember his father very well. Edwin Ross was such a charming gentleman, and extremely astute. And Daniel, I feel, has grown into his image in both looks and character.'

Somehow managing to suppress a snort, Katherine made a supreme effort to concentrate on the book lying open on her lap, and ignore the ensuing conversation between mother and daughter. Unfortunately she was only moderately successful, and one interesting disclosure had her and her equally astonished cousin exchanging startled glances.

'I didn't realise that Major Ross was Grandpapa's godson,' she freely admitted.

'Oh, yes, dear,' her aunt confirmed. 'Your grandfather and Edwin Ross had been friends since boyhood, and Daniel was very fond of dear Papa. Papa frequently mentioned in the letters he wrote how much he missed his godson's visits when Daniel went out to India.'

This appeared to capture Caroline's attention in a big way, for she immediately set aside her sewing. 'Major Ross has been to India? Oh, what exciting lives gentlemen lead!'

'I do not know whether Daniel himself found the experience so very rewarding,' her mother countered, 'in view of what took place during his absence.'

Although Katherine doggedly refused to betray further interest, she was not unduly sorry when her cousin demanded to know what precisely had happened during Daniel's travels abroad.

'His father passed away just a year after Daniel had set sail for India. Although his uncle, Sir Joshua Ross, did write promptly, informing him of the tragic news, it quite naturally took some time before the letter reached him. And if that was not bad enough, when the poor boy did eventually return, it was to discover that his childhood sweetheart, Julia Melrose, had married Sir Joshua's son Simon just a few months before.'

'Oh, poor Major Ross!' Caroline exclaimed, and Katherine, much to her surprise, found herself experiencing a twinge of sympathy too, and could not resist asking whether there had ever been anything official between them.

Lavinia Wentworth shook her head. 'I do not believe Julia's parents were averse to a match. Daniel, after all, was the son of a wealthy landowner, and therefore quite eligible. I believe the Melroses considered that it wouldn't hurt to wait a year or two before giving their consent to a marriage. Daniel himself had only just turned twenty when he set sail for India. I suppose he considered it would occupy his time until he could officially ask for Julia's hand.'

Caroline cast a puzzled glance across at her mother.

'But if Julia Melrose was truly in love with Daniel, why on earth did she agree to marry Simon Ross?'

'That I couldn't say, my dear. I do know that Julia, Simon and Daniel had known one another all their lives and had frequently played together as children, but from what I have gleaned over the years from the many friends I still have living in the area, Julia always showed a preference for Daniel's company. Most people, including your grandfather, expected them to tie the knot one day.' She shrugged. 'One can only imagine pressure was brought to bear on Miss Melrose to marry Simon. After all, he was the one who had been destined to hold the title, not Daniel.'

Mrs Wentworth sighed and shook her head. 'Whether the marriage was happy or not, I couldn't say, but it certainly proved fruitful. Julia gave birth to a son some five or six years ago, if I remember correctly. One cannot help but feel saddened that the union was brought to an abrupt end. Simon Ross, sadly, was killed whilst hunting in the Shires.'

'Which leaves the field now open for the Major, as it were,' Katherine remarked, with just a touch of cynicism that made her aunt smile.

'It is certainly a possibility that their love will rekindle,' her aunt acknowledged. 'He has, so I understand, never betrayed the least interest in marrying anyone else, even though his name has been linked with several— er—females over the years.'

Out of the corner of her eye Katherine saw her cousin glance in her direction, as though expecting her, now that the opportunity had arisen, to pass some remark, and she swiftly decided not to disappoint her. 'I clearly remember that, when I resided in Dorsetshire for those few short months, Captain Ross, as he was then, betrayed an interest in a close neighbour of Grandpapa's—Helen Rushton.'

'Helen Rushton?' her aunt echoed, frowning slightly. Then her brow cleared. 'Ah, yes, I remember—Hermione Rushton's girl!' The frown returned. 'Are you positive he was interested in her, Katherine? She must have been a mere child at the time.'

'She was seventeen.'

Mrs Wentworth's expressive brows rose this time. 'Yes, I suppose she must have been. So very sad, her dying so young. I remember Mrs Rushton very well—a sweet woman, but something of a dreamer and not very bright. I recall your grandfather mentioning once that Helen had become very like her mother.'

Until that moment Katherine had never considered that Helen had been very immature for her years. Looking back now, however, she was silently forced to own that her friend had been something of a dreamer and might well have imagined that Daniel Ross had been betraying an interest in her.

Swiftly thrusting this traitorous thought aside, she said, 'I also recall, Aunt, that he was displaying marked attention towards a young widow in the locale.'

'Very likely, my dear. He could only have been twenty-three or -four at the time. I doubt his intentions were serious. Gentlemen rarely are at that age. And you must remember he had suffered a grievous blow over Julia Melrose. When I spoke to him at the party I gained the distinct impression that he is more than ready to settle down now, however. He is quite wealthy, so should have no difficulty in finding himself a wife.'

Caroline's soft brown eyes glowed with a distinctly hopeful look. 'Although it is unlikely that Major Ross will ever inherit the title, it is not impossible that he and his childhood sweetheart might one day find happiness together.'

Whether or not it was because she had never fallen in love herself, or that she simply didn't possess her cousin's romantic streak, Katherine was not sure, but her interest had already swiftly begun to wane. The ex-Major's present romantic inclinations were of absolutely no interest to her. Consequently she experienced no compunction whatsoever in changing the subject by voicing something which was of far more concern to her, if a trifle mundane.

'I sincerely hope the weather improves by tomorrow. I do not relish the prospect of returning all the way to Bath in the pouring rain.'

'I wish you were not going back so soon, Katherine. Cannot Mama and I persuade you to remain a little longer?'

Katherine, smiling fondly at her cousin, shook her head. 'I should dearly love to stay another week or two, Caro, but my conscience will not permit it. I have already left poor Clarissa Mountjoy to her own devices for two weeks.'

'I think it was highly unfair of Aunt Augusta to foist that distinctly foolish female on to you, Katherine,' Lavinia Wentworth announced, with a rare show of annoyance. 'She is engaged as a companion and resides in your home for the sole purpose of ensuring that you, an unmarried female, are suitably chaperoned at all times. Yet I swear it is you who takes care of her. It is a fine duenna indeed who cannot bring herself to travel more than a mile or two because she fears becoming queasy!'

A further fond smile touched Katherine's lips as she looked across at her aunt. 'Believe me, Aunt Lavinia, I am not sorry that Mountjoy is afflicted with travel sickness whenever she steps inside a carriage.' She couldn't prevent a sigh escaping. 'I am forced to admit too that I do find her company excessively tedious, for she is undeniably an extremely foolish woman, but she does try so very hard to please. And I would never go back on the promise I made to Aunt Augusta and turn Mount-joy off. The poor woman put up with Great-aunt Augusta's megrims and ill humours for twenty years. I believe she has earned a little peace and contentment in a house where not too much is expected of her, and she can more or less come and go as she pleases.'

A further sigh escaped Katherine as she finally abandoned her book and set it to one side. 'I must admit, though, as chaperons go, she could never be described as diligent. I cannot say that I would feel in the least sorry if she did decide to leave, and I could employ someone of my own choosing.'

'I doubt there is much chance of that,' her aunt warned. 'I fear, my dear, that you have made the woman's life far too agreeable since Aunt Augusta's death for her to wish to take up another post.'

'You are possibly quite right,' Katherine agreed. 'But there is just a glimmer of hope on the horizon. Mountjoy received a letter from her widowed sister a month ago, inviting her to make her home with her. Needless to say I would be delighted if she does decide to leave, but I am resolved that it must be her decision.'

'You would have no need of a chaperon if you chose to make your home here with us,' her aunt reminded her.

Katherine had wondered how long it would be before the subject was once again raised. Her aunt had asked her on several occasions to make her home in Hampshire, and Katherine had always neatly avoided giving a firm answer. It was not that she felt she would be un-happy living with her aunt and uncle, for she was fond of them both, and adored both her cousins. Nor was she afraid that the little independence she had acquired would be drastically curtailed, for her aunt was such an easygoing soul who would willingly allow her to do more or less as she pleased. No, stupid though it might be, she was afraid to take up permanent residence under this roof; afraid that, as had happened so often in the past, she would bring ill fortune to the household if she were ever to remove here.

'That is certainly true, Aunt,' she agreed, her warm smile concealing quite beautifully those deep-rooted fears that had continued to torment her in recent years. 'But I would never dream of inflicting Mountjoy on you. And even if I should be lucky enough to persuade her to accept her sister's kind offer, there is still Bridie to consider. There is not the remotest possibility that I shall ever be able to persuade that fiendish woman to take up another post. I know I shall be cursed with her company for life! She is the most self-opinionated, domineering creature imaginable! If once she takes up residence here, you'd swiftly find her ruling the roost in the servants' hall, and your own staff leaving your employ.'

Mrs Wentworth frankly laughed. 'Oh, I know Bridie can be a little outspoken on occasions, and is certainly not what one might describe as a conventional domestic, but I for one, as I've mentioned before, have always felt very relieved that she has been there to take care of you, Katherine.'

She looked up as the door opened to see her butler enter the room, carrying a small silver tray. 'Yes, what is it, Meldrew?'

'A letter from Osborne House for Miss O'Malley,

ma'am,' he answered, presenting Katherine with the tray. 'The footman is still here, awaiting a reply, miss.'

Surprised, Katherine removed the missive, which did indeed bear her name in bold, elegantly constructed letters, and broke the seal. 'Good heavens!' she exclaimed, after running her eyes over the few lines. 'I've been invited to take tea with Sir Giles and his sister this afternoon at three o'clock.'

She handed the note across to her aunt. 'Have you anything planned for the afternoon, Aunt Lavinia?'

'As a matter of fact, dear, Lady Charlesworth plans to call. But, in any event,' she added, after scanning the brief missive, 'it would seem the invitation is for you alone.' She did not appear in the least offended, as her next words proved. 'I'm rather relieved. I should not have wished to cause offence to either Sir Giles or his sister by refusing. In the circumstances, however, I feel I must remain here, as I have already assured Lady Charlesworth that her visit will be most welcome.'

Katherine was far from convinced that her aunt's assertion was one hundred per cent true. If her cousin's expression of comical dismay was any indication, poor Caroline certainly wasn't looking forward with any real conviction to her future mother-in-law's proposed visit. Caroline, of course, had little choice in the matter; Katherine, on the other hand, most definitely had. She considered she had more than fulfilled her role as dutiful niece on the night of the engagement party, and had no intention of enduring the formidable Dowager's company for a further lengthy period.

'Would you mind very much, Aunt Lavinia, if I accepted the invitation to take tea with the Osbornes? I rather liked Sir Giles—a highly intelligent man who possesses a rather dry sense of humour.' She chose not to add that she had been less favourably impressed with his sister.

'Of course I do not object, my dear,' her aunt assured her before turning to Meldrew. 'Inform Sir Giles's footman that Miss O'Malley will be delighted to accept.'

'My, my, Katherine! You must have made a favourable impression on our reserved neighbour,' Caroline teased, the instant the butler had withdrawn. 'Sir Giles is not renowned for socialising to any great extent. He generally keeps himself very much to himself when in the country.'

'Oh, I do not think that is strictly true, Caroline,' her mother countered. 'Sir Giles has always been a most genial man. I do not deny that since his wife and his younger son died, he has tended to be less sociable, but that is only to be expected. Furthermore, his work for the government keeps him in London a good deal.'

Caroline frowned a little at this. 'Do you know, Mama, I've never perfectly understood the nature of Sir Giles's work. I do not think even Papa understands precisely what duties Sir Giles performs.'

'Our esteemed neighbour has always been a little vague about it, certainly,' her mother agreed. 'I believe he mentioned once that it was something connected with the War Office. I do happen to know that he numbers among the Regent's close friends. So perhaps one of his duties is to keep our future King abreast of events, though why he should feel the need to spend so much time in the capital now that monster is on Elba, and the war is thankfully at an end, I cannot imagine.'

She frowned as a thought suddenly occurred to her. 'In fact, I understood your father to say that Sir Giles accompanied Major Ross to the capital on the morning after the party.' She shrugged. 'Evidently he must have

returned… At least for Katherine's sake I sincerely hope
he has, otherwise she will find herself having to endure
his far less sensible sister's company for an hour or two.'

It required a monumental effort, but Katherine managed to resist the temptation to declare that if it was a
choice between spending time in the company of Lady
Charlesworth and Sir Giles's sister, she considered Miss
Mary Osborne most definitely the lesser evil!

The Wentworth carriage having been kindly placed at
her disposal, Katherine set off on the short journey to
Osborne House in good time to reach her destination at
the appointed hour. She was looking forward to visiting
the home of the man whose company she had very much
enjoyed on the evening of the party. She was pleased
too that the rain had ceased and the afternoon had been
blessed thus far with brief glimpses of an early February
sun. She was not, however, precisely overjoyed at being
denied the opportunity to make this perfectly respectable
visit unaccompanied.

Bridie had taken it upon herself to follow her out to
the carriage and had plumped herself down on the seat
opposite, that mulish expression Katherine had glimpsed
so often in the past taking possession of the homely features.

Katherine turned her head to stare out of the window,
lest her own expression betray the mingled resentment
and annoyance rippling through her. These were feelings
she had experienced increasingly during these past
twelve months. Augusta Fairchild might have been an
irascible old lady, sharp tongued, and not disposed to
consider the feelings of others, but she had not been
bound by convention, and had allowed Katherine freedom to do more or less as she pleased. Since her aunt's

demise, however, Katherine had discovered that treasured independence, which one might reasonably have expected to increase now that she had become mistress of her own establishment, had been gradually curtailed by the two females whom she employed.

And it was utterly ridiculous! She inwardly fumed, resolved to do something soon about her far from idyllic domestic situation. These past two weeks in Hampshire had, if nothing else, shown her that one attained far more freedom from living in the country. Weather permitting, she had gone for a walk, sometimes accompanied by her cousin Caroline, and sometimes alone. It was true that on the occasion they had visited the local town they had taken the little housemaid with them. Yet Katherine had hardly known the servant was there. Walking a few paces behind, the maid had barely uttered a word, and had merely carried the few purchases both Katherine and Caroline had made back to the carriage.

How different from the life she had led in Bath! Not once since her great-aunt's demise had she visited the fashionable shops without having to suffer Mountjoy's incessant prattling, as she scurried alongside like a timid mouse. Always eager to please, poor Mountjoy more often than not had only succeeded in irritating her so much that Katherine had come perilously close on numerous occasions to releasing her pent-up frustrations by administering a sound box round the ears, and only the promise she had made to her aunt had checked the words of instant dismissal she so longed to utter.

Smothering a sigh, Katherine turned her attention to the woman in the seat opposite. Even if she did manage to resolve the problem of her less than ideal companion, there still remained the even greater dilemma of what to do about the woman who had taken such loving care of her throughout her life. Although she had never been afraid to speak her mind where Bridie was concerned, which had resulted in numerous battles of will over the years, and many harshly spoken words, not for the world would she deliberately hurt the person to whom she was so genuinely attached. Yet somehow she must find a way of convincing Bridie that her one-time charge was no longer in need of leading-strings, but a young, independent woman, quite capable of making her own decisions and, more importantly, of taking care of herself. And there was no better time to embark on this crusade for total independence than right now!

'I cannot imagine why you felt the need to accompany me on this journey,' she remarked in a level tone, determined to deny Bridie the opportunity of accusing her of being in a 'naughty' temper, which she so often did when Katherine had taken her to task over something.

The mulish expression returned to the homely face. 'And who would have taken care of you if I hadn't come along, may I ask?'

'My aunt's groom is more than capable of ensuring that I come to no harm.'

'Pshaw! The great lummox didn't even think to provide you with a few necessary comforts,' Bridie retorted, lovingly tucking the fur-lined rug, which she had carried out to the carriage, more securely about her young mistress's slender legs. 'I promised your sainted mother on her deathbed that I would always look after her little girl. And I shan't go back on my word. Bridie will always be here for you, Miss Kate.'

Oh, dear Lord! Katherine inwardly groaned. Although moved by this touching declaration, she was very well aware that the task ahead of her was going to be far from easy. Yet somehow there had to be a way of convincing Bridie that she was now a capable young woman, and no longer a child in need of constant care and attention.

Determined not to be defeated in her objective, Katherine adopted a different tack, as the coachman drew the well-sprung carriage to a halt before the front entrance of the impressive mansion. 'As you have taken it upon yourself to play nursemaid, you had better accompany me inside. No doubt you will be invited to take tea with the more senior servants.' She paused after alighting to cast a cautionary glance over her shoulder. 'So kindly maintain a guard on that unruly tongue of yours for the duration of our visit.'

Bridie, both surprised and incensed at what she considered to be quite uncalled-for strictures, was denied the opportunity to retaliate by voicing her opinion of her young mistress's frequently caustic utterances by the prompt appearance of the very correct manservant who admitted them to the house.

'Sir Giles is expecting you, Miss O'Malley. If you would kindly step this way?' The butler paused, before leading the way across the chequered hall, to cast a faintly superior glance in Bridie's direction when she appeared about to follow her mistress. 'I shall ensure that your maid receives refreshments below stairs.'

Hardening her heart against the hopeful expression in those loving, dark eyes, Katherine swept past the door the butler held open. Only then did she begin to wonder if she had not been a little foolish in not insisting that Bridie remain with her, when she noticed that the book-lined room's sole occupant was Sir Giles.

Rising immediately from behind the desk, he came forward to take Katherine's hand briefly in his own. 'My dear Miss O'Malley. My sister and I were delighted that you were able to accept our invitation,' he announced, before dismissing his servant with the faintest nod of his head. 'Come, take a seat by the fire.'

A glimmer of amusement flickered in the baronet's grey eyes as Katherine hesitated. 'My dear child, I am old enough to be your father, if not your grandfather. Be assured that my sister will be joining us, once she has returned from her trip to town.'

Feeling rather annoyed with herself for so obviously betraying unease, while at the same time thinking it most strange that Miss Osborne should visit the local town when she had invited a guest to take tea, Katherine seated herself in one of the comfortable chairs by the hearth. It was strange too that the butler had shown her in here. Evidently he had been obeying his master's instructions. But surely it was more usual to invite guests to take tea in the parlour?

After watching her host move across to a small table on which several decanters stood, Katherine glanced about the room. It was a wholly masculine sanctum, which put her in mind of her grandfather's library in that charming house in Dorsetshire, the main difference being that this room had a second door, left slightly ajar, which possibly led to a small ante-room.

'Can I tempt you to a glass of Madeira, my dear?' Again there was a moment's hesitation on her part which drew a brief smile to Sir Giles's lips as he poured out a second glass. 'You came to take tea and yet your host is attempting to ply you with strong liquor. What sinister motive can there be in that? I hear you asking yourself. You are wise to be cautious, child, for this world of ours holds many sinister pitfalls for the unwary. And I did have a specific reason for wishing to see you alone.'

More intrigued than unnerved by this surprising admission, Katherine accepted the glass held out to her, observing as she did so that those shrewd grey eyes, alert and acutely assessing, were regarding her no less keenly than they had on the evening of the engagement party almost two weeks ago.

'You have striking colouring, Miss O'Malley,' he remarked, surprising her still further, as he settled himself in the chair opposite, his gaze never wavering from her face. 'Inherited from your Irish-born father, I should imagine.'

'Yes, sir,' she responded, wondering what he would remark upon next. She was not left to speculate for long.

'I am reliably informed that you and your father were very close. It was a tragedy that he lost his life in the service of his country… But it was a tragedy that was destined to take place long before he had set sail from Ireland.' Sir Giles saw the slender fingers tighten momentarily round the stem of the glass, and a look appear in the turquoise-coloured eyes which was no less penetrating than that in his own. 'Ill fortune played no part in your father's demise. The French had been informed that three vessels loaded with urgent supplies would be setting sail for Portugal on a certain date, and they were lying in wait.'

'How—how did you discover this?' Katherine demanded. The heartache she had suffered when she had first learned of her father's death had never left her, but now a completely different emotion, far stronger than the lingering pain, had swiftly gained supremacy. A despicable traitor had been responsible for the death of her father!

'I make it my business to know, child,' Sir Giles responded, smiling grimly. 'One does not need to don a uniform in order to serve one's country. And not all one's enemies are as visible as those on the field of battle.' The look in his steely-grey eyes grew noticeably harder. 'Napoleon is in exile on Elba. But my war is far from over, and shall not be so until I have unmasked the heartless devil who, during these past years, has been passing information on to the French.'

Taking a moment to refresh himself, Giles continued to regard her steadily over the rim of his glass. 'I shall not insult your intelligence by attempting to suggest that the person I am determined to unmask is the very traitor responsible for tampering with the document sent to the Admiralty requesting an escort for the convoy in which your father was destined to sail. There have been a number of agents working for France during these past years. I have a particular interest in uncovering the identity of just one of them, mainly because I was foolish enough once to underestimate him, and in so doing was responsible, in part, for the death of a young Frenchwoman whose knowledge would have proved invaluable in unmasking a cell of agents working in this country.'

Katherine's gaze remained as steady as her host's. She now knew precisely why Sir Giles, the secret spy-catcher, had invited her here. 'You believe that I might prove useful in helping you achieve your objective?'

'Yes, child, I do. From the moment I first set eyes upon you I was aware of the striking resemblance you bear to the young woman who was murdered whilst under my so-called protection,' he admitted, his voice surprisingly betraying a hint of regret. 'I failed her, and that weighs heavily on my conscience. I have no intention of repeating my error. I shall do everything within my power to minimise the risk, but should you agree to assist me it is as well for you to know at the outset that your life would be in danger.'

Leaning back in his chair, Sir Giles regarded her in silence for a moment. 'Now, before I divulge more, I need to know, Miss O'Malley, whether you are willing to undertake a very great service for your country, which, if successful, might go some way to avenging your father's demise?'

Katherine didn't need to take even a moment to decide, but was somewhat startled, after voicing her desire to help in any way she could, when the door leading to the small ante-room was thrown wide and a sparse man in his early forties, accompanied by a woman of similar age, walked calmly into the room.

'Do not be alarmed, my child,' Sir Giles advised gently. 'I wish you to meet Mr Arthur Ashcroft, and his sister Miss Margaret Ashcroft, two of my most trusted associates. They will play a small but vital part in the plan I am about to outline to you. There is one further key player with whom I must make contact, but that can wait for the time being. What we must do now is put our heads together and come up with some scheme whereby you may leave Bath again, and quite alone, in the very near future without arousing the least suspicion.'

A plump, middle-aged figure suddenly appeared before Katherine's mind's eye. 'That, Sir Giles, might prove more difficult than you imagine!'

Chapter Four

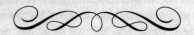

Major Daniel Ross laid his head against the back of
the chair, and stretched out his long legs in order to rest
his feet upon the fender. His time here in Curzon Street,
enjoying the hospitality of his good friend Harry Dan-
vers, must soon come to an end. These past few weeks
had proved to be highly pleasurable, and some recom-
pense, he supposed, for the many privations he had perforce to endure in recent years.

Undeniably London had much to offer any bachelor
of comfortable means. He would have been the first to
admit that he had been content to while away the hours
in the company of many of those who, like himself, had
known the hardship of life out in the Peninsula. There
was no denying too that the highly satisfying association
with that delicate vessel, short on brains but infinitely
skilful in other ways, had assuaged his physical needs
and provided a most pleasurable way of passing several
evenings and nights. None the less, a totally idle existence was not for him. It was time he returned to his
Dorsetshire acres to put into effect those improvements
he planned for his house and lands.

After sampling the contents of his glass, he began to

contemplate a future that would be in stark contrast with his past. Yet he had no regrets about the decision he had taken to sell his commission and leave the army. He believed he was more than ready now to take charge of his inheritance. The love of the land had taken time to come to him, but it was there now. Which was perhaps just as well, he mused, for there was precious little else in his life at the moment upon which he might shower attention and affection, least of all a woman.

A wry smile tugged at one corner of his mouth before he reduced the contents of his glass still further. Although he certainly hadn't lived the life of a monk in recent years, no female had succeeded in capturing his heart since Julia had held a place there in his youth. Even now, after all these years, he could well remember how utterly devastated he had been when he had discovered that his childhood sweetheart, the female whom he had considered so perfect in every way, had betrayed his love and trust by marrying his cousin. Had the bitter experience left him hard and cynical, and disinclined to trust another member of her sex? He could not help wondering. Or was it merely that he had searched in vain for a replica?

A slight frown creased his brow. If that was so, why then had he felt nothing within him stir when, after so many years, he had seen Julia again, a few months ago? He would have expected to feel something more than just a faint twinge of nostalgia for the happy hours they had spent together in their youth. Undeniably, time had been kind to her and she was still very beautiful. Graceful and serene, she remained for him the epitome of womanhood. Not like that damnable little shrew who had crossed his path just a few weeks ago! He inwardly fumed, his frown deepening dramatically as the pleasing image of golden locks and limpid blue eyes was unexpectedly thrust from his mind's eye by a set of quite different features, framed in a riot of deep auburn curls.

He shook his head in a vain attempt to dispel the vision which had too frequently plagued him during his stay in town. That unpredictable little virago typified everything he most despised in her sex! Contrary and sharp-tongued, she was just the type to lash out at a poor, unsuspecting male without the least provocation. Any man who was ever stupid enough even to contemplate taking that ill-mannered minx to wife would deserve all he got! he told himself, wondering why on earth he had been singularly unsuccessful in forgetting her very existence.

The door-knocker echoing in the hall brought these less than charitable musings to an abrupt end, and a minute later his friend's very correct manservant entered to apprise him that he had a visitor. A quick glance in the direction of the mantel-clock informed Daniel that the hour was well advanced. He had an appointment early in the morning, and had no intention of delaying too long before he sought the comfort of his bed.

'Did the caller give a name?' he asked after a moment's deliberation.

'He did not,' a smooth voice answered from the open doorway. 'But he felt certain that our long and—er—not uneventful association would be sufficient to grant him admittance.'

'Oh, you did, did you?' Daniel muttered, before dismissing the servant.

In one lithe movement he rose from the chair and moved towards the decanters. 'So, to what do I owe the pleasure of this unexpected visit? I thought you had returned to Hampshire?'

'I did…briefly,' the caller responded, accepting the glass of wine, before seating himself in one of the chairs by the hearth. He then waited for Daniel to settle himself in the seat opposite before adding, 'But I have been back in town for nearly three weeks.'

Frowning suspiciously, Daniel studied his companion over the rim of his glass, before demanding somewhat abruptly, 'Spit it out, Osborne! Why are you here?'

The baronet's thin lips curled into an appreciative smile. 'Always so delightfully brusque!' he quipped. 'Surprisingly enough, I consider it to be one of your most endearing qualities, my dear fellow. One always knows where one stands with you, Ross.' A faintly menacing gleam hardened his grey eyes. 'You are so refreshingly different from so many of those with whom I have been obliged to associate in recent years.'

'Nobody forced you to take up such work,' Daniel reminded him. 'It was done through choice.'

'Through necessity,' Sir Giles corrected, 'though I cannot deny that I have always displayed a certain aptitude. But my task is not yet complete.'

'But mine is,' Daniel returned, unable to prevent bitterness from edging his voice. 'Years of conflict… thousands dead…and for what?'

'So that we in these islands would continue to speak the King's English, and not French. Which you, of course, do so remarkably well… And that is precisely why I'm here, Major Ross. Once again I find myself in dire need of your undoubted talents. I am here in an attempt to persuade you to take charge of a little commission which has already begun across the Channel.'

'No!' Daniel's response, sharp and uncompromising, cut through the air like a knife as he rose once again to his feet. 'My war's over, Osborne. You cannot order me to go, not this time.'

A sigh escaped the older man as he stared intently at the impassive figure, solid and resolute, now standing before the hearth, staring intently down at the burning coals. 'No, I cannot order you to go, Major,' he concurred. 'But should you agree to do so, you might attain some justice for those many friends who needlessly lost their lives throughout the campaign.'

'Damn you and your spying games, Osborne!' Daniel exploded, unable to quell the bitter resentment and anger which had steadily increased throughout the years of conflict, and continued to fester even now, like some open sore that refused to heal. 'Justice for whom? Curse you!'

Daniel cast a glance over his shoulder in time to see the baronet's bony fingers tighten fractionally about the stem of his glass. 'Whose death are you so determined to avenge—your son's? He was a soldier and, like so many others, was prepared to die for his country. He's just another of those poor wretches who now lie buried in nameless graves scattered throughout Spain and Portugal.' His eyes narrowed. 'Or is it perhaps Justine Baron's demise which continues to prick your conscience?'

Sir Giles held the hard-eyed gaze steadily. 'Yes, I do feel that I owe it to Justine to bring her murderer to book.'

'You owe her nothing, Osborne,' Daniel countered, totally unmoved by the hint of remorse so easily discernible in the baronet's voice. 'She knew the risks she was taking. She and the traitorous devil who has plagued your dreams all these years were two of a kind, and both gained considerable financial rewards from indulging in their despicable trade.'

'Very true,' Sir Giles concurred, the composure for which he was justifiably famed seemingly having been fully restored. 'As I remarked before, Justine loved only one thing more than money—her sister. And it is the young woman who has agreed to pose as the former Mademoiselle Louise Baron who just might, if everything goes according to plan, avenge so many needless deaths.'

'Dear God!' Daniel muttered, his expression clearly disdainful, as he once again sought the comfort of the winged-chair. 'Don't you ever give up? Napoleon is on Elba. It's over at last.'

'Perhaps,' Sir Giles conceded, before his eyes hardened once more. 'And this is why my elusive friend has possibly begun to drop his guard. He may have severed all communication with many of his contacts, and now thinks himself safe. But he is at his most vulnerable. What will his reaction be when I make it known that, during these past months of Napoleon's exile, I have worked tirelessly and have managed to locate the whereabouts of Justine's sister? What if I also make it known that Justine left certain documents in the safekeeping of a lawyer whose identity is known only to the sister, and that the aforementioned sister has every intention of travelling to England in order to retrieve them? What if I were to suggest that the documents might prove interesting reading, and that the girl has agreed to let me study them before she takes her property back to France?'

Sir Giles smiled faintly at Daniel's openly sceptical expression. 'Oh, it will undoubtedly trouble him, Ross. He knew of the existence of this sister. But we managed to get to her first, did we not, my dear friend?' A hint of gratification just for one moment flickered in the baronet's grey eyes. 'I promised Justine that I would never disclose her sibling's whereabouts to another living soul. I also promised that I would never involve her in any of my exploits in the future. And I have kept my word, and shall continue to do so. Justine's old maid, Marie Dubois, is a different matter entirely, however. I did make contact with her, and she is more than willing to help in my attempts to uncover her late mistress's murderer. It is none other than Marie herself who is at present taking care of our delightful little impostor across the Channel.'

Daniel arched one dark brow. '*Our* little impostor?'

'Of course you must go to France in order to accompany your—er—lovely wife to England. Naturally you must not cover your tracks too well, as it were. However, by the time our intended victim has managed to alert his erstwhile associates to the hitherto unforeseen danger to his continued anonymity, I shall have the child safe.'

'As safe as Justine was in your care?' Daniel queried, not slow to remind his visitor of past errors of judgement.

Sir Giles was silent for a moment as he stared down into the contents of his glass once again. 'It will be different this time. Once you have brought the girl safely back to Dover, your part in the plot ceases. You'll be free to return to Dorset, and forget the whole business. Naturally you will receive your share of the reward, if we are successful in uncovering this traitor.'

Again Daniel's lips were curled by a smile of unalloyed contempt. 'Was that the inducement you used to persuade this idiotic female to take part in such a damnably foolhardy escapade—money?'

'No, it was not,' Sir Giles assured him. 'She knows

nothing of the reward. She has her own personal reasons for wishing to see this traitor brought to justice.'

Daniel's bark of derisive laughter echoed round the small salon. 'If she supposes for a moment the man will ever stand trial, she is a gullible little fool!'

Sir Giles's eyes were softened by a flicker of admiration. 'No, she is not a fool, Ross. She's an immensely brave young woman who is very well aware that what she has agreed to do is not without personal risk should things go wrong. The least I can do is try my utmost to ensure nothing does go wrong.' He gazed levelly across at the man for whom he had always had the utmost respect. 'And that is why I need you…someone I can trust implicitly. As you have already pointed out, I cannot order you to go, Major Ross. I can only ask you…one last time…to serve your country.'

Sir Giles made a point of visiting his club early one evening towards the end of the week, and was highly satisfied to discover several very interesting persons present, all seated together at a large table in one corner. Sauntering over, he did not hesitate to avail himself of the only vacant chair, before instructing a waiter to bring him wine.

'I didn't realise you had come up to town, Osborne,' the gentleman seated directly opposite remarked, briefly raising his eyes from the cards in his hand. 'Are you acquainted with young Gifford here, a distant relation I'm sponsoring this Season?'

'No, I've not had the pleasure, Waverley,' he responded, before acknowledging the young gentleman seated beside the portly baron, and receiving a stuttered salutation in response.

'You may not be acquainted with a near neighbour of

mine either,' the gentleman seated on his left put in. 'Sir Joshua and I travelled up to the capital together a couple of days ago.'

'We are acquainted, Cranford,' Sir Giles enlightened him, before turning to the baronet. 'How are you, Ross? Haven't seen you in town for a number of years. I do run across your nephew on the odd occasion, though.'

'Ha! Do you, b'gad!' Sir Joshua barked. 'Well, that's more than I do. Seen the boy only once or twice since he sold out. You'd think he'd settle down now that he's left the army, but he's forever gadding about. No repose, no repose at all!'

His sigh was distinctly mournful. 'Don't get about much myself now,' Sir Joshua continued in the same booming voice, which induced several other members, seated at tables nearby, to frown dourly in his direction. 'Health ain't so good. That's why I took the opportunity to travel with young Cranford here, when I discovered he was planning to come up to town. Daughter-in-law kept plaguing me to consult one of these fancy London practitioners about my hearing. Complete waste of time. Stone deaf in my right ear, and my left ain't much better, so you'll need to speak up a bit.'

As Sir Giles did not relish the prospect of shouting himself hoarse, he turned once again to the gentleman on his left. 'By the by, Cranford, I received your letter inviting me to the party next month. Providing nothing unforeseen crops up, I should be delighted to attend.'

He received a piercing gaze from the bright blue eyes of the last member of the party. 'What's likely to stop you now? Your work's done, Osborne, surely?'

'Yes, Davenham, to all intents and purposes, I suppose it is.'

'Well, what's stopping you, then?' the Viscount persisted. 'We'll all be there. You'll be among friends.'

A ghost of a smile hovered momentarily about Sir Giles's lips. 'I cannot tell you how relieved I am to here you say so, Davenham. Unfortunately, there is just a possibility that my presence will be required in town. I'm not quite certain when she'll be arriving, but I should imagine she has reached Paris by now, and is merely awaiting the arrival of her escort.'

Several brows rose at this. Since the death of his wife, several years before, Sir Giles's name had never been linked with that of any female. 'Don't tell me you've found yourself a French charmer, Osborne!' Lord Waverley exclaimed, laughing heartily. 'I'd like to meet her. She must be something out of the common way if you've gone to the trouble of having her escorted across the Channel.'

'Indeed, she is special.' Sir Giles reached for the wine, which a waiter had deposited on the table a few moments before, and filled his glass. 'She is none other than Justine Baron's sister, the former Mademoiselle Louise Baron.'

Viscount Davenham frowned. 'Should we know her? I can't recall hearing the name before.'

'No?' Sir Giles arched one silver-grey brow. 'Then let me refresh your memory—Justine Baron was a French spy who worked in this country a few years ago. She had a sister living in France, and although the girl was not involved in espionage herself, she mysteriously disappeared around the time of Justine's death. I managed to locate her whereabouts a few months ago, and wrote to her. She sent a very interesting letter back. Now that the war is over, she intends to travel to England to visit Justine's grave. She also informed me that Justine left some papers in the safekeeping of a London notary whose identity is known only to Louise. She has agreed to let me peruse the documents when she has retrieved them. So you can appreciate why I'm so keen to ensure that she arrives here safely, for I'm certain those papers will make enthralling reading. Naturally, she and the person I have engaged to escort her will be travelling under assumed names, posing as man and wife.'

The short silence which followed this astonishing disclosure was broken by Sir Joshua Ross who, gathering together the cards and reshuffling the pack, asked Sir Giles if he wished to be included in the game.

'Why not?' he responded. 'I'm feeling distinctly lucky tonight.'

This proved to be the case, and Sir Giles won several hands in quick succession before four of those assembled, making various excuses, rose from the table, leaving only one gentleman to bear him company.

'Dear me,' he murmured. 'Do you suppose it is my skill at cards or something I said? Surely they weren't all alarmed by my purely fabricated tale?'

'You had me almost believing it myself,' his companion admitted, a gleam of admiration flickering in the depths of his grey eyes. 'You can only hope that your—er—intended victim believed it.'

'I'm not so foolish as to suppose that, my dear fellow. No, he probably doesn't believe it. But he will need to be sure. And that is when I'll have him at last.'

'You know who it is, then?'

'I'm not one-hundred-percent certain, no,' Sir Giles admitted softly, 'but I believe I know. I need proof, though. And I'm relying on my little impostor to provide me with the proof I need.'

His companion's eyes widened fractionally. 'So, you have in truth a young female coming over from France.'

'Oh, yes, my dear. And she is indeed being escorted by…by someone I hold in the highest regard. He'll be across the Channel by now, if everything has gone according to plan, and will have the girl safely back in England before our traitorous friend has alerted his French associates. Undoubtedly at this moment our victim is frantically making arrangements for someone to go over to France. I, on the other hand, am for my bed, so I shall bid you goodnight. Come and dine with me tomorrow evening if you're free.'

Sir Giles remained at his club only for the time it took to collect his outdoor garments and then, declining the hall porter's kind offer to hail a hackney carriage, set out on foot and arrived at his home a short time later, feeling very well pleased with how smoothly events had progressed thus far.

Extracting the key from his pocket, he was on the point of inserting it into the lock, when a carriage pulled up outside the front of his house, and a familiar figure alighted.

'Ashcroft! What the deuce are you doing here?'

Not waiting for a reply, Sir Giles quickly unlocked the door and led the way into the house. He had never encouraged his servants to wait up for him, and the house was as silent as a tomb. Even so, he took the precaution of ushering his unexpected guest into the library and quietly closing the door.

'Don't tell me Ross has arrived in Paris already?' he said, going about the room lighting various candles.

Dishevelled, and looking decidedly weary, his faithful

associate availed himself of one of the chairs. 'He hadn't arrived when I left, sir, no.'

'Your orders were to keep watch over the girl until he did arrive, and then report straight back to me.' Sir Giles noticed that his unexpected visitor was looking deeply troubled. 'What's happened, Ashcroft? Was there some hitch during your journey to Paris?'

'No, sir. Everything went smoothly. It was two days after our arrival in the capital that I first learned of it. I advised Miss O'Malley to return to England at once, but she wouldn't hear of it, sir. She said that we couldn't be sure that the rumour was true, and that if it did turn out to be correct, your uncovering the identity of the traitor was even more necessary.'

'What rumour, Ashcroft?' Sir Giles demanded to know, surprisingly betraying signs of losing his iron self-control.

'You haven't heard then, sir? It will surely be all over London by morning… Napoleon has escaped from Elba and is, as we speak, marching on Paris.' He waited in vain for a response, and then added, 'There will be some, I dare swear, who will attach no importance to the event, believing that Napoleon will prove no threat. But others think differently. Panic has already begun to spread throughout the French capital, especially among foreign visitors, and those who openly welcomed the return of the Bourbon King.'

Ashcroft remained silent as Sir Giles, suddenly grave, went to stand before the hearth, then asked, 'What do you wish me to do, sir—return to Paris and bring the girl back here? She could travel under her own name. No one would pay much attention to an Englishwoman wishing to flee the city. I dare swear hundreds are doing so by now.'

A long silence, then, 'No. You will remain here in town. We must now place our trust in Major Ross. He has never failed me before… Pray God he does not do so this time!'

Katherine stared through the rapidly fading light at the street below her window. There were far fewer carriages and people about on foot now; less signs of the panic which had been steadily increasing during the past days. That, she supposed, was because so many had already fled the city, and many more, so she had been informed, were planning to go.

Had she been foolish to remain? She had asked herself that self-same question dozens of times since Mr Ashcroft's departure two weeks before. Having given it as his opinion that, with the unforeseen turn of events, their mission would of necessity have to be abandoned, he had urged her to accompany him. Yet she had chosen to remain, certain in her own mind that Sir Giles would have wished her to see his plan through to the end if it was at all possible. With every passing day, however, success seemed less likely. Had the person chosen by Sir Giles to escort her back to England arrived at the inn, there might have been a chance of carrying the plan through to a triumphant conclusion. Sadly, now, that seemed highly improbable.

The door behind her opened, and Katherine turned to see the middle-aged woman who had taken care of her since her arrival in France enter the bedchamber. Marie Dubois was not given to smiling much, and she was certainly looking far from happy now. None the less, the ice-cool reserve with which she had treated Katherine at the start of their association had swiftly diminished, and relations between them were now very cordial, each having acquired a deal of respect for the other.

'I have bespoke dinner, Madame Durand,' she announced clearly for the benefit of any inn servant hovering within earshot, 'and have requested yet again that it be served in here.'

Although beginning to feel something of a prisoner, Katherine could well understand her companion's continued caution. Marie never forgot the role she had been requested to play—that of a loyal maid to the wife of a prosperous French merchant. Katherine, on the other hand, was forced to own that she had been less successful in her portrayal of the devoted wife, longing for her husband's return from the south so that they could continue their journey to their home. There had been several occasions when she had failed even to remember that she was supposed to be French, and had reverted to her native tongue without having been aware of it.

There was some excuse for these frequent lapses, she supposed. So much had happened in so short a time that she hardly knew whether she was standing on her head or her heels. From the moment she had agreed to take part in Sir Giles's plot her quiet and faintly tedious existence had been brought to an abrupt end.

She clearly recalled the time she and the baronet had spent together on that early February afternoon, planning how they could spirit her away from Bath, unaccompanied, and without giving rise to the least suspicion.

After having divulged the name of a young woman with whom she had struck up a particular friendship during her time at the seminary, and with whom she had continued to correspond on a regular basis, Katherine had needed to do nothing further except try to carry on as normal. She had returned to Bath the following day as planned, and a week later had received a letter, undoubtedly written in a female hand, inviting her to stay with her friend. Miss Ashcroft, pretending to be her good friend's maiden aunt, had then arrived at the door a few days later, and had announced in a very authoritative tone that, as she would be accompanying Katherine throughout her stay, there would be no need for either a chaperon or a maid, as her own servants were more than capable of catering for both their needs.

Bridie, of course, had not wished to be excluded, but Miss Ashcroft, having been forewarned of Bridie's stubbornness, played the part of a dictatorial maiden aunt quite wonderfully, and had foiled each and every one of Bridie's attempts to be included in the trip.

Katherine had then been escorted to France without delay. In Calais they had been met by yet another player in the game, Marie Dubois. Miss Ashcroft had returned to England, and Katherine, having adopted the guise of a prosperous Frenchman's wife, had travelled on to Paris with Marie and Mr Ashcroft, where all that remained was to await the arrival of her 'husband'.

Everything had proceeded so well up until then, she reflected. Sir Giles had planned everything right down to the last detail. But he could not have foreseen the surprising turn of events that had taken place since her arrival in the French capital, and which, sadly, would ultimately foil his meticulously organised stratagem for uncovering the traitor.

Katherine sighed as she moved away from the window and took a seat at the table, where she had eaten all her meals since her arrival at the inn. 'I think we must now face the fact, Marie, that Sir Giles has possibly been forced to abandon all his well-laid plans. Tomorrow I shall commence the journey back to England.'

'I think that wise,' Marie whispered in English, as she joined her at the table. 'I did not like to tell you this, but whilst I was downstairs earlier there was talk that, even though the King had dispatched troops to intercept him, Napoleon entered Lyons without a shot being fired. He has many supporters in the army. Should they change allegiance…'

'Which makes it all the more imperative that you return to your home,' Katherine announced, knowing what Marie could not bring herself to say. 'If Napoleon does by some miracle manage to reach Paris and take control, then our countries will in all probability once again be at war. I do not wish you to be branded a traitor for protecting an enemy of your country.'

Marie's hard features were softened by a rare smile. 'I do not consider you an enemy, *mademoiselle*. But there are those who might should you remain. You will forgive my saying so, but you could never pass yourself off as a Frenchwoman, *petite*.'

Katherine was forced to acknowledge the truth of this. 'I did inform Sir Giles that my grasp of the Gallic tongue could best be described as adequate, but he insisted that that was of little importance, and that the person he had in mind to escort me back to England would have no difficulty in convincing anyone that he was French.'

The older woman's eyes narrowed speculatively. 'I wonder…?' she murmured.

'Wonder what?' Katherine prompted.

'I wonder if it is the same man who helped me rescue my late mistress's sister four years ago?'

Katherine was not at a complete loss to understand to what Marie was alluding. Before embarking on this exciting escapade, she had learned a little about the woman who had for two years passed on secret information supplied by the British traitor whom Sir Giles was determined to bring to book. More recently she had learned something of Justine Baron's early life from Marie who, Katherine had discovered, had been employed many years before as a maid in the Baron family's home on the outskirts of Paris.

Although not of the aristocracy himself, Justine's father had been a wealthy man who had made the mistake of speaking out against the injustices of the new regime, and in consequence had had his house and lands seized by those in power before he and his wife had been executed. Justine and her younger sister Louise had only just managed to escape with their lives. Spirited away in the dead of night by their devoted servant Marie Dubois, they had been taken to an isolated farm, owned by Marie's brother, deep in the French countryside, where they had remained safely hidden from the French authorities for several years. Unfortunately, by the time she had attained the age of eighteen, Justine had become utterly bored with the bucolic existence and, accompanied by the devoted Marie, had decided to find some means of supporting herself in the capital.

Having been the daughter of wealthy parents, Justine had received a good education, and had had little difficulty in acquiring a position in the establishment of a famous *modiste*. With her striking looks and superb figure, she had been perfect for modelling her employer's latest creations, and it had not been too long before Justine had fallen under the eye of a high-ranking government official. She had willingly become his pampered mistress, and for several years had lived in comparative luxury in a house overlooking the Seine.

During this period in her life, she had continued to visit her young sister regularly. Unlike Justine, Louise had been content to live a quiet life on the farm. Consequently Justine had been happy to leave her there, and had provided for her sister by sending sums of money to Marie's relations at regular intervals.

This act of generosity on Justine's part was to prove her downfall. When the time had come for her to find a new protector, she had chosen unwisely by agreeing to become the mistress of a sinister, shadowy figure who had close links with the man who four years previously had declared himself Emperor.

Her new lover had not been slow to make use of all Justine Baron's talents. By removing Louise from the farm and placing her in a secluded house, where she had become a virtual prisoner, he had attained the means by which he could force Justine to do precisely as he had wished.

Within weeks she had been despatched across the Channel, where she had swiftly found employment in the establishment of a famous Bond Street *modiste*. If the *modiste* had been faintly uneasy about her new employee's ability to obtain silks and laces at a much reduced rate, she had kept her suspicions to herself, and had not asked too many questions concerning Justine's frequent trips to the south coast. Which, of course, had allowed Justine to pass on the secret information obtained from the British traitor.

'I seem to remember you mentioned that you accompanied your mistress to England, Marie,' Katherine remarked as a thought suddenly occurred to her.

'Yes, *mademoiselle*. That was when I learnt to speak your language. We were there for a little over two years.'

'And in all that time you never once saw the man who sold my country's secrets?'

Marie shook her head. 'My mistress did not want me

involved. I cooked and cleaned in the little house we rented, and never went to the shop in Bond Street. It was at the shop, I think, that that devil passed on the information to my mistress, for no one ever came to the house, except Sir Giles on that one occasion.'

Katherine frowned. 'I suppose Sir Giles at some point must have become suspicious of your mistress's activities, Marie, and had her watched. But what I do not understand is why Justine remained in England when she might have given Sir Giles the information he required in return for her safe passage back to France.'

Marie betrayed surprise. 'Why, because of her sister, of course! She had had no contact with Louise in over two years. She was not even permitted to write to her, but she managed after several months to discover where her sister was being held, and wrote to my brother. He was permitted to see Louise on one occasion. He wrote and told us the poor child was treated badly, worked from dawn till dusk, and never allowed out of the house. My mistress was determined to get her little sister away from that dreadful residence, which was no better than a prison, and place her with people whom she trusted to love and care for her.'

'And Sir Giles was willing to offer his aid, providing she told him everything he wished to know,' Katherine remarked, when her companion fell silent. 'How, I wonder, did he manage to effect Louise's escape?'

Marie's harsh features were once again softened by a surprisingly tender smile. 'He did it, *mademoiselle*, by enlisting the aid of a very brave Englishman. I accompanied this man, who was a soldier, I think, over to France. Once he had achieved his objective, I returned with him, eager to impart the good news to my mistress, only to discover...'

'I know, Marie,' Katherine said gently. 'I'm truly sorry that the traitor managed to locate Justine's whereabouts.'

Marie must have believed the sympathy genuine, for she smiled wanly across the table. 'I know my mistress would have kept to her part of the bargain. She would have told him all he needed to know, and that is why, before I returned to France, I promised Sir Giles that if in the future he should ever need my help to catch the devil who murdered my poor mistress, he need only contact me.' She sighed as she gazed down at her work-roughened hands resting in her lap. 'I am a good French-woman, *mademoiselle*. I love my country. But I would do anything to avenge my poor mistress's death. I had great hopes too, for although I never knew the real name of that brave man who rescued little Louise, when I heard the name you were to use, I thought perhaps—'

Marie checked at the knock on the door and rose instantly from the chair to answer it. Supposing it to be the inn servant bringing their food, Katherine did not pay much attention, until she clearly heard Marie exclaim, 'Ah, *monsieur*! So it is you! Now we shall do very well!' Then she raised her head and for a moment was unable to believe the evidence of her own eyes as they focused on the tall figure, swathed in a voluminous grey cloak, peering over Marie's head from the open doorway.

Quite forgetting her role, she was on her feet in an instant. 'What in the name of heaven are you doing here?'

Chapter Five

Marie, looking from one to the other, would have been hard put to it to say which of them appeared more stunned by the other's unexpected presence. Or more angry too, come to that! Blue-green eyes, brightened by a dagger-look, were openly hostile, and there was a definite hint of menace in dark brown orbs too, before the gentleman whom she had been so pleased to see took a step into the room and quietly closed the door.

'It is good to see you again, Marie, after all these years,' he remarked in French, and Katherine, even in her intensely perturbed state, was forced grudgingly to own that anyone might have been forgiven for taking him for a native of France. 'I can only apologise for my late arrival, and trust that you have not found these past days being forced to endure my—er—oh, so charming *wife*'s company, too much of a trial.'

Marie clearly detected the half-smothered squeal as the young woman whose companionship she had found increasingly agreeable swung away to turn her back on the new arrival. 'On the contrary, *monsieur*,' she didn't hesitate to assure him, before she recalled the young lady's one grave failing. 'But I think I ought to warn you she does have a tendency to forget that she is supposed to be a Frenchwoman.'

'That,' he responded, removing his hat and gloves and placing them on top of a convenient piece of furniture nearby, 'isn't all she has a tendency to forget. She is wont to forget her manners too on occasions.'

Out of the corner of her eye Marie noticed two slender white hands curl themselves into tight, angry little fists. She had found her young friend courteous and charming. None the less, she didn't suppose for a moment that she had been blessed with that colouring for no reason, and decided it might be wise to intervene before 'Madame Durand' was tempted to deal her 'husband' a sound box round the ears, something which, Marie did not doubt, her young companion was more than capable of administering if sufficiently roused to anger.

'Have you eaten, *monsieur*? I have ordered dinner, but it would be no trouble to delay it a little to enable you to join us.'

'I have already dined,' he answered, his expression softening noticeably as he removed his gaze from the silent, slender figure whose taut features were clearly mirrored in the window and looked down at the older woman. 'There is no necessity to delay your meal on my account. I shall perhaps sample a glass or two of mine host's fine wine before I retire. But first I think it might be beneficial to have a little private conversation with my *wife*.'

Marie was inclined to agree. That the two had met before and were not upon the best of terms was abundantly clear. Therefore, it could certainly do no harm for them to attempt to settle their differences before they embarked on their homeward journey, she decided. 'In that case, sir, I shall return downstairs and attempt to hurry along our dinner.'

The instant Marie had departed, very tactfully closing the door behind her to enable them to clear the air without being overheard by any inn servants about their work, Daniel addressed himself to the woman who for the next few days would play the part of his wife, loving or otherwise. 'Well, this is a surprising turn up, is it not, Miss O'Malley?'

He noted the faint stiffening in the perfectly proportioned, slender frame. All the same, he had no intention of attempting to conceal the fact that he was not best pleased to discover that the female he had endured several days' hardship in order to rescue was none other than the infuriating little madam who, like some pestilential insect, had all too frequently returned to plague him, mentally if not physically, since their last encounter. 'I had been wondering who our mutual friend had managed to persuade to embark on such a ludicrous venture. It goes without saying that I was convinced it had to be someone with more hair than wit!'

'Oh, you were, were you?' Katherine managed to respond in a surprisingly mild tone. Only the glint in her eyes, when at last she turned to face him again, betrayed the fact that she was not as composed as she might wish to appear. 'Well, let me assure you, Major Ross, that, had I known that you were to figure as a key player in Sir Giles's plot, nothing in this world would ever have induced me to take part.'

Daniel studied her in silence as he removed his cloak and tossed it casually upon the bed. 'Ah, yes! I was forgetting your totally unfounded and quite infantile dislike of me. Tell me, Miss O'Malley, is it in an attempt to satisfy some puerile whim that induces you to display antagonism towards virtual strangers?' He could almost hear those small, perfect teeth grinding together, but steadfastly refused to spare her. 'I discovered on the evening of your cousin's engagement party that you were Colonel Fairchild's granddaughter, and that you resided with him for a short time. Would I be correct in thinking that your resentment stems from nothing more significant than my inability to recall that we had perhaps met in the distant past?'

Daniel noticed the strikingly coloured eyes momentarily stray in the direction of the porcelain vessel on top of the washstand. He didn't doubt for a moment that that small hand was just itching to reach out for the handle on the pitcher and then hurl the delicately painted piece of porcelain in his direction. Yet her voice when she spoke remained surprisingly calm and controlled.

'When I resided with my grandfather, we were never formally introduced, Major Ross. I did witness your arrival at the house on several occasions from an upper-floor window, however, and I believe we did once exchange a few words when I happened to be outside and you rode into the stable-yard one day.'

He frowned, endeavouring to remember, but swiftly abandoned the attempt. 'You must forgive me, ma'am, but I fail to recall the incident.'

'It is of no consequence, I assure you. I was little more than a child at the time, and quite naturally evinced no interest in you at all.' The faint twitch at the corner of her mouth was evidence enough that she had enjoyed delivering this mild insult. 'What I find hard to forgive,' she continued, when he refused to comment, 'or forget, for that matter, is that your callous behaviour was in part responsible for the death of my friend.'

For several moments it was as much as he could do

to stop himself from gaping across the room at her in astonishment. He would have been the first to admit that he had killed many during his years in the army, but as far as he was aware he had never been responsible for anyone's death off the field of battle. 'What the devil are you talking about, young woman?' he demanded, not attempting to moderate his language.

'I am referring to Helen Rushton, Major Ross,' she responded, not noticeably cowed by the barking tone. 'She and her widowed mother were close neighbours of yours, were they not? Helen and I became friends when I went to live in Dorsetshire towards the end of '08.'

This time he was more successful in his efforts to remember. 'Ah, yes! I recall her now. She was the daughter of Captain Rushton who died at Trafalgar.' He regarded her in frowning silence for a moment. 'But she was a mere child. She used to go about all the time carrying a rag doll, of all things! And if my memory serves me correctly, she and her mother unfortunately both lost their lives in a minor smallpox outbreak which occurred shortly after I had sailed for Portugal.'

Katherine's chin lifted. 'Helen was seventeen. Unlike her mother, she was young and strong and might well have survived had she not lost her foolish heart to a worthless profligate who gave her every reason to suppose his interests were engaged, only to cast her aside without so much as a second thought.' She paused to raise an accusing finger. 'After your treatment of her, she lost the will to live.'

Once again Daniel regarded her in silence, his expression totally unreadable, then he bridged the distance between them in three giant strides, and before she could do anything to avoid it, had imprisoned her chin in one long-fingered hand.

'And it is this upon which your dislike of me is based—my thoughtful attentions to the daughter of a man I admired, which were obviously totally misconstrued?'

Although Katherine remained stubbornly silent, she found herself unable to hold his openly contemptuous gaze, and lowered her eyes, but not before Daniel had glimpsed the look of mingled doubt and self-reproach she failed to conceal.

He tightened his grasp on the pointed little chin, forcing her head up and giving her no choice but to raise those delicate lids. 'Retain your infantile dislike of me if you will, Miss O'Malley, but if you possess any degree of sense at all you will refrain from permitting your misguided judgement to induce you to behave foolishly during the time we will be forced to endure each other's company.'

The warning was clear, and all the more menacing because it had been delivered in a surprisingly soft voice. 'If we stand the remotest chance of successfully returning to England unscathed, we must work together. Therefore I shall brook no childish acts of defiance on your part.'

Smiling grimly, Daniel watched the play of different emotions flitting over the delicate features before finally releasing his hold on her chin. He wasn't fooled by the seemingly silent acceptance of his dictum. Unless he was gravely mistaken, nothing would have given her greater pleasure than to place a well-aimed kick on his shin, before telling him to go to hell.

He cast a brief glance over the neat arrangement of fiery curls. No, he mused, he would be foolish to suppose that she would always be so quietly submissive. Beneath the quite lovely surface trappings was a determined and spirited young woman who was not lacking intelligence. Unless he much mistook the matter, she had already been forced to accept the fact that she needed his protection in order to return to England.

'I do believe that we are beginning to understand each other at last,' he could not resist adding. 'If you should continue to exert such admirable self-control, I believe we shall deal tolerably well. And now, Miss O'Malley, I shall leave you alone to ponder over the wisdom of what I have said, whilst I repair downstairs for an hour or so.'

With which he swung round on the heels of his decidedly dusty boots and, head held high, strutted from the room, like a combatant leaving the field of battle in the certain knowledge that he was the clear victor.

The instant the door had closed behind him, Katherine closed her eyes, and somehow managed to quell the temptation to reach out for that pitcher whose handle was invitingly close, and hurl it at the exact spot where the Major's arrogant head had been only moments before. How glad she was now that her grandfather had insisted that she spend a year at that superior Bath seminary! One schoolmistress of whom she had been particularly fond had endeavoured to teach her to control her temper, and to consider any forceful display of emotion faintly vulgar. She had certainly needed to heed those excellent teachings during the past few minutes, and attempt to behave in a dignified manner. Whether she would be able to continue to do so during the days ahead was a different matter entirely!

Suddenly feeling incredibly weary, Katherine slumped down on the bed, and began to consider her present predicament. Unpalatable though it was, she had to face the fact that she would, perforce, need to spend a consid-

erable amount of time in the Major's company. Like it
or not, she did require his escort to return to England.
He had not said as much, but she was acutely aware that
she desperately needed him, whereas he did not really
need her. It certainly put her at a distinct disadvantage,
and she was honest enough to admit that she very much
resented the fact.

She very much resented, too, having to acknowledge
that he had been right to stigmatise her dislike of him
as childish. If the truth were known, her own conscience
had begun to prick her over the attitude she had adopted
towards him on the night of the engagement party. Yes,
he had been right, curse him! Dear Helen had been rather
immature in her ways, and, although Katherine had completely forgotten the fact until he had remarked upon it,
Helen had frequently been seen in possession of the rag-
doll her mother had given to her.

One of Helen's favourite pastimes had been sewing.
She would spend hours creating fashionable outfits for
that wretched doll which she herself longed to wear. It
had created a very odd impression, all the same, to see
the toy so often in her hands.

Yes, it was little wonder that Major Ross had looked
upon Helen as a mere child, Katherine reflected, experiencing once again a pang of regret for the way she had
behaved towards him. She had been grossly at fault to
condemn him as heartless. That did not mean, of course,
that she could ever bring herself to like him. Arrogant
and overbearing, he epitomised everything she most dis-
liked in her sex. Yet somehow she was going to have to
learn to tolerate him until her feet were firmly planted
once more on British soil.

A light scratch on the door forced her to abandon her
unsettling reflections, and Katherine raised her head to

see Marie enter. She thought she detected a glimmer of sympathy in the older woman's eyes before Marie turned to the two serving-maids, bearing trays, and instructed them to enter.

Whilst the servants busied themselves placing the various dishes on the small table tucked in one corner of the bedchamber, Marie maintained a flow of inconsequential chatter, remarking that the evening had turned chilly, but that the landlord had predicted a fine day for tomorrow. She had never once forgotten the role she had been instructed to play—that of a devoted and conscientious lady's maid. She was always alert and remarkably astute, which made her obvious regard for Major Daniel Ross all the more puzzling.

Even in her own highly disturbed state, Katherine had realised by Marie's reaction to his unexpected appearance that Major Ross was none other than the man whom Sir Giles had engaged a few years before to effect Louise Baron's escape. What she quite failed to understand, however, was why Marie held the odious creature in such high esteem. It was perhaps understandable why she should retain feelings of gratitude. But she had greeted him like some long-lost friend, for heaven's sake!

Determined to have her curiosity satisfied, Katherine didn't hesitate to broach the subject the instant the servants had completed their tasks and had left them to enjoy their dinner in private.

'Major Daniel Ross.' Marie repeated the name Katherine had just divulged as though it were a benediction. 'Yes, *mademoiselle*. It was indeed he who succeeded in helping little Louise Baron,' she added after a moment's thoughtful silence.

'You evidently hold him in high regard,' Katherine

prompted when Marie turned her attention once again to the food on her plate.

'Indeed, I do, *mademoiselle*.' Marie raised her eyes to gaze at some spot behind her dinner-companion's head. 'His orders were to secure Louise's release. But he put his life at further risk by aiding me to escort her to a place of safety.'

Marie was silent whilst she subjected Katherine to a prolonged, searching stare. Then, seemingly satisfied with what she detected in the delicately featured face, she said, 'I believe I told you that the Baron family was once very wealthy. Monsieur Baron employed a steward, a man who had worked diligently for the family. Some years after her parents were killed, whilst she was residing in Paris, Justine discovered where her late father's steward and his family had fled, and it was in their care Justine wished her sister to be placed. Major Ross, as I have mentioned, ensured that we arrived at our destination safely. We should never have succeeded without him, that I know.'

'And does Louise still reside with the family?' Katherine enquired gently.

Marie nodded. 'With one of them.'

'And is she happy?'

'Oh, yes, *mademoiselle*. Within a short time she married the eldest son, Pierre, and they have now two lovely children. With the money Justine left her sister, Louise and Pierre bought a vineyard, and have prospered. I too live with them,' she added, before her gaunt features were softened by a gentle smile. 'Until you revealed it a short while ago, I never knew the real name of the man to whom we owe so much. I only ever knew him as Antoine Durand.'

Her expression suddenly turning grave, she reached

across the table to clasp Katherine's left hand. 'Set aside your differences, *petite*,' she urged gently. 'Believe me when I tell you that you could do no better than to put yourself in that man's hands. He will guard you well.'

Later, after she had changed into her night-wear, Katherine sat on the edge of the bed, and began absently to pull a brush through her long auburn tresses as she turned over in her mind what Marie had disclosed during dinner.

Yes, she could well appreciate now why the Frenchwoman thought so well of Major Ross. Yet when it had been suggested that she could do no better than to place herself in his care, she could not bring herself to agree. But why?

A bitter smile tugged at one corner of her mouth. Oh, yes, she knew well enough why she had been so willing to blame him for poor Helen's death; why she had been so contented to allow Major Daniel Ross to figure as the villain of the piece all these years. But that, she silently reminded herself, did not explain why now—now, when she had acknowledged how incredibly unjust and foolish she had been—she was still so determined to dislike him, to keep him at a distance.

It could not be denied that he possessed many of those traits she abhorred in his sex. None the less, she had been acquainted with several arrogant and dictatorial gentlemen during her lifetime, her grandfather to name but one, and she had experienced no difficulty whatsoever in tolerating their peccadilloes. So why was she so set against a more companionable relationship developing between her and the Major? After all, there was absolutely no danger at all in just liking someone. It was only when—

'Ahh, what a delightful sight! The dutiful wife remaining awake in order to welcome her lord and master
to bed.'

Katherine started so violently that the hairbrush shot
out of her hand to land on the wooden floor with a clatter. It was as much as she could do to stare in horrified
silence as the smugly smiling Major Ross entered the
room and calmly closed the door. Just how long he had
been standing there in the doorway, watching her, she
had no way of knowing, for she certainly hadn't detected
the click of the latch, but she could not fail to hear the
grating of the key now as it was turned in the lock.

'What on earth do you imagine you are doing, sir?'
she demanded in a voice which had suddenly risen by
an octave, making her sound more like a frightened child
than the self-possessed young woman she had wished to
appear.

'What the devil do you imagine I'm doing, madam
wife?' he responded, sounding distinctly bored, as he
proceeded to slip the key into the pocket of his tight-
fitting breeches. 'I am about to retire.'

For a moment Katherine was too stunned by this almost blasé pronouncement to notice that he was calmly
appraising her modest night-attire, from the ties at the
base of her throat to where her unshod feet protruded
from beneath the hem. Then she detected that unmistakable predatory gleam which she had glimpsed all too
often in recent years in many pairs of masculine eyes.

She was on her feet in an instant, almost tripping over
the edge of the rug in her haste to scramble into the robe
which she had left hanging in the wardrobe. If the sudden smile which pulled at the corners of an attractive
mouth was any indication, her actions appeared to have
afforded him no little amusement, a circumstance which

served to strengthen her resolve to be rid of his unwanted presence without delay.

'I too wish to retire, sir, so I would be obliged if you remove yourself forthwith. Anything you have to say to me can quite easily wait until morning.'

'For once we are in complete agreement, m'dear,' he announced, surprising her somewhat, but the hope that she might be rid of him so easily was swiftly dashed when he plumped himself down on the bed, and began to remove his jacket.

Katherine could only gape in astonished disbelief as cravat and waistcoat were added to the coat which he had flung over the back of the chair, and it was only when he tossed one boot into the corner of the room that the full import of his actions hit her with frightening clarity. 'You do not imagine surely that you are going to sleep in here?'

After removing his other boot and sending it the way of the first, he bent a look of mild surprise in her direction. 'Where the deuce do you suppose I'm going to sleep?'

'Anywhere but in here,' she returned, silently cursing herself for foolishly forgetting to lock the door after Marie had returned to her own room. 'I recall the landlord mentioning only yesterday that the inn is half empty now.'

'Yes, I dare say it is. Most British visitors to this city have made a bolt for the Channel ports. Why do you suppose it took me so long to get here?'

Momentarily diverted by this snippet, she asked, 'Was the journey here so very arduous? I wondered why you were delayed.'

There was more than just a hint of reproach in the glance he cast up at her this time, as though he considered her in some way to blame for the delay. 'I was left kicking my heels in Dover for twenty-four hours because of rough conditions in the Channel.'

He sounded genuinely peeved which, perversely, amused her, though she managed to suppress the wicked smile of satisfaction threatening to curl her lips.

'When I eventually arrived in Calais the *diligence* to Paris was full,' he continued in the same highly disgruntled tone, 'and I had perforce to wait two days before I could manage to acquire a seat in one of those pestilential vehicles, which I might add lost one of its wheels when we had travelled no more than twenty miles from the port. I was then compelled to put up at one of the most uncomfortable hostelries it has ever been my misfortune to enter, was refused a seat on the next coach to Paris on account of its being full, and tooled by the only driver I have ever come across who flatly refused to accept a bribe. Consequently I was obliged in the end to leave most of my belongings at the inn, purchase the landlord's misbegotten gelding, owing to the fact that he wouldn't entertain the notion of hiring it out, and then complete the journey on a horse that could not be induced to go above a sedate trot. So as you can appreciate, my dear, I am somewhat fatigued.'

'Quite understandable,' she was forced to admit, but steadfastly refused to concede more than this.

Now that she had overcome the initial shock at seeing the impertinent rogue walk brazenly into her bedchamber, Katherine found herself experiencing mere irritation at his continued presence, but certainly no fear. Which was most odd in the circumstances, considering that if he was determined to remain she would need to seek the assistance of the landlord and perhaps two burly ostlers in order to have him forcibly removed.

She swiftly decided that maybe a more tactful approach would serve her purpose better. 'All the more reason for you to enjoy a good night's rest in another room. I'm certain the landlord will be only too willing to oblige you.'

He didn't attempt to move, and merely regarded her, much as he had done earlier in the evening, as though she were some irritating and unruly child who was best ignored. Katherine succeeded in controlling her rising ire, even though with every passing second it was becoming more of an effort.

Without considering the wisdom of her actions, she moved towards him, holding out one hand. 'Give me the key at once, Major Ross!' she demanded in a voice which clearly betrayed that she was fast approaching the end of her tether, 'otherwise I shall create such a commotion that I shall rouse the entire inn.'

For a tall, powerfully built man, Daniel could move with lightning speed when he chose, a fact which Katherine was swiftly to discover to her cost. One moment she was standing with her bare feet planted firmly on polished wooden boards, and the next she was lying, supine, on the bed, arms pinned above her head. She was conscious of the stone-hard chest pressed against her breasts, and acutely aware too of the muscular leg clamped over her lower limbs, effortlessly pinioning both to the mattress.

She did not need to see the unholy gleam of satisfaction in the dark eyes staring down at her to know that she was now his prisoner, incapable of escaping. Yet, oddly enough, she felt more indignant than afraid, and thoroughly nettled for so foolishly placing herself in a position whereby she could be so effortlessly seized.

'Release me at once, you loathsome creature,' she ordered, stubbornly refusing to concede defeat, 'otherwise I shall scream my head off!'

The gleam in the dark eyes grew distinctly more ominous as he encircled her throat with one shapely hand. 'I could render you senseless in a trice, you provoking little witch,' he warned, sounding as though he would not have found the exercise wholly distasteful. 'But perhaps,' he added, his strong teeth flashing in yet another of those distinctly predatory smiles, 'there is a more effective means of ensuring your silence.'

Katherine watched those dark eyes widen fractionally as they focused on her mouth. His intent was clear, and she braced herself for the onslaught. Only for a moment, though, did she experience the punishing force of masculine lips as they clamped down over hers, successfully smothering the cry for help which too late rose in her throat; then his mouth became surprisingly gentle, exerting only sufficient pressure to induce hers to part, and evoking peculiar sensations which she was ashamed to own were not altogether unpleasant.

Although acutely aware that it would be altogether a waste of energy to attempt to free herself, and that she was completely at his mercy, she was astonished not to discover an expression of smug satisfaction over his obvious mastery when at last he released her, and hurriedly rose from the bed. No, amazingly enough, he appeared, if anything, slightly shaken and not just a little puzzled too, although his voice when he spoke was as infuriatingly self-assured and dictatorial as before.

'Let that be a lesson to you, young woman, to think long and hard before you embark on any such foolish escapades in the future.' He towered above her, arms folded across his chest, every inch the dominant male. 'It wasn't likely, I'll admit, that Sir Giles would have placed your well-being in the hands of someone whom he did not wholeheartedly trust,' he freely acknowledged. 'None the less, gentlemen do not always behave as they ought on occasions. Think yourself very lucky that I'm not disposed to ravishing innocent maidens. Nor do my tastes run to bedding sharp-tongued viragos.'

If he expected a show of gratitude for this assurance, he was doomed to disappointment. Katherine was hard put to it not to respond in kind by informing him in no uncertain terms that he was not to her taste either, but wiser counsel prevailed. She therefore contented herself with flashing him a further speaking glance, before rising from the bed and fastening her dressing gown, which at some point during his recent assault upon her had become undone.

'So you have nothing to fear from me, providing you do as you're told,' he continued, swiftly suppressing a smile as turquoise eyes favoured him with a further dagger-edged look. 'Be assured, Miss O'Malley, that I find our present situation as disagreeable as you do. Unfortunately we are supposed to be man and wife, and we have no choice but to maintain the pretence, at least for the duration of our stay in Paris. And married couples, let me remind you, are inclined to share the same room.'

The fact that the maddening creature was absolutely right did nothing to improve her state of mind, and when he calmly slid between the sheets, patting that portion of bed beside him invitingly, as though he expected her to play her part to the full, the tenuous hold she had maintained over her temper finally snapped, and she whisked the top coverlet off the bed.

He neither made the least attempt to stop her from taking it, nor, which was more infuriating still, did he offer to do the gentlemanly thing and suggest that he spend the night in one of the easy chairs by the hearth. He merely bade her an infuriating 'Goodnight,' before slipping further between the sheets.

Muttering under her breath, Katherine went about the airy chamber extinguishing the candles. For all his protestations to the contrary, she strongly suspected that Major Ross was attaining much amusement out of her evident discomfiture in having to share this room with him.

She shook her head, marvelling at her own stupidity. How on earth she could have imagined that there was the remotest possibility of her ever liking him she would never know. Without doubt he was the most maddening, detestable creature it had ever been her misfortune to meet!

Chapter Six

The following morning, when finally she had managed to prise open her eyelids a fraction, Katherine felt as if she had taken a punishing tumble from a horse. There didn't seem to be an inch of her that didn't ache abominably, and her poor back felt as if it might break if she attempted to move. Discovering bright morning sunlight surprisingly streaming through the bedchamber window did little to improve her overall discomfort, and she swiftly closed her eyes against the sun's smarting rays, but was prompted to open just one again a moment later when she clearly detected a strange rasping sound emanating from the general direction of the washstand in the corner of the room.

'Oh, God!' she groaned, when at last she had brought that nightmarish figure dragging a razor across its chin into focus, and her one and only hope that the events of the evening before had all been some fiendish bad dream had been wholly dashed.

The muttered exclamation carried, and Daniel paused in his shaving to stare through the mottled glass on the washstand at his companion's pained expression. A few minutes before, whilst still soundly asleep, she had looked utterly adorable, with those auburn locks in enchanting disarray framing her lovely face. It was quite evident that her mood had not improved to any significant degree during the night hours, and he could not in truth say that he was in the least surprised. The winged-chair might be comfortable enough to sit in for an hour or two of an evening, but it hadn't been fashioned to afford its occupant a good night's repose.

He managed with precious little effort to suppress a smile, but was not nearly so successful in ignoring that imp of pure devilment which induced him to say, 'Good morning, sweetheart. I trust you slept well?'

The darts of antipathy discharged from the depths of turquoise-coloured eyes very nearly sent him into whoops of laughter and in grave danger of taking a slice off his chin with the razor. Controlling himself with an effort, he glanced at her again through the mirror before concentrating on his own reflection. She was a termagant, right enough, stubborn and headstrong, and not every man's idea of a comfortable companion. Yet, in truth, he could not be sorry that she did possess an abundance of spirit, for he very much feared that she would require every ounce of mettle she possessed if they were to come through this venture unscathed.

Deciding to keep these reflections to himself for the time being at least, he concentrated on preparing himself for the day ahead. When at last he had arranged his cravat neatly about his neck, he slipped on his jacket, and turned at last to face her.

'There is sufficient hot water left in the pitcher to cater for your needs,' he remarked, successfully bringing to an end what appeared to be her idle contemplation of the dead ashes in the hearth. 'I'll go downstairs and order breakfast. You'll feel better for having some food inside you.'

His considerate gesture to leave her to undertake her toilette in private did little to alleviate Katherine's disgruntled mood, and she darted yet another vitriolic glare in his direction. 'My spirits are only ever likely to improve, Major Ross, when we part company... permanently.'

His lips twitched. 'Believe me, m'dear, it would afford me the utmost pleasure to oblige you. Unfortunately I'm unable to do so, at least not for several days.' He made to move across to the door, then checked and looked down at her again, a frown between his eyes. 'Let me hear you say something in French. Say anything you like to me.'

How Katherine wished her command of the language was such that she could do precisely that by consigning him comprehensively to the devil! Unfortunately it was not and she had to be satisfied with telling him politely to withdraw immediately, to which his response was to utter a protracted groan and clap a hand over his eyes.

'Dear God! Bath seminary French! Marie was right— you would never pass for a Frenchwoman in a million years!' He removed his hand to bestow a faintly exasperated look upon her. 'None the less, we must strive to maintain the pretence of a happily married French couple as best we can. Meet me downstairs when you're ready. You cannot remain skulking in the bedchamber now that your husband is here to protect you. We'll eat in the coffee-room. But kindly leave all the talking to me.'

'Insufferable oaf!' Katherine couldn't resist muttering the instant he had departed.

'I heard that,' a deep voice informed her from the other side of the door.

Aches and pains instantly forgotten, Katherine flew out of the chair to lock the door. From what sounded suspiciously like a rumble of deep masculine laughter floating down the length of the passageway outside the room, she strongly suspected that his sharp ears had also detected the grating sound of the key turning in the lock. The confounded man had the acute senses of a cat! And could move as silently as a feline too! She would have sworn she had been awake throughout most of that wretchedly uncomfortable night, striving to combat the very natural desire to part company with the Major at the earliest opportunity, and yet in all honesty she could not say she had heard him return the key to the lock.

She turned her attention to her small trunk, which had sat in the corner of the room since her arrival at the inn. Nothing would have afforded her more satisfaction than to begin to re-pack it at this very moment with her belongings, and persuade Marie to accompany her at least as far as Calais. Her wretched conscience, however, simply wouldn't permit her to attempt this course of action. She had pledged to do all she could to help Sir Giles in his endeavours to unmask that British traitor who had eluded him for several years. So she must strive, somehow, to overcome her quite understandable antipathy and collaborate with the Major. Their mission was the important thing, not her disinclination to work with someone whom she found an utter bane, and she must never lose sight of this fact, she reminded herself.

Consequently she swiftly made use of the pitcher's remaining contents, and after dressing herself in one of her modest, high-necked day dresses and arranging her hair in a neat chignon, she made her way down the stairs to the coffee-room, where she discovered the Major seated at the table by the window, staring intently out at the street.

Not surprisingly he detected her light footfall almost at once, and rose from the chair to place his lips lightly on one cheek before Katherine could do anything to avoid the fleeting contact with that much too attractive masculine mouth. She would have derived a deal of pleasure from stamping on one of those large feet encased in boots that since the previous night had received a polish, but as there were several other patrons present she refrained and merely betrayed her resentment of the chaste salute by flashing a speaking glance, which he blithely ignored.

As this was the first time she had eaten downstairs since her arrival at the inn, Katherine gazed about her with interest, and although the Major maintained a flow of conversation to which she only needed to contribute the occasional 'yes' or 'no', she did notice his attention straying as the meal wore on, his keen gaze alternating between a spot beyond the window, quite outside her own field of vision, and a certain area in the coffee-room beyond her left shoulder.

She realised at once that something was not quite to his liking, and was not unduly surprised, after they had both eaten their fill, that he seemed disinclined to linger. 'I fear, my dear, that I must leave you to your own devices this morning,' he remarked in a carrying voice, which the bearded man seated alone at the table nearest the door must surely have heard. 'I have an appointment with my bankers, so I'm afraid we must delay our departure until tomorrow. Annoying, I know, but it cannot be helped.'

Had Katherine not known that the Major was acting the part of the loving, considerate husband, she might have supposed the smile of gentle warmth he bestowed upon her as they made their way towards the stairs was perfectly genuine. 'Why not enjoy a last spending spree and treat yourself to a new bonnet?' he suggested. 'It might be some little time before we have a chance to visit Paris again, my love, so take advantage of a last browse round the shops.'

After accompanying her back up the stairs, he followed her into the bedchamber, where he remained only for the time it took to collect his outdoor garments. Then, without uttering anything further, not even a word of farewell, he left her, closing the door quietly behind him.

Katherine clearly detected a murmur of voices from the room adjoining her own, which Marie had occupied throughout their time at the inn. She could not hear precisely what was being said, and even if she could she doubted very much whether she would have understood half of what was being uttered, because the conversation quite naturally was being conducted in rapid French. Even so, there certainly seemed an urgency about the whispered exchanges.

Some few minutes elapsed before she heard a firm tread along the passageway, and several minutes more before she saw, from her bedchamber window, Major Ross leave the inn, and set off at a brisk pace towards the centre of the city. Almost at once a figure emerged from one of the doorways on the opposite side of the street and made off in the same direction. Mere coincidence, or something more sinister? She could not help wondering.

Her faintly troubled thoughts were interrupted by a knock on the door, and a moment later Marie entered, dressed in her outdoor clothes. 'Ah, *madame*!' she announced cheerfully, immediately perceiving Katherine by the window. 'Your husband has instructed me to bear you company in your quest for a new bonnet. How lucky you are, *madame*, to have such a generous husband and one who, moreover, panders to a lady's every whim.'

Katherine's response to this piece of arrant nonsense was to give vent to an unladylike snort of derision. She couldn't help thinking that poor Marie was allowing those lingering feelings of gratitude to cloud her judgement when it came to assessing Major Ross's true character.

She chose not to argue when it was suggested that it might be wise to don her heavy, fur-lined cloak before venturing out on what promised to be a very mild, almost spring-like day. Nor did she attempt to discover why Marie should consider it essential for her to place all the funds in her possession, enough to purchase a dozen dresses, let alone bonnets, in her reticule before setting off. It was only after they had left the inn, and Marie for once chose to dawdle along the streets, while maintaining an inexhaustible flow of small talk that Katherine began to suspect her companion had a very good reason for behaving in such an uncharacteristic way.

This suspicion was confirmed when, idly glancing in a shop window, she happened to catch sight of the man who, earlier that morning, had been seated alone at a table in the coffee room. His grey hair and beard suggested that he was not in the first flush of youth, and yet his gait was remarkably sprightly, and his hard, dark eyes, she noticed, before he stopped to study the goods on display in another shop window, appeared youthfully clear and direct.

'Marie, am I imagining things, or are we being followed?'

Katherine feared the worst when her companion's fixed smile began to crack. 'Yes, *petite*,' Marie admitted, as they continued their stroll. She did not, however, attempt to quicken her pace. 'Major Ross suspected that there were people watching the inn. But do not be afraid. He is at this very moment organising your removal from the city. All we need do is successfully lose our shadow. And I believe I know how this can be achieved. Endeavour, *petite*, to behave normally, and on no account be tempted to keep checking if he is still behind us.'

Resisting the temptation to glance over her shoulder proved to be more difficult than Katherine might have imagined. Strangely enough, though, she did not feel alarmed; in fact, she felt more intrigued than anything else, wondering how the traitor's henchmen had managed to locate their whereabouts.

Of course she realised that Sir Giles had intended to make it known that he had managed to discover the whereabouts of Justine Baron's sister, and that Louise would be travelling to London under an assumed name. It was also possible that Sir Giles had made it known that the person whom he had engaged to escort Louise to England would be adopting the role of her husband. But what had made them suspect that she might be Justine's sister? Did she truly bear such a strong resemblance to the Baron sisters?

This might possibly be the reason, Katherine supposed. Yet it still did not account for the fact that the traitor's associates had managed to locate her so easily. Paris was littered with inns. It would take some considerable time to visit them all in order to search for their quarry. Had it been pure chance which had prompted them to stumble upon the inn at which she and the Major were putting up?

Marie's unexpected exclamation of delight induced Katherine to abandon her puzzling conjecture for the present, and she turned her attention to the creation in the shop window which appeared to be holding Marie so enraptured. She suspected at once that there was something more to her companion's display of enthusiasm, and so offered no resistance when Marie insisted on entering the premises in order to view the fussily adorned bonnet more closely.

No sooner had they stepped over the threshold to find the establishment surprisingly empty except for one sales assistant than Marie's demeanour changed dramatically. She insisted upon seeing the proprietress, and after a few moments' haranguing the young assistant was persuaded to go in search of her mistress.

Not appearing best pleased at having her daily routine disrupted, the *modiste*, like a fearsome Amazon prepared to do battle, suddenly appeared between the plush red velvet curtains. Surprisingly enough, however, after one startled glance of recognition, she clasped Marie to her ample curves, for all the world as if she were some long-lost bosom friend.

A hurried and whispered exchange swiftly followed, the result of which had Madame throwing up her hands in a despairing gesture, casting a sympathetic glance in Katherine's direction and voicing the fervent hope that all hardhearted males would suffer the torment of eternal perdition.

Although faintly puzzled by this pronouncement, Katherine didn't hesitate to follow the *modiste* when she beckoned imperiously with one podgy, beringed hand. Having once passed between the velvet curtains, she found herself in a dimly lit passageway, from which, she swiftly discovered, one gained access to an enclosed, narrow yard.

Extracting a bunch of keys from the pocket of her severe black gown, Madame unlocked the gate set in the high, stone wall, and then surprised Katherine again somewhat by enveloping her in her plump arms.

'You may place your trust in Madame Pérot, *petite*. I shall send that fool who follows about his business if he should dare to enter my shop,' she announced, before utterly confounding Katherine by adding, 'Now go, *petite*. And God speed! You shall soon be safe in the arms of your lover.'

Before Katherine could gather her wits together sufficiently to demand of Madame precisely what she meant, Marie grasped one of her wrists and, after checking no one was lurking in the alleyway beyond the gate, commenced to lead the way hurriedly along a series of narrow, twisting streets. It was only when they eventually arrived at a much wider thoroughfare, running parallel to the Seine, that Marie slackened her pace.

Finding herself in a part of the city where she had never ventured before, Katherine looked about with interest, but eventually her mind returned to the brief encounter with that larger-than-life *modiste*. That Marie was well acquainted with Madame Pérot was obvious. What wasn't quite so clear was what she had imparted during that hurried and whispered exchange which had taken place in the shop.

Curiosity got the better of her at last and she found herself asking, 'How long have you been acquainted with Madame Pérot, Marie?'

'Do you not recall my mentioning that Justine Baron worked for one of Paris's most fashionable dressmakers, *petite*? That was Madame Pérot. She was fond of Justine.

She admired very much her spirit. After I returned to France, I kept in touch.'

That, of course, explained why Madame Pérot didn't hesitate to offer her aid, Katherine mused. It did not, however, explain Madame's curious parting words. 'What did you tell her about me?'

Marie's harsh features were once again transformed by one of those endearing smiles. 'I told her you were my new mistress, and that you had been very good and kind to me.'

'And?' Katherine prompted, when she surprised a mischievous glint in those world-weary eyes.

'I told her you had fallen deeply in love with the most brave and charming man, but that your papa stubbornly opposed the match. I told her you had been forbidden to leave the house, and had been denied all contact with the man you love, so you had been given no alternative but to agree to an elopement. Unfortunately your papa, guessing what you might do—'

'Stop! Stop!' Katherine beseeched her, both amused and slightly resentful at being cast as one of those idiotic, lovelorn heroines too frequently found between the covers of those books to which her companion, Miss Mountjoy, seemed addicted. 'I believe I can guess the rest.'

Katherine cast the woman beside her a fond smile. Undoubtedly in the normal course of events they would have viewed each other as enemies. Yet Fate had decreed that their paths should cross in exceptional circumstances and, even though their countries were probably in imminent danger of once again being at war, she and Marie had, against all the odds, become friends. How Katherine wished that Marie was in truth her companion,

for she doubted she could ever find one to suit her half
so well.

'You have the most fertile imagination, Marie,' she
could not resist telling her. 'And you are the most convincing liar to boot! I dare swear that Madame Pérot
believed every word of your ridiculous tale!'

'But, *petite*, it was not a complete lie,' Marie pro-
tested. 'I am taking you to a gentleman who is both
brave and charming, and you are about to fly with him
far away from Paris.'

This succeeded in wiping the fond smile off Katherine's face. Foolishly, up until that moment, the fact that
it would be impossible to return to the inn simply hadn't
occurred to her. But of course they could not! There was
bound to be someone watching the inn, awaiting their
return.

'Will you be accompanying us?' she asked, clinging
to the faint hope that she might rely on Marie's unfailing
support at least until they reached one of the French
ports, but deep down knowing what the answer would
be even before she detected the slight shake of her
trusted companion's head.

'No, *petite*. Major Ross does not need the added burden of taking care of me too.' She shrugged. 'Besides,
there is no need. I shall be perfectly safe. I know this
city well. I have several friends here and can hide myself
easily enough until I find some means to travel south.'

They turned off the main thoroughfare into yet another of Paris's many side roads to discover a one-horse
gig waiting halfway down the street, and an unmistakable tall figure standing beside the decidedly battered
conveyance.

Katherine felt the touch of fingers on her arm, and
turned to see a look of mingled concern and affection in

grey eyes. 'My task is almost complete, *petite*. But yours has only just begun. Do not allow your dislike of Major Ross to prompt you into foolish actions,' she advised in an urgent whisper. 'Do what he tells you and I have every faith that you will come through this unscathed.'

The advice had been kindly meant, and Katherine refrained from dismissing it out of hand. Even so, she was not prepared to commit herself. 'I have never made a promise which I thought I would be unable to keep, Marie, and I do not intend to begin by doing so now. But be assured that I shall not go out of my way to make difficulties, and shall, as far as possible, attempt to work with Major Ross and not against him.'

Even though Katherine had meant every word, resentment at his behaviour the night before remained and she could not bring herself, when at last they approached him, to acknowledge his presence with more than a cursory nod of the head.

Daniel regarded the frigid set of delicate features for a moment before turning his attention to the older woman. 'As you are late, Marie, I assume that you also were followed.'

'Yes, *monsieur*. It was as you suspected—there were two of them watching the inn. We managed to shake off our shadow, as you evidently did yours.'

'It might not be so easy next time, should they locate us again,' Daniel warned. 'I do not doubt that before too long there will be others scouring the streets of Paris for us. So we must not delay.' He reached for her fingers, and held them briefly. 'You are an old hand at this game, Marie, so you need no advice from me, save to say, God speed. If the outcome of this venture should prove successful, I shall ensure that you are apprised of the fact.'

Daniel refused to linger over protracted farewells, and

gave Katherine only sufficient time to receive a surprisingly warm embrace from the older woman, and then placed his hand under her elbow, giving her no choice but to take her seat in the gig.

'You have evidently found favour in the austere Marie's eyes, Miss O'Malley,' he remarked, after Katherine, peering round the side of the gig, had watched Marie turn and walk back along the narrow street.

'For several days she remained aloof,' she admitted, faintly relieved that he considered it safe enough to converse in their own language. 'Gradually, though, she became more friendly,' she went on, wondering if there was the remotest possibility that their relationship might follow a similar course. She did not hold out much hope, but was determined to keep the hostility which lingered towards him under control. 'I quickly grew very fond of her. She took very good care of me.'

'As I fully intend to do, Miss O'Malley.'

Out of the corner of his eye, Daniel noticed the suspicious glance she cast him, as he turned the gig into a much wider thoroughfare. Yes, she was certainly wary of him, and he was forced silently to own that, after his behaviour last night, perhaps there was good reason for her caution. Undoubtedly she was as innocent now as she had been on the day of her birth, a gently nurtured, chaste young woman. Which made her willingness to involve herself in such a perilous venture all the more mystifying, for he felt sure that she must have been aware from the start that there would be more than just an element of risk involved. From something her aunt had disclosed on the night of the engagement party, he had gained the distinct impression that Miss O'Malley was, if not extremely wealthy, a young woman of comfortable means, so he doubted very much, as Sir Giles himself had intimated, that the prospect of attaining a substantial reward would have played any part in her decision to become involved.

He was intrigued, and was determined to discover precisely what had persuaded her to embark on such an undertaking, but decided not to attempt to satisfy his curiosity at this juncture. Instead, he chose to be brutally frank about their present situation, and could not help but feel a deal of admiration for the calm way she accepted the unpleasant state of affairs.

'Yes, I had already realised that returning to the inn was out of the question,' she admitted, before a slight frown marred the perfection of her forehead. 'I wonder what made them suspect us?'

As Katherine kept her eyes firmly fixed in the direction they were heading, she missed completely the frowning glance he cast the errant curls showing beneath the rim of her fashionable bonnet. 'A pity really,' she went on. 'During my many ventures with Marie about the city during the past couple of weeks, I purchased several items of clothing, one of which was a rather pretty day dress.' Her faint sigh betrayed slight resentment over the garment's loss. Then she shrugged. 'The poor landlord is more out of pocket. We cannot even return to pay him for our food and board.'

'Save your pity, Kate. If I know anything, the old rogue will sell your belongings to recoup his losses.'

'Yes, I expect you're—' She caught herself up abruptly, when at last she had digested fully his every word. 'I cannot recall giving you permission to address me by my given name, Major Ross.' There was no response. If the slight twitch she perceived at the corner of his mouth was any indication, however, it was quite evident that he would take no account at all of her disapproval. She had no wish for them to be at odds at this early stage in the proceedings, and so reluctantly decided to compromise. 'But if you must resort to making free with my Christian name, you'll oblige me by calling me Katherine and not Kate. I only ever permit my personal maid to address me in that fashion.'

'Why, don't you like it?'

'I much prefer Katherine.'

He didn't attempt to hide his surprise. 'I think Kate's a pretty name, myself. Besides, it suits you. My name is Daniel, by the way. People will persist in still calling me Major, but it's a courtesy title only.'

'I'm aware of that, Major Ross.' She had not meant to sound quite so frigid, so haughtily formal. Yet it was as well that he should be made aware at the outset that she had no intention of allowing a friendlier relationship to develop between them, she told herself, while at the same time wondering why, perversely, she should feel piqued because he made no attempt whatsoever to persuade her to use his given name.

Katherine's thoughts were soon turned in a new direction when she became aware, a few minutes later, that the road they were using to leave the capital was not the one by which she had arrived in the city almost three weeks before.

'We are not making for Calais,' Daniel responded in answer to her question. 'I would be very surprised if there were not already people stationed at each of the major Channel ports awaiting our arrival. Just as I suspect that, now we've been—er—rumbled, as it were, there will very soon be those posted on every major road leaving the city on the lookout for us.'

This immediately called to mind her earlier thoughts. How on earth had they managed to arouse suspicion?

Apart from passing the time of day when venturing out of the inn in order to take a little daily exercise, she and Marie had not fraternised with the other people putting up at that hostelry. Daniel had arrived only yesterday. So when and how had they managed to betray themselves?

He shrugged one broad shoulder when she echoed her puzzling thoughts aloud. 'We don't know what Sir Giles saw fit to reveal. I suspect he would have disclosed enough information into certain receptive ears to ensure that our trail wouldn't be hard to follow. Of course, he hadn't bargained for the surprising turn of events which have overtaken us. By this time he would have expected to have had you safely back in London. The traitor must have viewed Napoleon's escape from Elba as nothing short of a godsend. It has offered him ample time to instigate a search for you.'

'True. But why on earth did those two men watching the inn suspect that I might be Louise Baron? Do I resemble her so closely?'

Brown eyes regarded her quite dispassionately for a moment or two. 'As far as I can remember—yes, there is a certain similarity. And of course you're about the right age. It's quite possible that Justine herself might have disclosed certain facts about her sister to the traitor during the time she worked with him. And you do have red hair.'

'Ah, I see!' Katherine could now appreciate just why Sir Giles had chosen her for the task. 'So Louise has red hair?'

'Yes, and so too did Justine Baron, although, if my memory serves me correctly, theirs was somewhat lighter than yours—more Titian.'

Katherine nodded. 'Red hair frequently runs in families, although it is not always the case.' She was silent for a moment, then revealed her disappointment at the unexpected turn of events by releasing her breath in a despondent sigh. 'Poor Sir Giles. Napoleon's escape couldn't possibly have come at a worse time for him.'

'It couldn't have come at a worse time for us, come to that,' Daniel reminded her, smiling to himself.

Their present situation was anything but rosy, and he suspected the young woman seated beside him knew this very well. It was, he mused, much to her credit that she had accepted the loss of her belongings and this impromptu flight from the capital with a quaint and dignified resignation, and he couldn't help but admire her for this present display of admirable self-control. Whether she would continue to behave in such a commendable manner during the days ahead was another matter entirely. He very much feared that, should the mood take her, she could prove to be a handful, fiery and stubborn. One thing was certain, though, during the next few days he was unlikely to be afflicted by the boredom which, unfortunately, all too frequently plagued him when in the company of most members of her sex for any length of time.

'Ideally I would have preferred to remain at the inn for a few days,' he remarked, surprising her somewhat. 'Those men watching us would in all probability have dropped their guard had we gone about the city displaying a lack of concern. Unfortunately, that was not possible with the Corsican on the loose once more. Last night I learned that Napoleon is not coming up against much resistance as he heads towards the capital. All he needs is to win the support of the army, then I'm afraid...'

'Do you think that is possible?' she prompted when his voice trailed away.

'I very much fear that it is, Miss O'Malley. His soldiers love him.'

'Oh, that wretched little man!' Katherine exclaimed, able to express her feelings more fully now than she had when in Marie's company. 'After all these years of conflict, has he not had enough of war? God forbid that it begins again!'

'Amen to that, m'dear,' he concurred, as they approached the outskirts of the city, and he turned his attention to what was going on about him, watching intently for any suspicious characters loitering by the roadside. He noticed no one, but he refused to be lulled into a false sense of security, for he very much feared that before the end of the day there would be someone, or possibly several, hot on their trail.

Fortunately his companion, continuing to behave with commendable restraint, didn't plague him with questions that he could not or might prefer not to answer. She didn't bore him to tears by trying to maintain a flow of small talk either. In fact, apart from generously praising him for his foresight in providing them with a basket of food, tucked away under the seat, she said very little, not even when they were obliged to stop on several occasions throughout the day in order to rest the horse. Only when, early in the evening, he turned off the main highway into a narrow country lane did she betray an interest in precisely where they were bound.

'Normandy.' Daniel didn't hesitate to enlighten her, and Katherine, in turn, didn't attempt to hide her surprise. 'I have a good friend living there.' His lips curled into a secretive little smile. 'I know I can rely on this person to aid us. Needless to say I do not expect to reach the town where my friend resides tomorrow, or the day after, come to that. So, in the meantime, we must make do as best we can. I'm afraid, though, that you are not going to find this journey particularly comfortable.'

'Do not concern yourself over me, Major Ross,' Katherine responded, feeling unaccountably resentful because he no doubt considered her some pampered ninnyhammer who couldn't do without her creature comforts for a few days. 'I cannot deny that I had not planned to leave Paris in such a fashion, but I do not hold you in any way responsible for that. Be assured that I shall do my utmost not to be a burden, and have no intention of causing you the least concern.'

She turned her head in time to catch a second rather secretive little smile playing about his mouth before he astounded her by admitting, 'You have been causing me no little concern for quite some time, Miss Katherine O'Malley.'

Before she could enquire precisely what he had meant, he changed the subject by informing her that he dared not risk putting up at an inn that night.

'I do not doubt that there are those already hot on our trail,' he continued. 'I strongly suspect that they will begin by searching for us in the inns along the main road we have just left. Which will buy us a little time, but not very much, I'm afraid. It will be dark in an hour, so we must find some form of shelter soon, for I have no intention of travelling at night and running the risk of getting us lost.'

It was then that he caught sight of billowing smoke in the distance, and turned off the road on to a deeply rutted track. 'There is some form of dwelling just up ahead, possibly a farm. With any luck there might be a village nearby. I'll have a scout around and see what I can find.'

Just for a second she thought she glimpsed a flicker of unease in his expression, before he handed her the reins and then jumped to the ground. 'Can you by any chance handle firearms, Miss O'Malley?'

'Yes, Major, I can,' she assured him. 'My father taught me, though not since I lived with my grandfather have I used one.'

Even in the rapidly fading light she could easily detect the glint of amusement in his eyes, and what might have been a hint of respect too. 'In that case I shall leave this in your care,' he announced, delving into the pocket of his cloak and drawing out a pistol. 'Do not hesitate to use it if you feel at all threatened.' There was a flash of white teeth. 'But I would be grateful if you do not mistake me for one of our pursuers. I shall give a low whistle to announce my return, just to be on the safe side.'

It was as much as Katherine could do to suppress an angry retort, and yet the instant he disappeared from view she experienced fear for the very first time since setting out on what she was now beginning to view as a madcap venture. Given the choice, she might not have wished Major Daniel Ross to have been designated her protector. There wasn't a doubt in her mind that he would continue to irk her unbearably during the days ahead. Yet she was forced to own that she experienced a most comfortable feeling of security when he was near, which was singularly lacking now.

She shivered and drew the rug that the Major had had the forethought to supply more closely about her legs. She was already feeling the loss of warmth which that large, muscular frame so close to her own had provided throughout what had been a mercifully dry day. She could only place her faith in the Major to find them some form of shelter, for she certainly didn't relish the prospect of spending a night under the stars.

A rustling sound emanating from the small clump of trees off to her left caught her attention, and she instinctively felt for the pistol which she had placed on the seat beside her. She derived a modicum of comfort from having the lethally formed piece of metal clasped firmly in her hand, but she couldn't deny that it was no substitute for a certain someone's presence.

A further noise reached her ears, then another and another, each sounding much closer and more menacing than the last. She had never been afraid of the dark, not since she was a child, but as dusk arrived, she came perilously close to crying out in relief when at last she detected that low whistle.

No one would have supposed for a moment that she was overjoyed to see him, least of all Daniel himself, when he finally clambered up beside her again, and she demanded to know where he had been and why it had taken him so long to return.

Strong teeth flashed more brilliantly in the dark when he turned his head to bestow a wicked grin upon her. 'Did you miss me, sweetheart?'

'I certainly did not enjoy being on my—' Stopping mid-sentence for the second time that day, Katherine favoured him with an angry look, her eyes flashing no less brilliantly than his smile. 'And don't call me sweetheart, you impudent rogue!'

She could feel that comforting frame shaking with suppressed laughter as he reached for the reins. 'It's a relief to know your spirit hasn't deserted you completely, Miss O'Malley. And I apologise for taking so long, but at least I was successful in my endeavours.

There is a village a couple of miles up the road. So you'll no doubt be relieved to know you shall attain at least a modicum of comfort this night.'

Katherine was beginning to feel so weary after the many hours they had spent travelling that she would have been quite happy to sleep on a dirt floor. Daniel swiftly proved he was able to offer her something more comfortable than that, however, when they reached the outskirts of the village and he drew the gig to a halt outside a blacksmith's premises.

After a swift glance up and down the deserted street to ensure that no one was about, he jumped nimbly down from the gig. Katherine saw him extract something from his pocket, and was rather surprised to see the large wooden door swing wide a few moments later. She succeeded in curbing her curiosity until they were safely inside and Daniel had provided further evidence of his resourcefulness by finding a lamp and lighting it.

'How on earth did you manage to remove that padlock, Major Ross?' she demanded to know, making herself useful by releasing the horse from its harness and leading the gelding into a stall.

After draping a piece of sacking over the one and only grimy window, Daniel satisfied her curiosity by extracting a cunningly fashioned thin piece of metal from the pocket of his jacket which, even in the dim light, she had little difficulty in recognising, for she clearly recalled being shown such an article several years before by a casual labourer who had worked for her father for a very short time.

Although she arched one fine brow, Katherine refrained from comment, and merely turned her attention once again to the gelding who was happily champing away on a substantial pile of hay. 'You are certainly no fiery steed, and definitely not in the first flush of youth, but you did us proud this day, old fellow.'

Daniel noted the affectionate way she both stroked and spoke to the animal. Evidently fear of horses was not one of her weaknesses, even if a dislike of the dark was. 'I'm afraid he and the gig were all I could manage to find in so short a time. I couldn't afford to be choosy.'

'You did very well in the circumstances,' she responded, surprising him somewhat by the mild praise. 'He's certainly strong and healthy, and has been well cared for.'

'Evidently you know something of horseflesh, Miss O'Malley,' he remarked, collecting the basket of food and rug from the gig, before lowering himself on the mound of hay piled in one corner of the stone building. 'We'll finish off the food and then get some sleep. We must be away from here at first light.'

Hunger swiftly overcame her understandable wariness, and Katherine joined him on the pile of hay, reflecting as she did so that this was the first time in her life that she had ever sought refuge in a smithy. She had no cause to complain though, she reminded herself, gazing absently at the fire, the ashes of which still retained sufficient heat to take the chill off the air. The bread and cheese might be simple fare, but it was wholesome, and her surroundings, though hardly palatial, certainly provided sufficient comfort and warmth.

The instant she had consumed the last mouthful of bread, Daniel rose to his knees and began to spread the rug over the hay. 'Come, let us settle ourselves for sleep. As I mentioned earlier, we must be away at first light, before the owner of this establishment turns up for work,' he remarked, before he noticed her staring down at the cover as though it were a hot bed of coals, and best avoided.

His lips twitched. 'What is the matter, sweetheart? Don't you trust me?'

Katherine transferred her gaze to those dark eyes glinting with sheer devilment. 'Let me assure you, Major Ross, that I consider it immensely difficult to trust a man who carries a picklock about his person.'

'Vixen!' he exclaimed, laughing in spite of the fact that he experienced a twinge of resentment because she obviously continued to mistrust him.

But perhaps he had given her reason enough to continue to remain a little aloof, he reminded himself, wrapping his cloak about him and settling himself on the hay at a discreet distance away from the rug. His behaviour towards her the previous night could hardly be described as that of a gentleman, though it had to be said in his defence that she had sorely tried his patience, and badly needed someone to take her in hand. Undoubtedly she had been allowed far too much licence to do and say exactly as she pleased. She wasn't spoilt, precisely, but was certainly accustomed to having her own way. Yet today he had glimpsed certain facets to her character that he couldn't help but admire. Blessedly her tongue did not run on wheels and she betrayed no signs of succumbing to a fit of the vapours if subjected to hardship. All in all, he was beginning to feel that Sir Giles Osborne, the cunning old rogue, had chosen well when he had selected Miss Katherine O'Malley for this venture. She might be an infuriating little madam on occasions, but by heaven she had certainly proved equal to the task thus far!

'I'm sorry, Kate, what did you say?' he asked, suddenly realising that she had spoken.

'I said—what's that noise?'

For a second or two all he could hear was the gelding contentedly champing away on the hay, then he clearly detected a scratching sound somewhere off to his left. 'A rat, I should imagine.'

'Heaven spare us!' he heard her mutter before she edged a little closer. 'And don't call me Kate!'

Daniel's response was merely to blow out the lamp, and then settle himself for sleep.

Chapter Seven

Although uncertain quite what had disturbed him, Daniel was suddenly wide awake and very conscious of something soft lying against him, and something softer still tickling his chin. Even in the dim light of early morning he could clearly see long tendrils of hair stretching across his chest and instinctively raised one hand to twist several of the gently curling strands round one finger; then just as quickly he released them and carefully edged himself away, before his suddenly aroused body tempted him to take further liberties, which at this early stage in their relationship would, he felt sure, be met with fierce resistance. The last thing he desired was for his soundly sleeping companion's understandable wariness to deepen into fear. No, it was her complete trust he must win, then maybe…

Refusing to allow his thoughts to dwell on what hopefully would be the very satisfactory outcome to a closer relationship developing between them, Daniel carefully raised himself on one elbow in order to study the perfect arrangement of delicate features now framed in a tussled mass of fiery curls: the small straight nose, the infinitely kissable and perfectly moulded lips above a determined little chin, which tended to lift so stubbornly on occasions. Undeniably she was a most desirable young woman, beautifully packaged and utterly feminine. Which made her single state rather puzzling, though he strongly suspected that this was entirely through choice.

He detected the slight movement of ridiculously long, curling lashes, and a moment later those striking turquoise orbs were gazing up at him rather wonderingly, before a suspicious frown drew finely arched, dark brows together.

'What on earth do you imagine you are doing hovering over me like some ravenous bird of prey, about to swoop, Major Ross?' she demanded to know.

'Spot on form again, I see.' Shaking his head in disbelief, Daniel rose to his feet. 'How is it possible, I ask myself, for someone to appear so beautifully angelic in sleep and yet possess the tongue of an adder?'

Katherine satisfied herself with flashing him an angry look, which only succeeded in igniting a rumble of masculine laughter. With narrowed eyes, she watched him walk over to the window and remove the piece of sacking. Tongue like an adder, indeed! She inwardly fumed. He had a crass nerve to criticise her when he wasn't above uttering some barbed remark himself! she decided, scrambling to her feet and giving her cloak a vigorous shake.

'You haven't time to concern yourself over your dishevelled state,' Daniel told her bluntly, turning in time to see her attempting to make use of the few pins that remained in her hair. 'We cannot risk being found here by the blacksmith when he arrives. Which, if I know anything, will be quite soon. It's already daybreak.'

Although she prided herself on her appearance, and never set forth unless perfectly groomed, Katherine appreciated that attempting to make herself presentable was hardly important in the circumstances, and merely thrust her reticule into her cloak pocket before swirling the fur-lined garment about her shoulders once more.

'As you appear to have a way with horses, sweet Kate, perhaps you'd be good enough to collect our trusted steed from the stall so that I can hitch him up to the gig?' Daniel requested, and received his second dagger-look of the morning.

'Willingly, Major Ross…and don't call me Kate!'

Grinning wickedly, he occupied himself, while Katherine went to do his bidding, by plumping up the pile of hay to hide all evidence of two people having used it as a bed. With his back towards it, he didn't notice the large wooden door open a fraction. Katherine too was oblivious to the fact that an unkempt rascal was stealthily entering, or that three equally villainous rogues were at their compatriot's heels. The first indication she had that they were no longer alone was when a shot rang out, by which time it was already too late to scream out a warning.

Katherine saw Daniel extract the pistol from his pocket and with unerring accuracy dispose of one of the intruders, before the other three, on him in a trice, knocked him to the ground, raining a barrage of kicks and blows down on him. Hidden by the gelding, Katherine looked wildly about for some weapon, and her frantic gaze swiftly fell upon a solid piece of wood. Without the least concern for her own safety, she joined in the fray, felling one of the attackers with a single blow to the head before anyone knew she was there.

'You damnable coward!' she screamed, delivering such a powerful blow to yet another assailant that he dropped the weapon he had been wielding, and made for the door with all possible speed, screaming in agony as he clutched his right arm.

Showing no mercy, Katherine scooped up the unwieldy firearm and gave chase like some avenging virago out for blood; while Daniel, having by this time managed to rise to his feet, easily disposed of the last attacker with a well-aimed blow to the jaw. He then turned in time to see Katherine, using both hands, striving to level the heavy weapon. Before he could yell out a warning, her finger had squeezed the trigger. There was the most almighty report, and a moment later, appearing dazed and not just a little embarrassed, she was sitting plump in the middle of the village street.

Galvanised, Daniel was beside her in an instant, demanding to know whether she was hurt. 'Only my pride,' she assured him, glancing at where she had dropped the firearm. 'What in the name of heaven is that thing?'

'The Lord only knows! Looks to be something between a blunderbuss and a ''Brown Bess'' to me. A ''Brown Bess'' is a musket,' he explained in response to her questioning look.

He cast her an impatient one in return as he helped her to her feet. 'Don't you know any better than to attempt to handle unfamiliar firearms, young woman?' he demanded sharply, continued anxiety over her well-being making him sound far harsher than he had intended. 'They can be notoriously unpredictable, not to mention downright dangerous. Though it appears,' he added, betraying a hint of admiration in his expression now, as he glanced at the spot directly in front of the inn, where the fourth attacker lay motionless on the ground, with something which Daniel couldn't quite make out lying on the road beside him, 'that you managed to discharge that monstrosity with remarkable accuracy. No mean feat, my darling, believe me!'

He quite failed to notice the swift and faintly sheepish look cast up at him through long lashes, for his attention was captured by a few villagers who had begun to emerge from their houses in order to investigate the commotion. To remain a moment longer would, he knew, be to court more trouble. There was every chance that others in search of them were in the area. Furthermore, he didn't relish the prospect of trying to explain to the French authorities just why they were being pursued across the country by a gang of hired assassins. Consequently he took a firm hold of a slender wrist and, before she knew what was happening, hauled Katherine willy-nilly out of the village towards a large stretch of rising pasture land, dotted with sheep happily grazing.

Katherine perfectly understood the reasons for their hasty departure. She could appreciate too why they could not have delayed in order to harness the horse to the gig. All the same, she felt that she might have been allowed the few seconds it would have taken to collect her bonnet from the blacksmith's barn.

The wind whistling across the open ground caught at her hair, lashing strands across her face. The cowl on her cloak was of precious little use, for unless she kept a firm hold on it the wind whipped it back in a trice. She refrained from complaining, however, for she needed all her breath in order to keep abreast of her companion.

Daniel set a cracking pace, and Katherine found herself almost having to run in order to keep up with that elegant, long-striding gait. Not until they had left the village far behind, and he seemed satisfied that no one was giving chase, did he attempt to walk at a more moderate speed; even so he did not suggest that they rest until quite some time later, when the open landscape had given way to a vast woodland area.

Settling himself on the grass, Daniel leaned his back against the substantial trunk of a conveniently fallen tree. Although he wasn't breathing particularly heavily, after their swiftly executed cross-country flight, Katherine wasn't slow to note that he was looking a little flushed. Initially she didn't give much thought to the unusual ruddy complexion, until she noticed him favouring his left arm, grasping it at frequent intervals beneath the folds of his cloak. Then, as he withdrew his right hand again, she clearly saw the telltale red stains between the long fingers.

'Daniel, you're hurt!'

Forgetting her own insignificant discomforts, she dropped to her knees beside him, and threw back his cloak before he had a chance to stop her. The instant her eyes focused on the charred portion of jacket just below the shoulder, and the dark stain surrounding the hole, she remembered the first shot fired in the barn. She had thought the attacker had missed his target entirely. Clearly he had not.

'Why on earth didn't you say something, you foolish creature!' she scolded.

Daniel assured her that it was nothing, barely a scratch, but made no demur when she insisted that he remove his cloak and jacket, and then his shirt, because the wound was too high up on the arm to reach by merely rolling up the sleeve.

Obligingly, he pulled the linen garment over his head, sending his dark brown hair into disarray. It was by no means the first time Katherine had seen a person of the opposite sex in a state of undress. Many a time when she had lived in Ireland she had seen men remove their shirts on warm summer days before they had attempted to groom one of her father's fine horses. So the sight of dark hair covering a well-muscled chest came as no surprise to her whatsoever. What sent a shock wave rippling through her, however, bringing her almost to the verge of tears, was the clear evidence of past suffering, and unmistakable bravery.

Without conscious thought, she reached out and began to trace the path of the longest scar, which ran from his right shoulder almost down to his pelvis, only to have her fingers swiftly captured in a firm yet gentle clasp.

'What is it, Katherine?' Daniel wasn't slow to detect long lashes moistened by tears barely held in check. 'What has occurred to upset you?'

'I-I feel so very ashamed.' Her voice was little more than a shaky whisper, but there was no mistaking the heartfelt contrition it contained. 'So very ashamed that I ever thought so badly of you; that I foolishly attempted to hold you responsible for dear Helen's death, when I always knew deep down that it wasn't your fault.'

Although she didn't attempt to draw her hand from his, she seemed unwilling, or unable, to meet his gaze, and her complexion had grown worryingly quite ashen. He didn't doubt her sincerity, but was puzzled by the admission. He had been inclined to dismiss her dislike of him as nothing more than a pampered young woman's childish spite. Now that he had come to know her a little better he was certain that that initial judgement had been sadly flawed. She was no foolish ninnyhammer prone to take a pet for no reason. Far more, he now realised, lay behind her former conduct towards him.

'Why were you so determined to dislike me, Katherine?' There was no response. Undeterred, he added,

'Come, do you not think that the man you've treated with such contempt on occasions deserves an explanation?'

This succeeded in drawing her eyes briefly to his, before she turned her attention to his most recent injury. 'Because it was far easier to blame you than myself,' she finally admitted, astonishing him somewhat.

Removing her hand from his at last, Katherine delved into the pocket of her skirt for her handkerchief, and proceeded to dab at the wound, which blessedly was little more than a scratch. 'I'm a scourge, Daniel. Everyone I have ever loved, or cared for deeply, every person with whom I have lived, has died. I tried to convince myself that Helen, at least, might have survived had she not lost the will to do so because she was mooning like a lovesick fool over you. It was grossly unfair of me to try to pin the blame on you. She was far too immature to capture a gentleman's interest. I suspect you were hardly aware of her existence…just as you were hardly aware of mine when I lived with my grandfather for those few short months. How I wish now that I had never resided in Dorsetshire!'

Not knowing quite how to respond, and feeling confused by these startling disclosures, Daniel remained silent as he watched her rise to her feet, and move in that graceful way of hers over to the tiny stream which gurgled its way through the woodland just a few yards from where he sat.

He didn't doubt for a moment that for some obscure reason she was determined to hold herself in some way responsible for the deaths of her grandfather and her friend, and possibly her parents too. He had no idea how Mr and Mrs O'Malley had met their maker, but there was no mystery about Colonel Fairchild's demise, and

Helen Rushton was by no means the only person to succumb to that outbreak of smallpox. Unless he was mistaken, her mother had perished too. So why was Katherine so determined to blame herself?

Although he would be forced to admit that, as yet, he didn't know her very well, he wouldn't have supposed for a moment that she was a young woman prone to indulging in foolish flights of fancy. So what deep-rooted fear was persuading her to believe such absolute nonsense? There was something…there simply had to be! And he was determined to discover precisely what that something was.

Deciding not to press her for an explanation quite yet, and thereby risk damaging the rather sweet rapport which had surprisingly developed between them, he changed the subject the instant she returned by remarking that he was relieved to see that the sight of blood didn't turn her queasy. 'Not that I'm unduly surprised,' he added, bestowing a look of the utmost respect upon her, as she began to dab at the slight wound with the handkerchief which she had soaked in the clear waters of the stream. 'Any young woman who possesses the courage to do what you did back there in that village isn't likely to flinch at the sight of a little blood.'

She cast him a distinctly rueful smile. 'You may as well know now that I have been cursed with an appalling temper, Major. I've learned to control it over the years…well, at least for the most part,' she added, incurably truthful. 'But the sight of those four men setting about you made me fume. Damnable cowards!'

'And you came to my aid without any thought for your own safety,' he murmured, experiencing a wealth of oddly contrasting emotions which left him not quite knowing whether he wished to kiss or shake her for doing such a foolhardy yet courageous thing. 'Wellington could have done with you out in the Peninsula, my girl. Who did you say taught you to handle firearms, by the way?'

'My father,' she reminded him, before asking if he had a handkerchief about his person.

He delved into the pocket of his breeches and drew out a square of linen, which she promptly pressed over the cleaned wound. 'You're a damned fine shot. You'd have made an excellent rifleman had you been a boy.'

This time he didn't miss the faintly sheepish expression, and was puzzled by it until she announced, 'It's no good. My conscience simply won't permit me to allow you to continue to view me as some sort of wonder woman. I've discovered today that I'm not that good a shot.'

He raised his brows at this. 'You managed to down that rogue who was doing his level best to get away,' he reminded her.

'Yes, and no,' she responded, confounding him still further, before once again casting him a glance from beneath long lashes. 'Did you not notice the inn sign lying in the road?'

'I noticed something, certainly.'

Katherine decided to confess before she had a chance to change her mind. 'Well, the truth of the matter is…I hit the sign, shattering its hinge, and the sign hit him, plump on the head.'

For several moments Daniel regarded her in silence, then he threw back his head and roared with laughter. The woodland area surrounding them resounded with the infectious sound, and Katherine found it impossible not to laugh herself.

'It isn't that funny!' she chided gently, regaining control first. 'I was mortified, I can tell you, when I saw that dratted sign fall. My aim has never been so awry before.'

'I doubt anyone would have stood the remotest chance of hitting his mark with that monstrous weapon,' he assured her, as she rose to her feet and blithely tore a strip off the bottom of her underskirt.

The sight of a neatly turned ankle, swiftly followed by the renewed touch of those gentle fingers on his arm, as she deftly wound the strip of material over his handkerchief, certainly put a further strain on his self-control. Desperate to turn his thoughts in a new direction, he searched about for something, anything, that might take his mind off earthy masculine desires, and his gaze swiftly fell upon her bloodstained handkerchief, lying on the ground.

Reaching for it, and earning himself a stern reprimand in the process for not sitting still, he studied the beautifully embroidered monogram in one corner. 'Is this your stitch-work, Katherine?'

'No. Bridie embroidered it. She was my nursemaid when I was a child,' she explained when he raised an enquiring brow. 'Now she's my personal maid… housekeeper…you name it.'

'What does the ''F'' stand for?'

A moment's silence, then, 'Fairchild.' She grimaced. 'I've Bridie to thank for that too!' she informed him, her disgruntled tone evidence enough that she wasn't best pleased. 'Apparently she took one look at me and announced that I was the fairest child she'd ever set eyes on. My mother, much struck by this, as it happened to be her maiden name, decided it would be most appropriate, and as Papa had chosen my Christian name he allowed her to have her way.'

'Fairchild,' he echoed. 'Yes, it suits you. It suits you very well.'

Half-suspecting him of mockery, Katherine paused in her tying of the makeshift bandage to cast him a suspicious glance. 'There, that should hold,' she announced, reaching for his shirt. 'Hurry and get dressed. I don't want you taking a chill on top of everything else.'

The garment was stained with blood, but he had no choice but to put it back on. Neither of them had a change of clothes, which, Katherine mused, didn't appear to trouble Daniel to any great extent; but she knew it would begin to irk her unbearably if she was forced to remain in the same garments for any length of time. She wasn't accustomed to going without meals either. Not a morsel of food had passed her lips since the previous evening, and she was now beginning to feel decidedly peckish.

Refraining from bringing this to his attention, she merely seated herself on the fallen tree. Despite the fact that Daniel's injury was, as he had stated himself, only slight, and she didn't suppose any complications would arise as a result of it, he was still looking slightly flushed, so it could do no harm to let him rest for a while.

Evidently he was of a similar mind, for he made himself more comfortable, and very soon afterwards closed his eyes. Katherine sat quietly beside him for a while, content to gaze at their pretty surroundings, which were thankfully betraying clear signs that spring had arrived. Then her stomach elected to remind her quite noisily that she required something to eat, and she decided it was time to do something about it.

Chapter Eight

The glade was pleasantly sheltered from the gusty wind that earlier had gathered strength across the open countryside, hindering their flight from the village. The March sun too was surprisingly warm, and Daniel had found little difficulty in dozing. The slight dizziness that had induced him to rest for a while seemed mercifully to have passed, and he was sufficiently restored now to recommence their cross-country trek to Normandy.

He turned his head, expecting to see his darling companion once again sitting on the trunk of the tree beside him, and was faintly surprised to discover no sign of her. Earlier, when a slight sound had disturbed him, he had opened one eye to catch her slipping quietly away. He had resisted the temptation to call out and ask where she was going. She might be a damnably brave little soul to have come to his aid, he reflected, but he suspected that, for all her innate courage, she would find it acutely embarrassing to admit that she was forced to answer a call of nature.

Women! Smiling to himself, he shook his head. He would never understand them. A jumbled mass of contradictions was what they were. At least, he silently amended, that red-haired little darling most certainly was. One moment snapping a fellow's nose off for absolutely no reason; the next a ministering angel, touchingly concerned and tending to his every need. Yet, for all her contrariness, he could think of no other female of his acquaintance whom he would prefer to have with him on this assignment. Come to that, he could think of no other woman, with the possible exception of his late grandmother, who would have possessed sufficient courage to do what Katherine Fairchild O'Malley had done that morning. Not to put too fine a point on it, she had in all probability saved his life—foolhardy, perhaps, but worthy of the utmost admiration.

And where the deuce had the damnable little firebrand got to? Sitting upright, Daniel consulted his pocket-watch. How much time did it take a female to perform some simple bodily function? She had been gone twenty minutes or more, for heaven's sake!

He rose to his feet and began to scan the surrounding woodland area, his sharp eyes searching for any slight movement that could not be attributed to natural rustling resulting from the wind. All seemed still and silent, except for the singing of birds, and occasional scurrying noises in the undergrowth.

His first instinct was to go in search of her, but wiser counsel prevailed. If she returned to find him gone, he very much feared that she wouldn't hesitate to go wandering off again, looking for him, and get herself hopelessly lost or, worse still, walk straight into the hands of those whom they were trying their utmost to avoid, if indeed she had not done so already.

Concern increased with every passing second, and he had almost reached the point where he felt he had no choice but to search for her, when his sharp ears caught the sound of humming, and a moment later he glimpsed her weaving a path through the trees, appearing as if she hadn't a care in the world.

'Where the hell have you been?' he demanded, resorting to the fierce tone he had adopted when dealing with any foolhardy, raw recruit under his command. She regarded him in mild surprise, but didn't appear unduly chastened which, perversely, only served to stoke the fires of his wrath. 'Haven't you more sense, girl, than to go wandering off by yourself? You might easily have walked straight into the hands of those villains engaged to capture us!'

Intrigued rather than incensed by this display of ill humour, Katherine held the hard-eyed gaze. She strongly suspected that this surprising show of annoyance on his part stemmed from anxiety over her well-being, and she was faintly moved by his evident concern.

'Oh, come now, Major Ross, be reasonable,' she urged gently, in an attempt to placate him. 'How many spies do you suppose there are in France? It was highly unlikely that I would have come across any more.'

'God give me strength!' Daniel clapped a hand over his eyes. 'You don't imagine for a moment that those four villains we encountered back there were spies, do you?'

'Were they not?' Katherine couldn't in all honesty say that she'd given the matter much thought. 'Who were they then, do you suppose?'

'Rogues hired to search for us, you damnable little idiot!' he snapped, which clearly proved that her soothing manner had not achieved the desired result. He removed his hand to glower down at her yet again, as she calmly seated herself on the trunk of the fallen tree. 'Be under no illusions, girl,' he warned. 'Should you fall into their hands, they won't be over-nice in their dealings with you.'

Her shrug of indifference wasn't likely to improve his state of mind, but Katherine was beyond caring. She considered that she'd had reason enough to venture forth on her own. 'Well, I don't suppose it's very likely that any others who might be in search of us would be able to pick me out amongst the throng.'

For a moment it was as much as Daniel could do to stare down at her in open-mouthed astonishment. 'Not be able to…?' Words failed him, but not for very long. 'I've been unfortunate enough to come across several harebrained females in my time, Katherine Fairchild O'Malley, but without doubt you reign supreme! You've a head of hair on you like a flaming hayrick, girl! You stand out like a beacon!'

If there was one subject guaranteed to stir her own uncertain temper, then it was someone passing a disparaging remark about her hair. 'I didn't ask to be cursed with auburn locks, Major Ross!' she flared. 'And might I remind you that had you permitted me the few seconds it would have taken to collect my bonnet, instead of dragging me away in that odiously cavalier fashion, I might have been in a position to keep my cursed tresses well hidden!'

She watched the anger fading from those dark, masculine eyes as he cast them over her hair, which she had managed during her brief venture alone through the French countryside to confine neatly at the nape of her neck by means of a further strip torn from her underskirt.

'I considered that I had a sound reason for wandering off on my own.' From beneath her cloak, she drew out a loaf of bread and a goodly wedge of cheese. 'Though why I bothered to bring them back here to share with you, I cannot imagine,' she added, feeling quite out of charity with him now.

Daniel sat down beside her and, relieving her of the round loaf, proceeded to tear it in half. 'Where did you manage to lay your hands on this delicious fare, may I ask?' he enquired, secretly impressed by this display of self-reliance on her part. 'Is there some village nearby?'

Katherine shook her head. 'Didn't see one. There's a farm in the valley, though, just beyond the wood. The rear door to the main building was wide open. I didn't see anyone about, so I slipped inside and removed these from the kitchen table.'

He bent a look of mock severity upon her. 'That was stealing, my girl. Many in Wellington's army were hanged for less.'

'As I left some coins on the kitchen table, I do not consider I was stealing,' she responded, winning herself a faint smile of approval.

'In that case, I'll forgive you this time. But you're not to go wandering off again by yourself, understand? I can appreciate that there will be occasions when you'll desire a—er—little privacy,' he added delicately. 'As long as I can see the top of your head at all times, I shan't object.'

Katherine didn't pretend to misunderstand and glowered at him, the picture of indignant outrage. 'I'll take leave to inform you, Major, that you're an exceedingly vulgar man. Top of my head, indeed! I've never heard the like before!'

Although he found it impossible to suppress a smile, Daniel managed not to add to her obvious annoyance by laughing outright. 'One tends to forget the social niceties after years of hard campaigning out in the Peninsula, Kate.'

'Then it's high time you began to re-acquire a few, Major. And you can begin by paying me the common courtesy of remembering not to call me Kate.'

Clearly he was not prepared to begin his retraining quite yet, for he merely applied himself to the bread and cheese for several minutes, and then surprised her by remarking, 'For someone who places such store by correct behaviour, I'm rather surprised that you lent yourself to this outrageous scheme.' He studied her in silence for a moment, his gaze penetrating, but not unduly censorious. 'Why did you agree to aid that crafty old reprobate, Sir Giles Osborne?'

Katherine returned that searching gaze, reflecting as she did so that, had he asked her such a thing just twenty-four hours before, she wouldn't have hesitated to tell him to mind his own business. Now, for some obscure reason, she didn't object to his knowing in the least.

She transferred her gaze to the stream a few yards away, which put her forcibly in mind of the one that had rippled its way across her father's Irish acres. 'There were several reasons,' she admitted truthfully. 'The main one, I suppose, was because I wished to avenge in some part the death of Liam Patrick O'Malley.'

'Your father?'

'Yes, Daniel, my father. Had I been a boy I would have been granted the opportunity to do so by enlisting in the army. That, however, was denied me. Sir Giles offered me the opportunity to rectify this…and I didn't need to think twice about it.'

'How did your father die, Katherine?' he asked gently, as he detected the shadow of sadness flickering over the delicate features. 'Was he a soldier?'

She shook her head. 'My father owned a stud in Ireland. I doubt there has ever been—or ever will be, come to that—a man who has known more about horses than my father. His expertise was renowned, and his horses were much coveted. He was approached by someone attached to the War Office, I know not who, to acquire animals for the army, and to travel to Portugal in order to take care of them on the journey.

'He left Dublin with his prized cargo in the summer of '08 and joined up with two other vessels, carrying much-needed supplies, which had set sail from Bristol, I believe. The small convoy was supposed to receive protection from our Navy. No escort appeared; the captain in charge of the expedition decided to press on in the hope, I suppose, that before too long some naval frigate consigned to escort them would appear. It did not. The French, however, did. They were lying in wait off the Bay of Biscay.'

Katherine was silent for a moment, but her voice when she spoke again was as coolly controlled as before, betraying none of the searing heartache she continued to experience when recalling that time in her life when she had waited daily for the father who was destined never to return. 'There were no survivors. I did not discover until recently that the French were well prepared. They had received details from someone connected with the War Office.'

'And Sir Giles told you this?' Daniel was clearly more angered than anything else by what he had learned. 'He ought never to have disclosed such details. Damn his eyes!'

Evidently Major Ross was a man of strong emotions. Moreover, he was not reticent about voicing staunch disapproval if he felt inclined to do so. Katherine saw nothing amiss with this, for she herself was not above giving vent to her own feelings on occasions. She was faintly surprised, all the same, by this display of ill humour, and didn't hesitate to come to Sir Giles's defence. 'He didn't attempt to convince me that the traitor he is determined to uncover now is indeed the one responsible for my father's death,' she hurriedly assured him. 'In fact, he took great pains to inform me that it's highly unlikely it is the same person.'

How very magnanimous of him! Daniel thought, totally unimpressed, and more than moderately annoyed by the baronet's devious methods.

He at least was under no illusion about Sir Giles Osborne's true character. Although the baronet seemed to epitomise the perfect English gentleman, suave and dignified, he wasn't above preying on a person's vulnerability in order to attain his ends, and could be as ruthless in his methods to achieve his objectives as those he was determined to root out and bring to book for their treachery.

Daniel clearly remembered that his and the baronet's paths had crossed for the very first time in London, just prior to his setting sail for the Peninsula, when he himself had been at a very low ebb. Learning of his father's death whilst he had been out in India had been a bitter blow, and discovering, on his return to England, the heartless betrayal of the woman he had once wished to marry had added considerably to his distress. It was hard to imagine, now, that at the age of three-and-twenty he had been a very vulnerable young man, disillusioned and heart-weary. A grim smile curled his lips. Oh, yes, he had certainly been a highly prized fruit, just ripe for the picking! And Sir Giles had not hesitated to take full advantage of the young captain who, badly bruised in spirit, had betrayed scant concern for his own safety.

Daniel didn't doubt for a moment that it had been Osborne who had suggested that he be chosen so often for those perilous missions behind enemy lines in Spain and Portugal. His command of the French tongue, coupled with a complete disregard for his own safety, had made him a prime choice.

He knew for certain that it had been at Sir Giles's request that he had been sent back to England to effect Louise Baron's escape. He hadn't wished to desert the men under his command, but he'd been given little choice in the matter. The verbal order to do so had come from Wellington himself. His army days were now over, of course, and he wasn't obliged to take orders from anyone. So what the deuce was he doing here now, stuck in the heart of France, once again involved in that unscrupulous baronet's fiendish stratagems?

Daniel glanced briefly at the lovely young woman sitting beside him, who was daintily eating her way through the chunk of crusty bread and portion of cheese. Although his years out in the Peninsula had undoubtedly changed him from a vulnerable young man into a self-possessed, if faintly cynical, ex-army Major, he couldn't find it within himself to be in the least bit sorry that he had allowed that foxy old baronet to persuade him to take part in one last venture for his country, for he was beginning to feel increasingly that it would turn out to be the best decision he had ever taken in his life.

By the time evening had arrived Daniel judged that they had covered a good twenty miles. More importantly, he had discovered a deal more about his delightful companion and the idyllic life she had enjoyed in Ireland. If she had had one fault to find with her childhood, then it had been the lack of companionship of girls

her own age. Which, undoubtedly, was the reason why,
after suffering the loss of both parents in quick succession, and removing to England to live with her grandfather, she had swiftly struck up such a close friendship
with Helen Rushton.

Little wonder the foolish little darling had convinced
herself that she was some sort of curse, Daniel reflected,
as he at last saw signs of what appeared to be a sizeable
habitation just up ahead. It was utter nonsense, of
course—a fact that he had every intention of making
perfectly plain at the earliest opportunity. The underlying
reason for this foolish notion had become increasingly
clear to him too—she was determined never to form a
deep attachment to another living soul, simply because
she was desperate to avoid suffering the searing heartache she had all too frequently experienced in the past.

Sadly it was all so very understandable. Still, it was
no way to live one's life. It might take some time, but
he would eventually peel away those protective layers
in which she had shrouded herself, he thought determinedly, little realising that he had already begun to do
so.

As Daniel, ever alert, paused for a moment to cast his
eyes up the main street of the small market town they
had just entered, Katherine stared up at him, her eyes
resting for a moment on the square, powerful jaw, before
studying the other strong contours of a face that was
certainly not handsome, but full of character and ruggedly attractive. At least she found his physiognomy extremely appealing and, more surprisingly still, she was
beginning to find his nature very engaging too.

Strong willed and determined, Daniel certainly possessed the power to annoy her from time to time by
uttering some blunt remark. Yet beneath the brusque, no-

nonsense manner was a wealth of tenderness, which manifested itself in quite touching displays of gentlemanly consideration.

More than once throughout the day he had kindly offered a helping hand to clamber over some gate or stile, and on one occasion, much to her intense annoyance, he had gone so far as to toss her over one brawny shoulder, as though she weighed no more than a sack of grain, and had carried her across a wide stream to save her feet and clothing from becoming sodden.

Although still faintly aggrieved at having been manhandled in such an odious fashion, Katherine couldn't deny that, against all the odds, she was genuinely beginning to like and admire this occasionally infuriating man.

'I don't know about you, my little Amazon,' Daniel announced, resorting to one of those many colourful epithets by which he was wont to address her, 'but I'm feeling decidedly weary and in desperate need of sustenance. Are you willing to risk paying a visit to the inn up yonder?'

She didn't need to take even a moment to consider the matter. Not a morsel of food, or a drop of liquid, had passed her lips since the morning, and she wasn't in the least doubtful that she could do full justice to a substantial meal.

'Very well,' he added, after she had given several vigorous nods of assent, 'but you must remain on your guard. And do not forget you're supposed to be a native of this country. So for the Lord's sake don't relapse into English!'

Thus adjured, Katherine was quite content, as they entered the inn, to leave it entirely to Daniel to order their food, and left him to do precisely that whilst she seated herself at the vacant table in the corner of the room, well away from the other patrons who just might overhear her and guess her true nationality.

Fortunately the same would never be suspected of Daniel. She had discovered during the day that he had learned to speak the language fluently from his maternal grandmother, a Frenchwoman of immense character, according to Daniel, whom he had absolutely adored and then missed dreadfully after she had passed away shortly before he had embarked for India.

Apart from these few snippets Katherine had learned next to nothing about him. It wasn't that she had gained the impression that he was disinclined to talk about himself, and therefore out of common courtesy she had not attempted to pry; it was simply that he had seemed interested to learn about her, and she had found herself quite surprisingly divulging far more about her past to Daniel than she had to another living soul.

What an enigma the man was turning out to be! she reflected, gazing across at the spot where he stood deep in conversation with mine host. How she wished now that she had paid more attention to what her aunt Lavinia had disclosed about him, when she had stayed in Hampshire for those two weeks. She frowned in an effort to remember, and vaguely recalled her aunt mentioning something about his returning from India to discover the woman he had loved riveted to his cousin.

Katherine surprisingly found herself experiencing a deal of animosity towards this unknown female. How heartless she must be to have dealt such a crushing blow! Yet, to be fair, the young woman whom Daniel had hoped to marry had hardly been in a position to inform him that she had experienced a change of heart, Katherine reminded herself. A letter would have taken months and months to reach him out there in India. Yet

it was all so very sad. Daniel wasn't in the least light-
minded, and must have cared for the woman deeply to
have wished to marry her. It went without saying that
her betrayal must have been a bitter blow. Perhaps,
Katherine mused, that was why he had never married,
though it had to be said that he didn't appear to be suffering now from the pain of unrequited love. Nevertheless, she didn't suppose for a moment that he was the
kind of man to wear his heart on his sleeve.

Although she was keen to discover much more about
the man whom, against all the odds, she had begun to
regard in a very favourable light, Katherine was aware
that this was neither the time nor the place to satisfy her
curiosity. Her command of the language was not sufficiently good to conduct an inquisition in French. Besides
which, she didn't suppose that Daniel would wish to
satisfy her curiosity at a time when his prime concern
was to satisfy his hunger. So she merely asked, when he
eventually joined her at the table, what had taken him
so long and whether the landlord had been unwilling to
supply them with a wholesome meal.

Daniel cast her a mocking glance as he handed her a
glass of wine and slid into the seat opposite. 'Have you
ever known a landlord turn away custom? No, he was
more than happy to oblige, once he'd seen the colour of
my money. Which reminds me… How much have you
about you?'

Katherine delved into the pocket of her cloak, which
she had removed and placed on the settle beside her, and
without hesitation handed him the bulging purse.

Daniel tossed it in his hand, gauging its contents.
'We've done well today, my little darling,' he remarked,
consigning the purse to the safety of his own pocket.
'But we're going to need to cover more miles if we stand

the remotest chance of keeping one step ahead of those rogues out searching for us.'

Something in his tone put her immediately on her guard, and Katherine instinctively stared beyond his broad shoulders, taking swift stock of the other patrons. 'Would I be correct in thinking that you do not care for that ill-favoured rascal sitting alone at the corner table?'

Daniel didn't attempt to deny it. 'He appeared to be taking an uncommon interest in you when we first arrived, certainly,' he admitted, casting a frowning glance over her curls. 'Let me know if he leaves, or if someone joins him,' he added, before turning his attention to the innkeeper's wife, who arrived at the table bearing a tray laden with several dishes which exuded the most mouthwatering aromas.

It hadn't been difficult for Katherine to guess what had been passing through his mind when he had subjected her hair to a fleeting glance of irritation. Yet it was hardly her fault that she had been destined to inherit her father's colouring and in consequence was, as Daniel himself had tauntingly pointed out earlier in the day, easily picked out in a crowd.

Successfully suppressing a feeling of pique, she immediately set about the rewarding task of satisfying her hunger. During the time it took to consume a bowl of heart-warming broth, and work her way through a selection of meats and a variety of pasties, she succeeded in blotting from her mind the danger the man seated at the corner table might pose. Unfortunately, she just happened to glance in his direction, as she was about to consume the last mouthful of the most delicious fruit tart she had ever tasted in her life, and the very real possibility that he might indeed be one of those assassins hired to discover their whereabouts returned to cause her no small concern.

'I like to see a female with a healthy appetite.' Daniel approved, as he leaned back in his seat, totally replete himself.

For her part Katherine couldn't help but admire the way he always appeared so composed in the face of possible danger. However, he wasn't quite impervious to their present situation, as his next words proved. 'I think it is high time we were making tracks, don't you?'

He regarded her in silence for a moment, his dark eyes assessing as he contemplated the modesty of a dress now sadly creased and travel-stained, and the arrangement of fiery curls. 'You are by no means the only female in France to possess red hair, and it just might be that our friend over there in the corner admires your colouring. On the other hand, if he isn't an innocent local out enjoying his evening tipple, there's every chance that he'll follow us when we leave. And to be perfectly frank with you, I'd rather not leave a trail of corpses littered across France, clearly indicating in which direction we're heading, if I can possibly avoid it. So let us see if we can persuade him that we're not the pair he's been hired to locate.'

Katherine could find no fault in this course of action, until he calmly asked her to undo the buttons at the neckline of her dress, and release her hair from its restraining band. 'Whatever for?' she demanded, not unreasonably.

'Because you, my little darling, are about to become my doxy.'

He could not have startled her more had he tried, and it plainly showed when she gaped across the width of the table at him, not one hundred per cent certain she could have heard aright. 'I...beg...your...pardon?'

There was just a suspicion of a twitch at one corner of his mouth. 'For the love of God, Kate, don't go all missish on me now!' he ordered in a voice which contained a suspicion of a tremor too. 'I'm only asking you to act the part of a strumpet, not to take up the profession in earnest, for heaven's sake!'

Katherine regarded him in silence for a moment, half wondering if he had taken complete leave of his senses, but very much fearing that he was in deadly earnest. 'I shall take leave to inform you, Major Ross,' she said with careful restraint, 'that I am incapable of attempting such a portrayal. My experience of strumpets, and how they conduct themselves, is non-existent.'

'Fortunately mine isn't,' he countered, with what could best be described as an evil leer, and, reaching out, he tugged the strip of material from her hair, allowing the auburn tresses to tumble about her shoulders. 'All you need do is cling to my arm, and look at me as though you find me as delicious as that fruit tart you've just devoured with such relish.'

Although appalled at the mere suggestion, Katherine swiftly came to the conclusion that masquerading as a woman of easy virtue for a few minutes was a small price to pay in order to attempt to avoid a confrontation with a would-be assassin. Consequently she made no demur when Daniel slipped her arm through his, and proceeded to guide her across the inn towards the door, though she might have wished he had refrained from uttering a rather lewd remark in a carrying voice, the result of which induced several patrons to exchange knowing looks and several others to snicker behind their hands.

As they left the inn, still arm in arm, and began to retrace their steps along the street, Katherine was just beginning to think that the embarrassing little interlude had been entirely worthwhile when she clearly detected the sound of a door opening behind them. Before she knew what was happening, Daniel had her pinned against the stone wall of a house, and was smothering the squeal that rose in her throat by clamping his mouth down hard over hers.

For a few moments Katherine was too stunned by the speed of the assault to appreciate why he was behaving in this brutal and uncharacteristic manner, holding her so tightly that there was no possible hope of escape, and forcing an embrace upon her which was singularly lacking the persuasive tenderness she well remembered him displaying on that memorable night in Paris.

'For the love of God, Kate,' he muttered, dragging his mouth towards her left ear, and grazing her cheek in the process with the rough stubble on his chin, 'don't just stand there like a stock, girl! At least try to pretend you wish to bed me.'

A slight movement in the shadows succeeded in thrusting aside the last barrier of reserve. Reaching up, Katherine entwined her arms about his neck, and thought she detected a flicker of what might well have been surprise in his eyes before she took the initiative and forced his mouth down on hers in a kiss which began as little more than a mere meeting of lips, but which swiftly deepened as she instinctively parted her own, moving them back and forth beneath his. The fact that this was pretence, a mere show of passion for the benefit of inquisitive eyes, rapidly faded from her mind as a highly pleasurable but totally foreign longing began to spread swiftly through her limbs.

Without conscious thought she pressed her body closer until breasts, hips and thighs made contact with strong bone and well-honed muscle. They seemed to meld together so wonderfully, like two halves of a perfect whole, that she couldn't say with any degree of certainty whether the sudden tremor that rippled through her, or the low earthy moan which followed, emanated from her or the man who a moment later brought an abrupt end to the intimate contact by almost wrenching his mouth away.

For several moments his breathing seemed faintly laboured, and there was a flicker of something quite intense in his dark eyes. Then he seemed to collect himself, and took a hurried step away.

'Why, you're a passionate wench, and no mistake!' he announced, his strong teeth flashing in a sportive smile. 'Come, take me to your bed, otherwise I'll have you here and now!'

Like a cruel slap in the face, harsh reality returned with a vengeance, and was no less humiliating than the hearty smack he unexpectedly administered to the seat of her skirt, before linking her arm through his once more. Yet it took Katherine, still plagued by a wealth of unfamiliar sensations, several moments to come to terms with the fact that what had just taken place between them had been a sham, nothing more than mere pretence on his part. How she wished she could say with complete honesty that it had been likewise with her!

Wounded pride and bitter resentment was an explosive mixture. Yet Katherine steadfastly refused to give vent to her emotions and betray the fact that she was foolishly feeling unaccountably hurt by this display of seeming indifference on Daniel's part to that passionate interlude which had just taken place.

It certainly did nothing to improve her state of mind when the sound of a footfall close behind suggested very strongly that her humiliation might all have been in vain, and she was just about to suggest that they should confront the stalker, when Daniel's clasp on her elbow was suddenly increased and she was unexpectedly thrust down a side alley.

'Await me at the far end,' he ordered, releasing his grasp, and although she would have preferred to remain, she found herself automatically obeying the whispered command.

It was by now quite dark and Katherine, almost stumbling over the uneven surface, hurried along the narrow alley, not knowing whether it would offer a means of escape, and not caring very much either. She could not, would not, attempt to save her own skin and leave Daniel to face the threat of danger alone. She stopped and turned, clearly hearing the sounds of a scuffle, swiftly followed by a low groan. Then she almost cried out in relief, her former resentment completely forgotten, when she saw that tall, dependable being emerging from the gloom.

His grim expression, as he paused to slip an evil-looking knife inside the top of his boot, told her all she needed to know. He took no pleasure in taking a human life, of that she felt certain, and to do him justice he had done all he could to avoid the confrontation, so she chose not to ply him with unnecessary questions that would only add to his distress.

'Needless to say we shall be unable to remain in this town overnight.' He sounded quite matter-of-fact, but the flicker of anguish lingering in his eyes was unmistakable. 'I doubt our friend back there came here alone. I very much fear there may be others about the place searching for us. Therefore we must resign ourselves to yet another night without any creature comforts.'

Katherine frankly didn't care where they spent the night. A feeling of well-being, something that she had not experienced for several years, washed over her as they left the town and headed for the open countryside. As long as this man was with her she knew instinctively that she would never come to any harm.

Chapter Nine

Katherine awoke to find herself in unfamiliar surroundings yet again. Having had little choice but to lie on a dirt floor, with a thin pile of leaves beneath her, she had passed possibly the most uncomfortable night of her entire life. Yet she clearly remembered that, when they had quite by chance stumbled upon the woodcutter's rustic shelter, she had been too tired to care where she had bedded down, and had fallen asleep almost from the moment her head had touched the ground.

Easing herself into a sitting position, she glanced about the rough wooden structure, which, boasting three sides only, was open to the elements at the front, and was surprised to discover herself quite alone. She immediately experienced a moment's unease, not because Daniel was no longer propped in the adjacent corner, where he had settled himself the night before, but because she suddenly recalled that he had seemed strangely quiet, subdued almost, after they had left the small market town the evening before.

They had been obliged to walk quite some distance before they had chanced upon this shelter, nestling in the wood. Throughout the lengthy trek Daniel had not uttered above a dozen words. At first she had put his unusually subdued state down to the fact that he had been compelled to put a period to their stalker's existence in order to effect an escape. That, however, could not account for the fact that he had seemed disinclined to be near her, to so much as touch her. Why, not once had he offered a helping hand over the rougher ground, which he had not hesitated to do earlier in the day. Furthermore, when they had finally discovered this shelter, he had settled himself as far away as possible from her, when it would have made more sense to have lain side by side in order to share bodily warmth.

Sweeping her hair back from her face, Katherine stared through the wide opening at the surrounding woodland, wondering now if his odd behaviour was not a means to an end: an attempt to protect himself. Perhaps he had no intention of placing himself in a position whereby he would feel obliged to offer her the protection of his name?

She recalled with embarrassing clarity the passionate interlude outside the inn. She hadn't found kissing him, or holding his strong body next to her own, in the least distasteful. In fact, the opposite was all too embarrassingly true. Perhaps Daniel had sensed this and it had put him on his guard? Perhaps, also, he was afraid that she would expect him to do the honourable thing by marrying her once this venture was over? If so, she would swiftly disabuse him, she decided, experiencing a resurgence of that ever-present fear. She had made up her mind years before that marriage was not for her. She had no intention of ever putting any man's life at risk, especially one of whom she had grown so inordinately fond. It had possibly been a grave mistake on her part to become so friendly with Daniel, though she failed to see how she might have prevented herself from doing so. Nevertheless, it might help to ease his mind a little if she followed his recent example and attempted to remain a little aloof herself from now on.

Hurriedly rising to her feet, Katherine went outside to scan the surrounding woodland more intently, but worryingly could detect no sign of him. Where on earth had he got to? Surely he hadn't left her to fend for herself?

The instant the idea entered her mind, she dismissed it at once, ashamed for having had the mere thought. He would never do such an unchivalrous thing! Heaven only knew he could be the most irritating man on occasions—arrogant, overbearing and downright rude! But Major Daniel Ross was no coward. He was an exceptionally brave man who could be quite touchingly considerate on occasions. So where in the name of heaven had he taken himself off to?

Fortunately Katherine wasn't left worrying unnecessarily for very long. A minute or so later she detected the sound of hoof beats, and turned to see Daniel, astride a large bay and leading a second mount, negotiating a safe passage between the trees.

Instantly forgetting her resolve, she ran to meet him, her expression clearly betraying delight, and it was only as she reached his side that she recalled her resolution. His returning smile was just too spontaneous not to be perfectly genuine, and she couldn't help wondering whether she had merely read too much into his strange behaviour and that his former reserve might have stemmed from nothing more than mere fatigue.

'Well, sweetheart?' Looking very well pleased with himself, Daniel drew the horses to a halt. 'What do you think of our latest acquisitions? Not precisely high-stepping thoroughbreds, but I believe they'll serve their purpose by speeding up our journey.'

'Sturdy and, yes, capable of doing the job,' she announced, after a brief examination of both mounts, where she betrayed once more the knowledge she had gained from her father. 'How on earth did you manage to acquire them?'

'You might not have observed those two men propping up the counter at that inn. I, on the other hand, overheard one of them saying he would be bringing two horses to the market held in the town on Friday, and that there was no need for him to make an early start as he lived in a small village just four miles east of the town. That is why I came this way last night. The village is about half a mile away, just beyond the wood.'

Katherine couldn't help admiring his superb sense of direction. Even at night he never seemed to get himself lost. He was immensely capable, equal to any challenge. Why, not only had he managed to acquire horses, but saddles and bridles too!

When he apologised for not having been able to provide her with a side-saddle, Katherine dismissed it with a wave of her hand. 'Don't give it another thought,' she urged him, easily mounting without assistance. 'I frequently rode astride as a girl, and much preferred it. Unfortunately, when I reached a certain age Mama objected, and I was obliged thereafter to ride like a lady. Believe me, I shall enjoy the experience again.'

It took Daniel a few minutes only to appreciate her skill in the saddle. She was an extremely accomplished horsewoman who handled her mount with ease. 'Your father taught you well, Katherine,' he remarked, not reticent to voice his admiration, but could not resist adding,

'His only fault, I strongly suspect, was a reluctance to beat you often enough.'

Katherine wasn't slow to detect the provocative gleam in dark eyes. 'It might surprise you to know, Major Ross, that my father never once laid a violent hand on me. It might also surprise you to know he never felt that he needed to.' Her smile faded. 'He had a certain way of looking at me whenever I had displeased him, which always made me feel so guilty that I promised never to do it again.'

Anyone of the meanest intelligence couldn't have failed to appreciate how deeply she had cared for her father. But was a desire to avenge his death the only reason why she had agreed to involve herself in Sir Giles Osborne's machinations? Daniel couldn't resist asking.

'Good heavens, no! I did it as much for myself as anything else, I suppose,' she was honest enough to admit. 'I have become increasingly disenchanted with the life I have been leading in Bath. I am feeling increasingly restrained…suffocated, almost.'

Katherine released her breath in a resentful sigh, which matched quite beautifully the fleeting glance she cast him. 'It's all very well for you men. You can come and go as you please, but for a female it is quite different. I have inherited a companion who's a dear person, but faintly scatty, and on occasions something of a trial. And then, of course, there's Bridie, who will insist on treating me just as though I were still a child.'

Although he was smiling, he betrayed genuine sympathy as he said, 'There's one course of action which will enable you to sever those restraining ties. You could wed. Married women enjoy far more freedom.'

'True,' she agreed, 'but I do not consider a desire for freedom reason enough to take the matrimonial plunge, at least not in my case. Besides which,' she added, suddenly remembering her determination to put his mind at rest, 'I am resolved never to marry. Remember, I'm a curse, Daniel. I could never reconcile it with my conscience if I were to shorten any man's life.'

If she had expected this declaration to reassure him, and bring about a return of the wonderful camaraderie that had been surprisingly increasing between them, she was swiftly to discover her mistake.

'Don't talk such rubbish, girl!' he snapped, his expression no less harsh than his tone. 'You're no more a curse than I am. Your parents' deaths were tragic, but had absolutely nothing whatsoever to do with you. And how you can suppose you were responsible for your grandfather's heart attack when you were in Bath at the time beggars belief. And as for your aunt Augusta,' he went on, without granting her the opportunity to edge in a word, 'she was an elderly spinster who died of old age, and would have done so had you lived in the house or not. It is much more likely that you made her last years much happier with your presence.'

His expression, if anything, darkened. 'So I want to hear no more of such foolishness, understand? Otherwise I shan't hesitate to shake some sense into you!'

Stunned by the vehemence of the outburst, it was as much as Katherine could do to watch him steer a path through the last few yards of woodland towards the open countryside. By the time she had gathered her scattered wits together sufficiently to formulate a response, he was already some distance ahead.

She quickly discovered that, although her own mount was both healthy and strong, the gelding possessed a decidedly stubborn streak and was determined to progress at his own pace. Consequently she found herself always trailing those few yards behind, a circumstance which didn't appear to bother Daniel to any great extent, for apart from taking the trouble to inform her that they would stop somewhere for luncheon, and would risk putting up for the night at a village inn, he continued to ride on ahead, and remained in an unusually quiet mood for the remainder of the day.

The following morning, after the sheer joy of sleeping on a horsehair mattress, Katherine awoke feeling wonderfully refreshed. As she swung her feet to the floor, and padded across to the washstand, she couldn't help smiling to herself as she recalled the expressions on the faces of the landlord and landlady when she and Daniel had walked into their inn the previous evening, without an item of baggage between them, and looking travel-stained and altogether dishevelled, just like a couple of vagrants.

Daniel, once again proving himself equal to any situation, and improvising quite beautifully, had explained that they had been set upon by rogues who had deprived them of all their belongings, except for several items of jewellery which his sister had cunningly hidden in the lining of her cloak, and which they had subsequently been forced to sell to purchase mounts in order to get home. From that moment the landlord and landlady's attitudes had changed dramatically and they simply couldn't do enough for the poor, unfortunate siblings.

Katherine would have been the first to admit that she had grown increasingly impatient of her dear Bridie's incessant cosseting in recent months, but she had to own that she had been immensely grateful for the landlady's thoughtful attentions. Not only had the kindly woman provided her with a few basic necessities, including the loan of a night-gown, but she had also taken the trouble to wash and dry all Katherine's clothes. It felt wonderful being attired in freshly laundered garments once more, and no less satisfying being able to brush and arrange one's hair.

Once Katherine had completed this task to her satisfaction, she went downstairs to join Daniel for breakfast. She hadn't seen him since he had accompanied her upstairs as far as her bedchamber door the evening before, where he had informed her, prior to disappearing into the chamber opposite, that he had arranged for her dinner to be brought up on a tray. Just why he had taken it upon himself to organise this she had no way of knowing. Nor had she any idea how he had spent the evening. None the less, one glance was sufficient to convince her that he too had received the landlady's kindly attentions. His linen had been laundered, his coat had been sponged and pressed, and he had made excellent use of mine host's razor. The only thing that hadn't improved, she swiftly discovered, was his morose state of mind, for although he rose to his feet as she joined him at the table, and did not fail to ask if she had slept well, he displayed yet again a marked disinclination to indulge in small talk.

Throughout breakfast and later, after they had set off on the last leg of their journey to Normandy, Katherine racked her brains, trying to think of what might have brought about Daniel's strangely subdued state. She would have been the first to admit that there was much she still had to learn about him, but she wouldn't have thought that he was a man prone to brood unnecessarily. So she could only imagine that he was concerned that there might still be pursuers hot on their trail. It would be foolish to advise him not to worry. Besides which, she clearly recalled her mother saying once that gentlemen would share their troubles only if they wished to do so; if not, they were best left alone to resolve their concerns in their own way, for eventually they would return to normal.

And how right her mother had been! As the morning wore on Daniel began to betray definite signs of shaking off his strangely subdued mood, and by mid-afternoon, as they arrived at the town where his friend resided, his spirits had lifted noticeably.

'Except for crossing the Channel, the most arduous part of our journey, sweetheart, is now over,' he announced, sounding relieved.

'Are we so close to the coast?' Katherine asked, surprised that they had managed to cover so many miles.

'We're about ten miles away. We'll have no difficulty reaching it from here. The problem besetting us now is finding someone to take us across to England. And that is where I'm hoping my friend can help. At the very least we'll be offered a bed for the night.'

The certainty that he could rely on his friend ought to have offered some comfort, and to a certain extent Katherine didn't doubt that it had. So she couldn't quite understand what lay behind the troubled look he cast her before he swiftly turned his mount off the busy main street and into a fashionable thoroughfare, lined with large dwellings set a little way back from the road.

Drawing his horse to a halt in front of the last dwelling but one, he dismounted, and then helped Katherine to do so, before securing their mounts to the railings and leading the way towards the front door. Once again Katherine detected that fleeting look of concern before he raised the polished door-knocker and administered several short, sharp raps. They were forced to kick their heels for several minutes before the summons was eventually answered by a middle-aged woman, built on generous lines, who bore all the appearance of a housekeeper.

Grim-faced, she cast disapproving grey eyes over Daniel, before betraying surprise as she glanced in Katherine's direction. 'Yes, what is it that you want?'

Her openly hostile tone didn't deter Daniel from demanding to see the lady of the house. 'She'll see me,' he interrupted, when the woman attempted to inform him that her mistress did not receive callers at this time of day. 'Have the goodness to inform her that Major Daniel Ross is here and wishes to speak with her immediately.'

It was quite evident that the woman had never set eyes on Daniel before, but she certainly recognised the name, for her demeanour changed immediately, and she became almost reverential as she stood to one side and bade them enter.

'*Madame* usually does her accounts at this time of day, *monsieur*, but I'm sure she will see you. If you'd care to make yourselves comfortable, I'll inform her that you're here.'

Unlike Daniel, Katherine availed herself of one of the gilt chairs positioned against the wall, and looked about with interest. Directly ahead was an ornately carved wooden staircase that swept upwards in a graceful arc, and to the left was a wide archway, surrounded by plasterwork cupids, by which one gained access to a large, crimson-carpeted salon. There were several low tables dotted about the very spacious room, surrounded by numerous chairs and several *chaise-longues*, all of which were upholstered in the same shade of dull yellow velvet. The walls were covered with gilt mirrors and paintings of females in various states of undress, or wearing absolutely nothing at all, between which sconces in the shape of cupids held their candles aloft.

The furnishings were undoubtedly expensive, but far too ornate and faintly vulgar. The strong odour of perfume about the place was a trifle overpowering too, Katherine decided, before the door on her right, through which the housekeeper had disappeared a few minutes before, opened. A moment later a woman of about Daniel's age entered the hall, uttered a squeal of delight, and then cast herself upon his chest, planting full red lips upon his mouth.

After recovering from the shock of witnessing such wanton behaviour in a member of her sex, Katherine felt herself in the grip of an emotion quite foreign to her nature, before anger and acute resentment won control. For almost two days she had been forced to endure the humiliation of being virtually ignored for most of the time. But be damned if she would be overlooked yet again whilst he enjoyed an amorous woman's embrace! she decided, inwardly seething, and drew immediate attention to her presence by clearing her throat quite pointedly.

Large brown eyes, clearly betraying surprise, peered above Daniel's left shoulder. 'But what have we here, *mon cher* Daniel?' the woman enquired in a voice that was both silky smooth and seductively husky.

Suddenly appearing highly embarrassed, Daniel disengaged the slender arms from about his neck and held her away. 'Josephine, may I present Miss O'Malley... Katherine, this is my good friend Madame Carré.'

Katherine swiftly discovered that dark eyes could glint with seductive invitation one moment and become quite disconcertingly direct in the next, when *Madame* looked her over from head to toe, her gaze openly assessing and remarkably astute.

Her full lips curling into a provocative smile, *Madame* then returned her attention to Daniel. 'You naughty, naughty man! What have you been doing that you must bring this girl to me?'

'Not what you might suppose, Josephine,' he hurriedly assured her before she could give voice to further outrageous assumptions. 'But I do require your help. Katherine and I need somewhere to stay tonight. And, more importantly, we need to find someone who'll be willing to take us across to England as swiftly as possible. I shall explain everything to you presently. But first, have you a room where Katherine may go…where she'll be safe and—er—left quite undisturbed?'

A look clearly betraying immediate understanding flickered over the Frenchwoman's expressive features. 'Of course, my friend,' she assured him as she reached for the tiny silver bell on the table by her elbow.

Quite some time later, after having been plied with refreshments, and having experienced the sheer luxury of bathing and washing her hair in rose-scented water, Katherine's opinion of the formidable housekeeper had undergone something of a change. From the moment Madame Carré had instructed her servant to take good care of their unexpected guest, the housekeeper could not possibly have done more to oblige, and was even now taking the trouble to groom the long red hair which she had patiently dried on a fluffy towel.

'Your hair is beautiful, *mademoiselle*,' she remarked, at last setting the brush aside. 'Many women would give much to call it their own.'

Maybe, Katherine mused, smiling up at the surprisingly kindly servant through the dressing-table mirror. She knew, however, of at least one person who didn't hold her auburn mane in the highest regard.

'There will be time for you to rest a while before dinner, *mademoiselle*. I shall return presently to dress your hair and shall bring some suitable garments for you to wear. Your own clothes will be freshly laundered and will be returned to you by morning.'

Surprisingly light on her feet for a woman of her size, the housekeeper went over to the door, her expression clearly troubled as she turned back to add, 'Should you require anything further, please do not hesitate to make use of the bell-pull. But I beg of you, *mademoiselle*, under no circumstances leave this room. The house is large, and I should hate for you to lose yourself.'

Puzzled, Katherine watched the housekeeper withdraw. How on earth was she supposed to take that strange warning? she wondered. Was the woman truly concerned over her safety, or was she perhaps afraid that the unexpected guest might be tempted to purloin the family's silver?

What an odd creature the housekeeper was, to be sure! Bemused, Katherine shook her head, sending her long hair floating about her shoulders like a swathe of silk. It was almost as if the woman had a dual personality, not unlike the house in which she worked. One half totally at variance with the other, Katherine mused, as she gazed with renewed interest about the apartments into which she had been escorted some little time before. In stark contrast with the vibrant colours in the ground-floor salon, the bedchamber was charmingly decorated in subtle shades of primrose and cream. Foolish though it might be, it was hard to believe that she was in the same house.

Rising to her feet, she went over to the window, which offered a view of an enclosed garden. Madame Carré too, like her house and devoted servant, was something of an enigma. Who was she? More importantly, what part had she played—did she continue to play—in Daniel's life? The way she had greeted him in that over-familiar fashion suggested strongly that at some point they had been rather more than mere friends.

The cruelly stabbing thorns of that unfamiliar emotion once again made themselves felt, but Katherine stead-fastly refused not to face the very real possibility that at some period in the past the vivacious Madame Carré had been Daniel's mistress. But if that was the case, what had become of Monsieur Carré? Had there in truth ever been such a person and, if so, where was he now? More importantly, where was Daniel himself? And why had he left her here alone with only strangers?

A blessed surge of anger began to protect her from those wickedly stabbing barbs, and she swung away from the window, as bored with the restricted view as she was with the confines of this bedchamber. But what could she do? Her clothes had been removed for laun-dering, and she had been given the flimsiest of dressing robes to cover her modesty.

Suddenly feeling weary, Katherine glanced across at the four-poster bed, and after a moment's indecision de-cided to avail herself of its comfort. A book lay open on the bedside table, and she decided to make use of that too. Fortunately she could read and understand the French language far better than she could speak it, and was able therefore to follow the story of a pair of star-crossed lovers reasonably well. Eventually, though, the effort of translation became too much, and her eyelids grew increasingly heavy.

* * *

Katherine would have sworn she had dozed for a few minutes only. Be that as it may, when she opened her eyes it was to discover the drapes drawn across the window, the bedchamber bathed in soft candlelight, and to see a pile of clothes neatly placed at the bottom of the bed.

The position of the hands on the mantel-clock confirmed that she had, surprisingly, slept soundly for more than two hours. Hurriedly slipping her feet to the floor, she wasted no time in scrambling into the clothes, which were a perfect fit, and exactly to her taste, except for the slightly immodest neckline on the pretty muslin gown. This minor defect was immediately remedied by the donning of a silk shawl, which she arranged carefully about her shoulders as she crossed to the bell-pull.

She raised her arm, but her reaching fingers were stilled for a second or two by a disquieting sound, somewhere between a scream and a squeal. Then, clasping the velvet cord and tugging sharply, Katherine momentarily wondered what the noise might have been—the wind, whistling about the eaves, or perhaps two cats at odds in the garden? Then she clearly detected the noise again, clearer and more shrill this time, and definitely coming from somewhere inside the house.

Certain that someone must be hurt, and perhaps in need of help, she conveniently forgot the housekeeper's warning and immediately went to investigate. The long passageway outside the room had doors leading off at intervals on both left and right, but she judged the odd cry must have come from behind that single closed door at the very end. Beneath her guiding fingers its key turned easily in the lock and the wooden barrier swung wide to reveal the continuation of the passageway in a dazzling blaze of light, its floor, walls and ceiling dec-

orated in the same garish colours as were to be found in
the main salon below, its atmosphere heavy, too, with
the aroma of cheap perfume.

For a few moments it was as much as Katherine could
do to gape in wonder, in disbelief. It was like suddenly
finding oneself in another world, a totally alien place—
intriguing but unnerving, and undoubtedly littered with
unseen snares primed to entrap the unwary. Faint-hearted
she had never been, and yet some sixth sense kept her
rooted to the spot, as that cautionary little voice in her
head gave clear warning not to venture further.

Prudence won the day and Katherine was on the point
of retracing her steps to find the housekeeper, when a
door suddenly burst open, and a squealing female,
dressed only in a pair of frilly pantalettes, erupted into
the passageway, quickly followed by a balding, middle-
aged man, sporting only a pair of under-breeches, and
brandishing something suspiciously resembling a feather
duster.

As the ribald pair disappeared round the corner of the
passageway, the woman squealing with delight as she
received a thwack with the feather-ended stick across the
buttocks, stark reality hit Katherine with all the force of
a physical blow, and was no less disconcerting than the
fingers which suddenly grasped her arm and hauled her
backwards. The door was then firmly closed and re-
locked and she found herself confronted by the highly
disapproving housekeeper.

'I warned you not to go wandering about, *mademoiselle*!' Her tone was scolding, like that of a governess
reprimanding a disobedient child. 'Come, dinner is almost ready, and I have yet to dress your hair.'

In something of a daze, Katherine allowed herself to
be led back into the bedchamber, and made no demur

when requested to sit before the dressing-table. The housekeeper's demeanour changed the instant she began to set about the task of arranging the auburn curls, and she became once again that very obliging woman who had willingly catered for her unexpected guest's every need. Would that Katherine could summon up one ounce of gratitude now for all the care and attention she'd received!

A house of ill repute! A surge of anger swiftly mastered Katherine's searing sense of shame. It beggared belief that any man purporting to be a gentleman would ever think of housing a virtuous young woman in a brothel, let alone leaving her there to fend for herself. Yet her so-called protector, the unprincipled wretch, had done precisely that!

Like a bottle of warm champagne, vigorously shaken, Katherine was ready to explode. Had Daniel been present she would not have been responsible for her actions. Yet she somehow retained sufficient control and good manners enough to thank the housekeeper for the trouble she had taken over the arrangement of her hair, before obediently following her down to a room on the ground floor where a table had been set for just two persons.

She was conscious of a stab of disappointment only to find Madame Carré present, and did her utmost to convince herself that this was purely the result of being denied the sweet satisfaction of subjecting Major Ross to a blistering tirade.

'Ah, Katherine! I may call you Katherine, may I not?' Madame Carré greeted her with every evidence of delight, before she subjected her guest's attire to a swift scrutiny. 'I see the dress fits you very well. I was sure that it would.'

Until that moment Katherine hadn't given a thought

as to whose apparel she had donned. She was fairly certain that it had not been taken from the wardrobe of the woman who was now patting that portion of the *chaise-longue* beside her invitingly. Blessed with womanly curves, Madame Carré was below average height, and several inches shorter than Katherine. It was quite possible, however, that the flimsy garment belonged to one of those females working in this disgraceful establishment.

Cosseted and protected throughout her life Katherine might have been, but she was not completely ignorant of the ways of the world. She had been aware for quite some time that younger men were wont to seek the company of a certain type of female, and it was not unheard of for a married man to satisfy his carnal desires outside marriage either. She wasn't so bigoted as to condemn those poor unfortunates who, through no fault of their own, were forced to sell themselves in order to survive. Madame Carré, however, didn't appear to be under-nourished. And neither had that brazen hussy whom she had seen romping along the passageway been a half-starved waif!

Something in her expression must have betrayed her thoughts, and the fact that she was no longer ignorant of the nature of the establishment in which she had been temporarily housed, for Madame Carré, after a moment's thoughtful silence, lowered her deceptively dreamy brown eyes and smiled wryly.

'Oh, dear,' she muttered. 'My darling Daniel will not be best pleased with his little Josephine when he discovers that you know.'

Major Ross's views on the matter were of absolutely no interest whatsoever to Katherine. After all it was he, the unconscionable wretch, who had brought her here in the first place! she decided, at last availing herself of the invitation to sit beside her hostess on the *chaise-longue*. Outraged though she was, she was still not prepared to allow the housekeeper to be blamed for what had been in effect her own misdeeds, and didn't hesitate to make this point very clear, before casually enquiring the present whereabouts of the man who had plummeted in her estimation.

'After we returned in the carriage, he went into the town to see if he could find a buyer for your horses. I no longer enjoy that form of exercise and have no need for hacks. Furthermore, my stable is not sufficiently large to house them. He said he doubted he would be back in time to join us for dinner. But I am certain we can manage to entertain ourselves well enough without him.' Again there was a suspicion of a wry smile. 'As you might imagine, it is not often that I find myself in the company of such a refined and charming young lady.'

Striving not to allow lingering resentment or prejudice to cloud her judgement, Katherine attempted to view her hostess dispassionately as she watched her rise gracefully to her feet and move across to the table on which several decanters stood.

Madame Carré might not have been universally considered a beauty. Yet, blessed with a riot of dusky curls, a flawless ivory complexion, and a pair of sparkling dark eyes, she was certainly most attractive. She was not short on charm or sportiveness, traits which would undoubtedly appeal to the vast majority of the opposite sex, and for all her provocative smiles and dreamy-eyed glances, she was not lacking in intelligence either.

It was only when she accepted the wine held out to her that Katherine realised that, since entering the room, the conversation had been conducted in English and, intrigued, she didn't hesitate to discover where *Madame* had learned to speak the language so well.

'Josephine, please,' *Madame* insisted before subjecting Katherine to yet another of those swift and acutely penetrating glances. 'My parents were prosperous enough to afford the services of a governess for both my sister and myself.' Once again a flicker of a wry smile tugged at the corners of the full-lipped mouth. 'The dress you are wearing is a present for my widowed sister. I intend to pay her a visit in the not too distant future. Needless to say, I cannot invite her or my little niece to stay here with me, though I do try to help her as much as I can. Her husband died in Spain, and she does not find it easy to manage on the little she makes from taking in sewing. I help as much as I'm allowed, but she is very proud. One day I shall buy my house by the Seine, and invite them to live with me.'

Clearly detecting the slightly sombre, almost wistful, note in her voice, Katherine couldn't help thinking that Madame Carré was not altogether happy with her present situation. So why had she chosen such a profession in the first place when she was more than capable of earning herself a living in some genteel occupation? And where did Monsieur Carré fit into the scheme of things?

'And you, *Madame*…Josephine, have you ever been married?' Katherine found herself asking, curiosity having got the better of her a second time, and she quickly discovered that eyes which could twinkle with a wickedly teasing sparkle could harden in an instant and glint like chips of ice.

'Oh, yes, *petite*. Unfortunately I was once married. Both my sister and I married soldiers, the only difference being my sister chose wisely. My brother-in-law was a charming man, courageous and noble, not unlike your Major Ross in many ways; whereas Henri Carré, although possessing all the outward trappings of a gentleman, was a callous, manipulative blackguard who cared for nothing and no one except himself.'

Josephine's eyes, dimmed by bitter regrets, focused on a spot somewhere on the wall opposite. 'Young and foolish, I was beguiled by a handsome face and the silver tongue of an inveterate gamester. And not a very skilled one at that! It did not take me very long to realise the mistake I had made, but I was too proud to return to my family. When he had gambled away my dowry and our home, I had little choice but to accompany him out to the Peninsula, where I swiftly discovered just how vile and contemptible he could be, when he forced me to retrieve his IOUs from his friends and fellow officers in a way that only a woman can.'

Utterly appalled, Katherine was as powerless to prevent the gasp that rose in her throat from passing her lips as she was to conceal the heartfelt sympathy which sprang into her eyes. Yet surprisingly Josephine raised one hand in a dismissive gesture and, more amazingly still, even managed to smile.

'I do not deserve your pity, *ma chère*. I was too proud to return to seek assistance from my family and admit the mistake I had made. And my pride cost me my self-respect. Nevertheless, it also taught me something too. I know the depths to which men can plummet. But I have also been blessed to experience how honourable and chivalrous some quite exceptional men can be.'

The self-deprecating smile which had clung to her lips suddenly became very tender, as did her whole expression. 'When my husband was killed at Badajoz, it was not a Frenchman who came to my aid, but an English captain.'

Katherine gazed at her companion in dawning wonder, clearly remembering at least part of the conversation she had had with her cousin on that wet February day. So it was true! She had been foolish ever to doubt it.

'Yes, *petite*,' Josephine confirmed, expertly judging her companion's expression. 'It was your Major Ross who saved my life, who spared me the humiliation of being violated by several of Wellington's troops, little realising at the time that suffering painful humiliations was nothing new to me. His noble act very nearly cost him his own life. I remained in the British camp and nursed him back to health.' There was a suspicion of tears in the dark brown eyes as they lowered and focused on the contents of her glass. 'He demanded nothing from me during the time I remained with him. He gave me money so that I might return home and even went so far as to escort me as close as he dared to the French lines.'

She paused for a moment to sample the contents of her glass. 'My return to France was not altogether happy. On reaching Paris I discovered that my mother had died just a few weeks before. I didn't choose to live with my brother and his wife, who I had always considered a shrew, and I refused to be an added burden to my dear sister, whose husband had died at Talavera. So I came here to Normandy to take care of an ailing maiden aunt. She had little money, but she did leave me this house which, after my experiences in Spain, I was more than capable of putting to good use.'

Half an hour earlier Katherine would have found such a bold admission deplorable, but this was no longer the case. Now she could understand perfectly, and felt ashamed of herself for having been so naïvely judgmental as to stigmatise the woman sitting beside her as nothing more than an immoral trollop.

She didn't believe she could feel more conscience-stricken, but she was wrong. Her sense of shame spiralled when Josephine unexpectedly announced, 'Although I would never betray my country, I do not forget my friends. When I first settled here in Normandy I did write a letter to Daniel, which eventually reached him. He paid me an unexpected visit last year, in the summer, before finally returning home. Naturally, after Napoleon's abdication, we assumed the conflict between our two countries had finally come to an end. Sadly, this increasingly seems not to be the case. But I told Daniel once that if ever he should be in need of my help in the future, he had only to contact me.'

Slender fingers reached out to give Katherine's hand a reassuring squeeze. 'He brought you here, *petite*, because he knew you would be safe. And for no other reason.'

As the door opened and a servant entered, bearing a tray, Madame Carré rose to her feet. 'That, I think, should satisfy your curiosity about me. And now, while we eat our dinner, you must satisfy *my* curiosity and tell me all about yourself.'

Chapter Ten

It wasn't until later that night, as she sat once again before the dressing-table mirror, absently pulling the brush through her hair, that Katherine began to appreciate for perhaps the very first time the effect her experiences in France were having on her: changing her attitude to a great extent; forcing her finally to face the fact that, when eventually she did arrive back in England, she simply couldn't pick up the threads and continue that humdrum existence she had been leading in recent months, if she wished to bring even a modicum of contentment back into her life.

She might have been prompted by the purest of motives to agree to this venture. Yet she couldn't deny that she had seized upon the opportunity offered to sever those ties placed upon her by Bath society and its petty restrictions. What eluded her completely was why she had lacked the courage, the self-confidence to do so long before now.

Oh yes, when her aunt had been alive there had been some excuse for remaining in that once very fashionable watering place. Sharp-tongued and frequently contrary her great-aunt Augusta had undoubtedly been, but from the very first she had proved to be excellent company, and they had rubbed along together wonderfully well. Since the elderly lady's demise the previous year, however, the atmosphere in the Camden Street house had been for the most part sombre, alleviated only by those battles of will in which she and Bridie occasionally indulged.

Katherine shook her head, at a complete loss to understand why she had allowed herself to live such a repetitive, boring existence all these months, where all she had seemed to do was make and receive calls from the same circle of people. What on earth had happened to the spirited girl who had ridden at that next-to-nothing pace across the Irish countryside with her father, whose days had been filled from dawn till dusk with excitement and laughter? Oh, she was still there somewhere, hidden beneath that mantle of good manners and respectability which she had been forced to don in order to be accepted into the fringes of the polite world. How she longed to toss the restricting covering aside and just be herself again!

But had she not succeeded in doing precisely that in recent days? a tiny voice queried. Had she not, in fact, begun to reveal glimpses of that occasionally volatile and intrepid Anglo-Irish girl some time before embarking on this trip to France?

The second question, filtering through her mind hard on the heels of the first, induced Katherine to pause in her task of brushing her hair and to stare intently at her reflection, seeing not her own image in the glass but a scene in a crowded salon where she had confronted a tall, broad-shouldered ex-army Major, whose Rifleman-green uniform had set him quite apart from every other gentleman in the room. Dear God in heaven! Was it possible that she had *him* to thank for helping her to break through that repressive shroud of ladylike respectability? Or had Major Daniel Ross alone been responsible, without her having been aware of it, for slowly peeling away those layers of conformity and reserve to reveal increasing glimpses of the Katherine Fairchild O'Malley of yore?

A knock on the door interrupted these disquieting reflections. Assuming it must be the housekeeper returning her freshly laundered garments ready for the morning, Katherine didn't hesitate to bid enter, and was mildly disconcerted to discover none other than the subject of her former disturbing thoughts purposefully entering, with a pile of clothes held firmly in his large, shapely hands.

The niggling resentment at his behaviour, his almost total neglect throughout the entire day, swiftly surfaced, instantly restoring her composure. She rose to her feet, so determined to air her grievances that she never gave a thought to her less than respectable state of dress.

Daniel, on the other hand, was instantly aware that the borrowed raiment left little to the imagination, and it took a monumental effort to draw his eyes away from the clear outlines of perfect feminine curves and oh, so enticing shadows to inform her that he had brought her attire for the morning.

Momentarily forgetting her pique, Katherine cast a brief glance at the neat pile of unfamiliar garments which he had placed on the chair by the bed. 'Those are not mine. Am I not to wear my own clothes?'

'No.' An expression of rueful amusement flickered over his features. 'I acquired these garments especially for you, on account of the fact that tomorrow you are to take on a new role—that of my nephew.'

'Really?' Although the smile she cast him could not have been sweeter, it didn't quite disguise the return of the dangerous glint in her eyes. 'Well, let us hope you display a deal more consideration towards your nephew than you did the sister you abandoned in this—this disreputable establishment!'

He held her disdainful gaze levelly, not too pleased himself to discover that she was no longer ignorant of the nature of her surroundings. 'Who told you?' he demanded abruptly.

'No one told me,' she admitted, incurably truthful. 'I discovered it for myself.'

'You mean you went wandering about the place, you infuriating girl!' Hands on hips, he regarded her much as an irate father might an erring child. 'I cannot take my eyes off you even for five minutes without you getting into—'

'Had it been only five minutes,' she interrupted, her voice no less censorious than his own, 'I might possibly have remained ignorant of the fact that you, you unconscionable wretch, had abandoned me in a house of ill repute!'

'Damn it, you little shrew, I did not abandon you!' Sighing, he ran impatient fingers through his hair, clear evidence of a troubled mind. 'I discovered from Josephine, shortly after we arrived here, it's strongly rumoured that Louis XVIII has fled and Napoleon is now back in the capital. If it's true, then I very much fear our country will once again be at war, so it's imperative we get back to England as swiftly as possible. Josephine very kindly agreed to accompany me to the coast, where she made contact with a friend of hers who subsequently agreed to take us back across the Channel tomorrow.'

If this was meant to appease her it fell far short of the

mark, for she had already learned of this earlier from her hostess during dinner. All the same, Katherine was fair-minded enough to appreciate fully his reasons for not wishing her to accompany them. She could not have been of any use whatsoever, whereas Josephine had proved of immeasurable help. Furthermore, if there still happened to be those out scouring the countryside in search of them, and there was every reason to suppose that there might be, Daniel wouldn't have wished to put his good friend's life in jeopardy by being seen in their joint company. And neither would Katherine herself, come to that!

Amazingly enough Katherine couldn't help but feel a deal of respect for a woman who had suffered so much and yet had managed to withstand all the cruel blows life had dealt her. Despite the fact that the means by which Josephine was attempting to build a new life for herself, whereby one day she would be able to enjoy a comfortable and quiet existence in a modest house overlooking the Seine, could not but appal any virtuous young female with the least sensibility, Katherine couldn't find it within herself to condemn the woman for making use of the experience which she had been forced to acquire during her turbulent marriage.

Nevertheless, she retained a deal of resentment towards the being who had seen fit to place her in the hands of a brothel-keeper, no matter how certain he had been that the greatest care would be taken of her. Surely he must have known her every feeling must be outraged? Or was it, perhaps, that he had considered her so naïve, such a ninnyhammer, that she would never suspect for a moment that she had been lodged in a house of ill repute?

Perversely, this very real possibility annoyed her more

than all the rest, and she began to pace the room, striving to control her rising ire, and resist the very great temptation to hurl the hairbrush still clasped in her hand in the general direction of his head.

Daniel, watching her closely, was not slow to note the tense set of the perfectly proportioned, slender frame, nor the dangerous glint in those gorgeous eyes, before she had turned away to begin her angry pacing. Understandably, she was deeply offended, and not just mildly resentful too at being brought to such a place. But what other choice had been open to him?

Had she but known it, he had suffered the gravest misgivings, and even though his friend had assured him that every care would be taken, and Katherine would be safely placed in that totally private part of the building, where only Josephine's closest friends were ever invited to enter, he hadn't known one moment's peace throughout the entire time he had been away.

'Oh, come now, Kate, be fair,' he urged, in a voice clearly laced with exasperation. He was tired after the many tasks he had been obliged to perform that day. He had not eaten a morsel since breakfast, and if the truth were known he was not in the best possible humour himself. 'It isn't like you to be missish. Do you think I would have brought you to this place if I'd any other choice? I couldn't take you to one of the inns, and risk your being noticed. That hair of yours is an absolute bane on occasions. But at least I've managed to overcome that particular problem for the remainder of our travels. I had the forethought to acquire a hat.'

No response was forthcoming, and he began to grasp at straws. 'Look on the bright side, sweetheart. Your situation could be a devil of a lot worse.'

This pronouncement was sufficient to stop Katherine

in her tracks. She swung round to look directly at him, wondering whether she had misheard or he had taken complete leave of his senses.

'Worse…? Worse!' she echoed, regarding him in a mixture of outrage and disbelief. 'How in the name of heaven, you blockhead, could my situation possibly be any worse? Behind me lurks Napoleon, no doubt amassing an army as we speak. Awaiting me across the Channel is a traitorous wretch bent on putting a period to my very existence. And I'm stuck here in a Normandy brothel with the…with the most notorious rake ever to hail from the county of Dorsetshire!' She raised her eyes ceilingwards, as though seeking divine guidance there. 'Ye gods! How the deuce could my situation possibly be any worse?'

The grasp Daniel had managed to maintain over his mounting exasperation finally snapped. 'You damnable little virago!' he growled back at her, raising clenched fists to the whitewashed plasterwork above his own head. 'I'll teach you to maintain a guard on that viperous tongue of yours if it's the last thing I do!'

Only by the execution of some swift, side-stepping footwork did Katherine neatly avoid the long-fingered hand reaching out to grasp her arm. Daniel proved equally nimble in avoiding the hairbrush that she could no longer resist hurling in his direction a moment later, and which went harmlessly sailing past his left ear to hit the wall, narrowly missing the window. His growling threat of immediate reprisals sounded frighteningly sincere, for all that Katherine could clearly detect a slight tremor in his voice, though whether from laughter or anger she would have been hard pressed to say. And she wasn't about to wait around to find out either!

The room which only minutes before had seemed

wonderfully spacious appeared to have shrunk alarmingly, with the Major looming large and threatening within its walls. Her only means of escape was the door and she didn't waste a precious moment in making a beeline for it. She was within a yard or two of grasping the handle, when her toes became entwined in the hem of the negligée, and only the strong muscular arm that snared her waist saved her from falling. The next moment she was lifted quite off her feet, and before she could so much as cry out in protest, she had been tossed carelessly down on the four-poster bed.

The two hundred pounds of solid bone and muscle that were swiftly lying half on top of her, not to mention the one strong hand effortlessly holding both her wrists captive above her head, made any attempt at escape rather futile. Torn between indignation and amusement, she stared up into dark eyes brightened by a gleam that was no less predatory than the grin which hovered about that shapely mouth only inches above her own.

'Let me go at once, you great ox!' she demanded, nowhere near ready to admit defeat, nor reticent to continue doing battle with the only weapon left to her.

'Certainly, when you've apologised for your appalling behaviour,' he responded, with all the smug satisfaction of someone who knew he had the upper hand.

'My behaviour…?' Incredulity succeeded in stilling her tongue for all of five seconds. 'Fagh! That's rich, coming from you!'

One dark brow quirked. 'Are you going to apologise, young lady?'

'Never!' she avowed, stubborn to the last.

'I was hoping that would be your answer,' he surprised her by announcing before lowering his head, and masterfully preventing the unflattering string of epithets rising in her throat from passing her lips.

The instant his mouth touched hers, Katherine's defences crumpled, and she found surrender far too sweetly satisfying even to contemplate a resumption of hostilities. Something lurking somewhere in the deep recesses of her brain was desperately striving to peal out a warning, but the chime was too indistinct and too swiftly silenced by the demands of a body aroused by that wholly masculine and intensely special touch.

Not one inch of her skin seemed immune to the wealth of sensations prickling through her as he removed his mouth from hers to trail his lips down the length of her neck to explore the hollows at the base of her throat. The instant the grasp about her wrists slackened, she raised her arms and wrapped them about him, eager to acquaint herself with the contours of a strong back and powerful shoulders. The guttural sound that instantly followed was no less satisfying than the demands of the mouth which once again captured hers, or the hand which stole beneath her to hold her so fast against him that her breasts both ached and tingled with pleasure at the hard contact with the large expanse of chest for those few brief seconds before he repeated an action which was rapidly becoming all too frustrating. Releasing her abruptly, Daniel once again proved that he could move with amazing agility for a man of his powerful build and was on his feet within seconds, leaving Katherine, bereft and bewildered, to stare up at him. He returned her gaze for a few moments, his expression wooden, devoid of emotion except perhaps for a trace of what might have been regret, then he swung round on his heels and headed across to the door.

'I'll leave you now to get some sleep.' His voice

sounded so coolly matter of fact that he might have been addressing a complete stranger, not the person with whom he had just shared an all too brief but exquisitely intimate episode. 'There's no need for you to rise early. We do not need to leave here until mid-morning.'

Determined not to give way to tears that could serve no useful purpose, Katherine waited until, without so much as a backward glance or a gentle word of farewell, he strode from the room. Then she lay and stared at the canopy above her head, at a complete loss to understand why he should have called a halt to an occurrence that innate feminine wisdom assured her he had been enjoying every bit as much as she had herself. Yes, he had done so before, she reminded herself, on two quite separate occasions. Somehow, though, this time had been different. For all his threat of reprisals, he had been gentle from the first, swiftly extracting a response that— God forgive her!—was all too swift in coming.

Ashamed though she was to admit to it, she could no longer deny that when in Daniel's arms self-restraint and morality were all too easily forgotten, swept aside by a rapidly increasing yearning demanding fulfilment. Just the touch of his hand had the power to affect her like no other man's had done before. But so it had been from the very first, on that bitterly cold January day, when they had collided with each other in the doorway of that inn and he had prevented her from falling.

How strange that she should recall the incident now; recall too that his touch had put her forcibly in mind of her father's reassuring, protective hold. Yet there had been nothing paternal in the hands which had caressed her so gently not so very long ago, and honesty prompted her to admit that she was glad of it.

Drawing her eyes away from the lace-edged canopy,

she glanced about the tastefully decorated chamber, clearly recalling its owner's parting words after they had dined together. 'You may rest easy tonight, *petite*. This part of the house is entirely private. Be assured too that, although the bed you sleep in is indeed mine, no man has yet been invited to share it with me.'

Although Josephine might have spoken no less than the truth, Katherine was brutally aware that one might well have been sharing it this night if Daniel hadn't possessed the strength to call a halt before their mutual passion had taken them to a point beyond which there was no turning back.

For her sake, and most especially for his, it must never occur again, she thought determinedly, little realising that below, in the room which functioned as both dining and sitting-room, Daniel's feelings on the matter were vastly contrasting and that he was equally determined that it should.

His appetite having deserted him, he had managed to consume very little of the delicious supper the housekeeper had kindly brought to him, and he rose from the table, taking both bottle and glass over to a comfortable chair.

Scant compensation, he mused wryly, studying the bottle for a moment before refilling his glass. All the same, it would need to suffice for the present, though there were times, he was forced to admit, when he wished he might forget that he was born a gentleman. And never more so than tonight!

Yet, deep down he knew he had done the right thing, the only honourable thing, he reflected, leaning back against the soft fabric of the chair. No, he could never have reconciled it with his conscience if he had taken advantage of the situation in which they now found themselves. For all that she could match his passion with her own, she was a highly moral young woman. Furthermore she trusted him. How could he betray that trust, even though he now felt quite certain that she wasn't indifferent to him? When he did make her his own, and he would eventually, it would be on their wedding night and in his own bed, not in a room in a Normandy bawdy house. To have done so would have been to cheapen what he felt for her, and take cruel advantage of her vulnerability, not to mention her innocence.

No, there was not a doubt left in his mind now. Although at the beginning of this venture he might possibly have experienced no more than the desire to take her to his bed, that had swiftly changed. Katherine was the woman with whom he wished to spend the rest of his life. They were so right for each other in every way—almost kindred spirits. But first there was still that one huge barrier which needed to be demolished: somehow he must find a way to rid her of those foolish notions that she had allowed herself to believe in an attempt to protect herself from future hurt. He could not have her fretting unnecessarily, believing the worst every time he might be delayed in returning home, as most assuredly she would, unless he eradicated those fears completely and forced her to face the truth. Now was certainly not the time to make the attempt. Once they were safely back in England, once this foolish escapade was behind them, he would storm the citadel of her fears. In the meantime he must continue to maintain that control over his desires and emotions, which during the past couple of days he had succeeded in doing reasonably well, even though it had meant for the most part attempting to ignore her very existence.

'Ah, *mon cher*!'

Josephine, smiling at him from the doorway, effectively brought his musings to an end, and he even managed to return her smile, as she settled herself on the floor at his feet.

'I shall keep you company for a little moment. You have been up to see Mademoiselle Katherine and have assured yourself that she is well, no?'

Katherine's welfare had been the first thing about which he had enquired on his return to the house. 'Yes,' he muttered, as memory stirred. 'And all I received for my pains was a hairbrush thrown at my head. Damnable little termagant!'

Josephine's gurgle of laughter was infectious, and Daniel found it impossible not to smile too. 'Ah, yes, your Katherine certainly does not lack spirit.'

He stared down for a moment into the large brown eyes twinkling up at him, before transferring his gaze to the contents of his glass. 'What makes you suppose that she is *my* Katherine?'

Full lips curled into a knowing smile. 'If she is not already, then I suspect that it is your intention to make her so. And I am very happy for you, *mon cher*, even if it does mean that I have lost you.'

The small hand resting lightly on his knee did little to ease his frustrations, and brought vividly to mind a very satisfying interlude they had enjoyed the previous year. 'What makes you suppose that you have lost me?' The husky timbre of his voice betrayed clearly enough his mounting desire. 'Katherine as yet has no right to place demands upon me.'

'Her affection and her trust give her the right, my friend,' Josephine countered, before rising to her feet. 'I think you know that I could happily lie with you again. But I shall not. Even a woman in my profession has her pride. I have never yet shared my bed with a man who has left it regretting that he had been there.'

Daniel regarded her in silence for a moment above the rim of his glass. 'And what makes you suppose that I would?'

'Perhaps you would not until you had to face your Katherine again, and saw the hurt in her eyes, for she would know. She is no fool. Unless I am very much mistaken, she already suspects that you and I have found pleasure in each other, but she did not know you then. But she cares for you now. Do not hurt her needlessly. It would be better by far for you to face her with a clear conscience in the morning, so I shall place temptation out of reach.'

With a rueful smile curling his lips, Daniel watched her leave. 'You're a damnably astute woman, Josephine Carré,' he murmured, before returning his attention to the only solace he would receive that night, and finishing off the wine.

Chapter Eleven

'What the hell do you suppose you're doing?'

Katherine, who had been about to make the first judicious snip, almost jumped out of her skin, and was granted only sufficient time to recover from the shock of Daniel's unexpected presence in the room before the scissors were snatched from her fingers.

She had chosen to partake of breakfast in the bed-chamber in an attempt to delay the inevitable encounter with him for as long as possible, and had spent no little time pondering over what his attitude towards her might be this morning. She had half-expected him to distance himself, as he had done before, only speaking when it was absolutely necessary, and then in a voice which bordered on the icily polite. At the very least she had anticipated a little reserve in his manner, and yet he was behaving just as though nothing untoward had occurred between them, adopting the same high-handed approach which had not infrequently irked her during their short but highly eventful association. Somehow, though, it made facing him again after the events of last night so very much easier, so she swiftly decided to follow his lead by revealing her own faint annoyance at his imperious attitude.

'Well, I certainly wasn't about to lop off an ear,' she responded with thinly veiled sarcasm, while having no difficulty whatsoever in returning his angry gaze through the dressing-table mirror. 'And hasn't anyone ever told you that it is extremely rude to enter a lady's bedchamber without knocking first? Also that it is most impolite to snatch.

'I don't know why you are glowering at me like a bear with a sore head,' she went on when she quite failed to win an apology. 'You informed me that I was to adopt the role of your nephew. It might have escaped your notice, but boys don't generally wear their hair halfway down their backs.'

If anything his expression darkened. 'I cannot imagine why you are so out-of-all-reason cross,' she continued, taking little heed of the angry sparkle in his dark eyes. 'I thought you would be pleased that I was willing to sacrifice my hair for the role. After all, you dislike it intensely.'

This did at last manage to elicit a response. 'I'd like to know from where you gleaned that piece of utter nonsense,' he retorted, placing the scissors well out of harm's way and then reaching for the hairbrush. 'Your hair must rate as possibly the most beautiful I've ever seen,' he astounded her by admitting, before making use of the hairbrush and sweeping the rich auburn locks gently back from her face, and securing them at the nape of her neck with a length of ribbon.

It was the total sincerity in his voice that astonished Katherine as much as anything else, and in an attempt to hide her confusion she proffered a mild joke. 'You missed your vocation in life, Major Ross. You would have made an excellent lady's maid.'

'Any more remarks like that, young woman, and I shall apply this hairbrush none too gently to quite a different part of your anatomy,' he threatened, with a swift return to his former domineering manner. 'Which would be no more than you deserve, after hurling the wretched thing at me last night.'

Evidently he was not in the least reticent to allude to the incident, but Katherine wasn't so certain whether the memory of those more tender moments was one that he found difficult to forget, or simply did not wish to do so, for his expression was quite unreadable as he handed her the hat that he had acquired to complete her disguise.

'Yes, very neat,' he approved, after watching her secure her hair beneath the rim, and scrutinising her overall appearance. 'Providing no one looks at you too closely, you'd pass for a lad. Now, if you're ready, we'd best be on our way. Josephine has kindly put her carriage at our disposal. But first, she wishes to make her farewells.'

They discovered both the carriage and its owner awaiting them in the courtyard at the front of the house. None of them chose to linger long over the leave-taking, although Katherine did promise, before finally clambering into the carriage, to visit Paris again when Josephine had acquired her house overlooking the Seine.

'You sounded as if you genuinely meant that,' Daniel remarked as he made himself comfortable in the seat opposite, and they commenced the last stage of their journey through France.

'I did,' she assured him. 'Although I might not wholeheartedly approve of the way Madame Carré earns a living, I cannot help but admire her spirit and determination. What she was forced to endure during her marriage would have destroyed a lesser woman.'

'Possibly,' he agreed.

'Furthermore, it does not necessarily follow that, just because she runs a bawdy house, she need participate in any of the activities that take place beneath its roof. In fact, I gained the distinct impression last night that she spends most of her evenings entertaining guests in the card-room, though I do not suppose for a moment that she would refuse to be—er—private with a gentleman if he should appeal to her.'

Thankful now that he had spent the night alone on the couch, Daniel was able to return that penetrating turquoise-eyed gaze. No, Katherine was certainly no fool, he mused. She possibly did suspect that he and Josephine had enjoyed a closer relationship at one time. But that had taken place in the past, long before he had met her. How he conducted himself from now on was all that need concern her.

Katherine was not slow to note his look of smug satisfaction. 'Why are you smiling? Have I a smudge on my nose?'

'No, but it might be better if you had. You make a damnable pretty boy, my darling,' he informed her before, much to her intense surprise, he leaned back against the squabs and closed his eyes.

'Heavens above! Surely you don't propose to sleep?'

The indignant tone brought a further smile to his lips. 'You might have enjoyed a good night's repose. But I most certainly did not. I spent the whole night with my legs dangling over the end of that confounded *chaise-longue* in the parlour. And damnably uncomfortable it was too!'

Katherine hurriedly turned her head away to stare out

of the window, thereby concealing an expression of un-
bridled satisfaction. It ought not to matter a whit to her
where he had spent the night, but it did, and she couldn't
deny the intense pleasure it gave her knowing that he
had spent the night alone.

By the time Madame Carré's coachman had set them
down in the centre of a small habitation on the coast,
and they had visited several of the inns in a vain attempt
to find the man who was supposed to be taking them
across the Channel, Katherine's feelings towards Daniel
were far less charitable. He had been highly critical over
her behaviour from the moment she had stepped down
from the carriage and she was fast coming to the end of
her tether.

'I have not got a mincing walk. I'll have you know
that I have frequently been complimented on the ele-
gance of my carriage. And I do not simper like an idiot,
either!'

'But you're speaking in English again, you infuriating
little baggage!' he snapped, grasping her elbow, thereby
forcing her to halt in the middle of the street. 'Go and
await me on the quayside! And here…' delving into his
pocket he handed her a few coins '…go buy yourself a
pasty from the street hawker we just passed. If anyone
should attempt to hold you in conversation you can start
munching it, then with any luck they won't take too
much notice of your deplorable accent.'

Satisfying herself with casting him a dagger-look,
Katherine did as bidden, buying a pie before settling
herself on the wall by the quay. Although the afternoon
was dry and reasonably sunny, there was a stiff breeze
coming off the sea, and it wasn't too long before she
began to feel decidedly chilled. The rough woollen cloak

he had purchased for her was nowhere near as warm as the totally feminine, fur-lined garment she had been forced to leave behind at Josephine's house.

But of course the wretched man wouldn't have considered that, not when he's no doubt swigging down wine or brandy in some comfortable inn! she thought angrily, following the progress of a boat leaving the small harbour, before her attention was captured by a troupe of acrobats performing wondrous feats as they progressed along the street. So enthralled did she become that she didn't even notice a tall figure positioning himself on the wall beside her.

'You've been well entertained during my absence, I see,' that unmistakable voice remarked, thereby alerting Katherine to Daniel's presence at last. 'You'll no doubt be pleased to hear I was successful in my search, and we'll soon be leaving these shores.'

Katherine watched him glance about him. Ever vigilant, he was always on the lookout for any possible danger. 'You sound relieved,' she remarked, before taking a further bite out of her pie. 'Do you suppose there are people here searching for us?'

'Unlikely. But I shan't be completely easy in my mind until we've set foot again on English soil. Ah! And here's the very person who'll be making that eventuality possible.'

Katherine raised her eyes to see a man of about Daniel's age and build bearing down upon them. The breeze caught his long blond hair, whipping it back to reveal a face which was both bronzed and handsome. He nodded at Daniel before turning his striking blue eyes in her direction. Then he smiled faintly.

'Your nephew, *monsieur*, is ready to leave? Let us hope that—er—he is a good sailor, *hein*?' He raised his eyes and glanced out to sea. 'The wind is getting up. I fear the crossing will not be a smooth one,' he warned, before returning his gaze to Daniel, who was now looking decidedly thoughtful. 'I ask no questions, *monsieur*. I have been paid well to take you. Come, my boat is moored a little further along the quay, and my men are ready to set sail.'

'How on earth did you manage to pay him, Daniel?' Katherine whispered, as they followed the man whom she imagined pirates of old would have strongly resembled. 'Surely the money I gave you was not sufficient?'

'It is Josephine we must thank for his services,' Daniel didn't hesitate to reveal. 'He is a—er—close friend of hers. Even so, she was forced to dig deep into her purse before he would agree to her request.' His worried frown grew more pronounced. 'I do not doubt that he'll keep to his part of the bargain. But what does concern me is that he has already guessed your sex. Stay close by me, Kate.'

She hardly required the warning. It was an effort, but she did just manage to resist the temptation to cling again to that reassuring hand, once Daniel had helped her negotiate the narrow gangplank, and her feet were safely planted on the wooden deck. All the same, she followed him like an adoring puppy to the stern of the boat, where she settled herself as near as she dared beside him on a thick coil of rope, well away from those members of the crew who resembled nothing so much as a band of cut-throats as they continued about their duties.

Katherine experienced a tiny thrill of excitement as the vessel began to move away from the quayside. Unfortunately the pleasure was short-lived, for no sooner had they left the calm waters of the small harbour behind them than she realised that the captain's warning of a rough crossing had not been in jest. The wind grew very much stronger, and it wasn't long before she began to feel a little queasy at the constant rolling of the boat.

At first she tried to ignore the feeling of nausea, reminding herself that she had travelled by water on numerous occasions when, as a child, she had made frequent visits to England, and had never suffered any ill effects. Furthermore, when she had travelled over to France on the packet just a few short weeks before she had felt perfectly comfortable. None the less, she was eventually forced to face the fact that she wasn't going to be all right this time. Her head had started to throb, and she was beginning to feel hot and sticky, even with the chill wind full in her face.

'What's the matter?' Daniel had not been slow to note that she had become increasingly withdrawn. 'Do you feel unwell?'

She saw little point in trying to deny it. 'Yes, terrible. In fact, I think—'

She got no further, and made a frantic dive for the side of the boat, hanging her head over, while at the same time striving to keep a hold on her hat. Daniel was beside her in an instant, his firm clasp on her shoulders steadying her, before promptly handing her his handkerchief.

'Oh, you poor darling,' she thought she heard him mutter, as he very gently guided her back to their makeshift seat. 'Wait there. I'll not be a moment.'

Through streaming eyes, Katherine watched him making his way with amazing agility along the rolling deck to where the captain stood issuing instructions to his crew. She saw those striking blue orbs turn in her direction, before she closed her own in an attempt to stem the flow of tears rolling down her face. She felt so ashamed for succumbing to a feminine weakness that she had always despised, but she just didn't seem able to stop herself. She felt as helpless as a baby, and couldn't even summon enough strength to shake off the hand which suddenly grasped her arm just above the elbow, urging her to rise, when all she wanted was to be left alone to curl up and die.

'Come,' Daniel coaxed, when she managed to put up a feeble show of resistance at being led across the deck. He would willingly have carried her had he not needed one free hand to steady himself and prevent them both from stumbling. The Channel seemed to be growing rougher with every passing minute, but he somehow managed to maintain his balance and succeeded in getting them both down the few wooden stairs which led to the captain's private quarters, without either coming to grief.

Once safely inside the cabin, Daniel wasted no time in removing Katherine's outer garments. Which was perhaps just as well, for no sooner had he helped her on to the narrow cot-bed than he found himself having to snatch up a bowl.

'You'll feel better soon,' he tried to assure her, once she had made use of the receptacle, though he was far from certain himself. She looked deathly pale, even though her forehead felt clammy to the touch, but there was little more he could do for her except bathe her face with the fresh water he had discovered in a bottle, and then cover her with a blanket.

He very much feared that she wasn't over the worst quite yet, and his prediction proved all too accurate. Unfortunately he wasn't quick enough with the bowl the second time, and Katherine succeeded in badly soiling the front of her shirt.

It took him a few moments only to come to a decision. The captain, although undoubtedly a rogue of the highest order, had been generous enough to put his cabin and its contents at their disposal. Consequently Daniel didn't hesitate to rifle through a large chest, and take out a clean shirt. Whether Katherine felt too weak to put up any resistance, or simply in the throes of sleep was unaware of what he was doing, Daniel wasn't quite sure. However, she didn't attempt to open her eyes or voice any protest when he peeled the shirt over her head, gently sponged her body and then hurriedly dressed her in the clean linen.

He then wasted not a moment in taking himself back up on deck in order to empty the two bowls over the side, and to take some deep steadying breaths, before seating himself on the coiled rope and marvelling at his powers of restraint. He was certainly no stranger to feminine charms, but he couldn't recall setting eyes on a female form more perfect than that.

With a decidedly rueful grin on his lips, he gazed beyond the starboard side of the boat into the darkness. He could only hope that when she discovered what he had done, which assuredly she would, she would understand that his actions had been prompted by the purest motives, though he could not deny that it had been difficult to resist the temptation to look his fill.

'Your young friend is feeling better, I trust?'

Daniel raised his eyes in time to catch a roguish grin on their captain's lips. He had guessed at once, when Josephine had introduced them the previous evening, precisely in which profession her friend was engaged. A smuggler and out-and-out scoundrel the man might be, but he wasn't lacking sympathy, and he was certainly no fool.

'It didn't take you very long to guess my companion's a female,' he remarked as the captain appeared inclined to linger.

He received a shout of laughter in response. 'I am a Frenchman, *monsieur*. You no doubt had your reasons for attempting to conceal her sex. But she is far too enchanting to be a boy.'

Lovelier than you imagine, Daniel mused, as the tantalising image of that perfect, naked torso appeared before his mind's eye to torment him.

'I've been paid well by our mutual friend to take you across to England. I've always made a practice of minding my own business. It is safer that way.' The captain raised his blond head to stare out across the sea. 'The wind is dropping. We've made good time. You shall see your homeland again at dawn.'

Relieved by this assurance, Daniel settled himself more comfortably on the coil of rope. 'You do not envisage having any difficulty in landing us at the location requested?'

'I know your coastline as well as I know my own,' the captain assured him. 'And I'm a master at avoiding your patrolling vessels. No, I do not envisage any trouble. Why do you not go below and get some rest? You shall not be disturbed.'

A further rueful smile tugged at the corners of Daniel's mouth. 'I think it might be wise if I remain on deck, I thank you. I'm in need of a little air.' He chose not to add that he knew his limitations. He was a man, after all, and he didn't wish to be tempted into doing something of which afterwards he might well feel very ashamed.

* * *

Katherine opened her eyes to see the lamp suspended above her head swinging to and fro and, uttering a groan, quickly shut them again. She had hoped it might all have been some diabolical nightmare; that she could not possibly hear the creaking of timbers or be rocking to and fro as though she were in a cradle, but it was all too real. She was still on board that wretched vessel!

'Ha! So you're awake, are you? Good! It saves me the trouble of having to rouse you.'

Katherine forced just one eye open this time to see Daniel, appearing disgustingly hale and hearty, negotiating the last few narrow steps down to the cabin. 'No, I'm not awake. Go away!' she snapped pettishly, as a vague memory of his being here not very long ago and pouring something fiery down her throat filtered through her mind. 'I'm not having any more of that wretched draught you gave me.'

'It was brandy, young woman. And it wouldn't hurt to take a drop more. You must get up,' he announced with what she considered a callous lack of sympathy. 'The rowboat is already over the side, and two members of the crew are waiting to row us ashore.'

His last disclosure possessed the magical effect of some powerful restorative, and Katherine sat up, swinging her feet to the floor. 'Do you mean we're back in England?'

'Not quite, but we very soon shall be,' he assured her, helping her to don both hat and jacket, before swirling the cloak about her shoulders. Then, taking a firm clasp of her wrist, he led the way up on deck, where the captain stood waiting to help her over the side.

Daniel offered to toss her over his shoulder and carry her down the rope-ladder; a suggestion which she instantly declined. Her legs might still feel slightly wobbly and she certainly wasn't fully restored, but she had no intention of suffering the indignity of being handled in such a fashion with the captain and his crew looking on, though she was thankful when Daniel insisted on descending first.

Although they seemed a fair distance away from the shore, Katherine was amazed, once she had managed to scramble into the rowing-boat, just how quickly they reached the beach. The relief of stepping on to dry land almost restored her spirits completely.

'Where in the name of heaven are we precisely?' she asked, after watching the two sailors head back towards their vessel.

'We're on the Dorset coast.'

For a moment she thought she must have misheard. 'What possessed you to have us set down here? How do you propose we reach London...? Walk?'

'I'm not taking you to London. I've funds enough remaining to get us safely to my home, which is about twenty miles from here, where I'll be able to keep an eye on you.'

Puzzled, Katherine joined him on the huge rock a little further up the beach, where he had settled himself. 'I do not perfectly understand, Daniel. Sir Giles wished me to travel to the capital.'

'I know what that old rogue wanted, Kate. But I have no intention of placing you in his hands. I'll send him word that we're back safely, once I've reached home. But until I know precisely what he intends to do, I'm not letting you out of my sight.'

Arrogantly dictatorial his decision might have been, but it engendered such a warm feeling of contentment deep inside as she turned her head to see the rugged lines of his profile now set in hard determination.

What a complex mass of amazing contradictions Major Daniel Ross had turned out to be! she mused. He still did, and possibly always would, annoy her intensely on occasions. Yet there had been times during these past days when she had felt very moved by his displays of attention and thoughtful concern for her well-being. Although she thankfully retained few memories of that wretched sea voyage, she did recall quite clearly how he had helped her down to the privacy of the cabin, and had covered her with a blanket. She recalled too with humiliating clarity the way he had held the basin for her when she had been so helpless in the throes of nausea.

Her smile was distinctly tender. 'I have yet to thank you for taking such care of me last night, Daniel,' she said softly. 'It must have been no less a disagreeable time for you than it was for me.'

'I have enjoyed vastly more pleasurable experiences, certainly,' he conceded.

An understatement if ever there was one! Katherine mused, with a tiny shake of her head, still at a loss to understand why she should have succumbed to the malady. 'It really is most odd. I've never suffered from seasickness before. I can only imagine it must have been that pasty I ate.'

'Possibly,' he returned vaguely, as he raised his eyes to scan the cliff face, which Katherine privately hoped he had no intention of asking her to attempt to negotiate. 'If you feel sufficiently recovered now, I should like to begin the last stage of our journey. I have every intention of reaching Rosslair before nightfall.'

'Rosslare?' Katherine gaped up at him in astonishment as he rose to tower above her. 'But that's in Ireland, Daniel! Why in the name of heaven do you want to go there?'

Once again a wry smile clung to his attractive mouth as he helped her to her feet. 'Yes, I suppose I should have known from the very first,' he remarked somewhat enigmatically, just as a gust of wind sent several auburn curls whipping across her face. 'Rosslair is the name of my home, Katherine,' he enlightened her, as he reached out one hand to capture the errant strands and confine them beneath the hat once more. 'The spelling is different. It is a coincidence, all the same, that I should be taking to my Rosslair a half-Irish girl.'

The fleeting touch of those fingers brushing against her cheek was no less disturbing than the look of tenderness Katherine couldn't fail to perceive in his dark brown eyes. For several entranced moments she found it impossible to draw her gaze away. It was almost as if something tangible were binding them together, making each such an integral part of the other that they were becoming inseparable, becoming one. Then the spell was broken by a further gust of wind off the sea that caught at her cloak, sending it billowing about her. She grasped at the folds in an attempt to keep it about her shoulders, and her attention was captured by the long length of fine lawn almost reaching down to her knees.

Frowning slightly, she began to tuck the shirt front beneath the waistband of her trousers. The garment seemed much longer, and baggier than the one she had been wearing the day before. 'Daniel, this isn't the shirt you purchased for me, is it?'

He hurriedly turned away, but not before Katherine had detected the look of comical dismay which took possession of his features. Eyes narrowing suspiciously, she followed him towards the mass of large rocks which lined the base of the cliff. 'Daniel, where did this shirt come from?'

'You have our free-trading friend the captain to thank for your clean linen, Kate. You soiled your own shirt, and he was kind enough to give you one of his.'

'Free-trader?' Katherine swooped down on this interesting snippet. 'Do you mean he's a smuggler? I should have guessed,' she went on when he nodded. 'I thought it a strange fishing vessel. And I certainly didn't detect the aroma of fish.'

'No, but you'd have detected the aroma of brandy quickly enough if you'd been more yourself,' he responded, thereby returning her thoughts to the borrowed raiment, and inducing a frown.

'It's odd, but I cannot recall being given the shirt.'

There was no response.

'It's odd that I cannot recall putting it on, either.' Again there was no response. Furthermore he had suddenly quickened his pace, determined, it seemed, to remain just that short distance ahead—or determined to bring the conversation to an end. A horrendous possibility suddenly occurred to her. 'Daniel! I demand to know at once how I come to be wearing this garment!'

He stopped and swung round so abruptly that Katherine almost cannoned into him. 'All right, if you're so set on knowing… I changed it for you, as you were incapable of doing it yourself,' he admitted. 'Now, does that satisfy you?'

She could feel the searing heat slowly rising from the base of her throat. 'But-but…I'm not wearing anything beneath,' she squealed, cheeks now aflame.

'I'm well aware of that, strangely enough,' he admitted, before neatly avoiding the small fist which swung in a wide arc towards his left ear.

It wasn't so much the bold admission itself that had instantly replaced the searing humiliation with anger as the provocative gleam which had sprung into his brown eyes. 'Ooh, you—you lecherous wretch!' she screeched, frustration at missing her target only adding to her wrath. 'I trusted you! How could you have taken advantage of me in such a despicable way?'

Half-amused, half-exasperated, Daniel followed as she swung away and began to stride up the beach, her slender frame held rigid with indignation. He could quite understand her mortification and anger, though he found it difficult to maintain his countenance when she swiped his hand away as he reached out to assist her over the rocks.

'All I did was try to make you more comfortable, Kate,' he ventured gently.

'Kindly do not speak to me!'

'My actions stemmed from the purest of motives,' he assured her, sublimely ignoring the request.

The earnest admission won him a brief, considering glance. 'Maybe so,' she conceded in a tight little voice still throbbing with anger.

'Come, be fair, Kate!' he urged, determined to bring her out of her sulky mood, which was so unlike her. She might be a feisty little wench on occasions, hot-tempered and occasionally wilful, but sullenness was not in her nature. 'After all, it was no more than you did to me when I received that slight wound the other day.'

'That, Major Ross, was totally different, and you know it!' she countered, clearly unwilling to be pacified. 'You were fully aware of what I was doing the whole time. Furthermore, I don't suppose for a moment that I'm the first female to have glimpsed you in a half-naked state. Whereas you are most certainly the first man ever to have seen me.'

He hardly needed this assurance, but the totally honest

admission gave him a wonderful feeling of satisfaction all the same. 'No, I don't suppose I am the first, Kate. I expect your father was,' he teased gently, and she swung round, tiny fists clenched.

'Ooh, you really are asking to get your ears boxed!'

'If it will help you recover from your fit of the sullens, then go ahead,' he invited, screwing up his eyes in anticipation of the blow that never came. Consequently he risked opening just one again a moment later in time to catch the faintest of twitches at one corner of that delectable mouth.

'This conversation is becoming ridiculous,' Katherine announced, turning away in time to hide the smile that she seemed incapable of suppressing.

'Wrong,' he countered. 'This conversation was ridiculous from the first. So I would suggest that, instead of wasting our breath in fruitless argument, we channel our energy into something far more worthwhile—namely, getting off this beach.'

She couldn't help but agree with this. 'And do you happen to know of some way off this rock-fall, without having to get our feet wet?'

'There's a path up the cliff a little further along. My cousin Simon and I occasionally played here when we were boys.'

Memory stirred. Katherine was almost sure that the cousin to whom he had just referred was none other than the man who had married his childhood sweetheart. Consequently she tactfully refrained from comment. She had no desire for him to discover that she had already learned something of his past from her aunt. If he wished to confide in her he would do so, she decided, asking instead if they were close to any towns or villages.

'There's a sizeable habitation about three miles away,

where I'm certain we'll have no trouble in acquiring a mount. We'll be able to get something to eat there, if nothing else.'

She cast him an impatient glance. 'If you possess any sensibility at all, Major Ross, you will kindly not mention food to me, especially after what I've suffered.'

His shout of laughter might have held a callous ring, but his voice did not lack sympathy. 'I can understand your sentiments, my little love, but food is precisely what you do need, if only to maintain your strength. I'm determined to complete the last leg of our journey, for I have every intention of sleeping in my own bed tonight!'

Chapter Twelve

Rosslair was bathed in warm afternoon sunshine when Katherine caught her first glimpse of the greystone manor house, set in the gently rolling countryside she well remembered. It was a truly handsome building, not large by some standards, but undeniably the home of a gentleman of comfortable means.

As Daniel urged the weary mount into the courtyard at the back of the house, the sound of hooves on cobblestones brought a stocky individual of average height from one of the numerous outbuildings, which lined the yard on three of its sides. His craggy features were instantly softened by a broad smile of welcome, as his clear blue gaze rested upon the man about whose waist Katherine had clung for the past few hours, and a moment later her ears were assailed by an unmistakable accent.

'To be sure now, I were only saying to Janet this very morn she were worrying herself to no purpose, and that you'd return safe and sound in your own good time. And that happy I am to be proved—'

He checked as his gaze fell upon the delicately featured face peering at him round one broad shoulder.

'Now what have we here, Major, sir? Not another lad to help about the place, I'm thinking.' He peered more closely as Daniel assisted the slender figure behind him to the ground before dismounting himself. ''Tis not a lad at all, I'm thinking.'

'There's no fooling you, Sean McGann,' Daniel announced, before making Katherine known to the man who had served him loyally throughout the hard-fought campaign in the Peninsula.

'O'Malley?' Positively beaming with delight, the ex-sergeant grasped the slender fingers held out to him. 'Now, there's a fine Irish name for you!'

'And with a fine Irish temper to match,' Daniel assured him, much to his loyal henchman's intense amusement. 'Come into the house when you've taken care of the horse, McGann,' he added before leading the way into his home by way of the rear entrance.

In the large farmhouse-style kitchen he discovered his elderly housekeeper, seated at the table, busily occupied in repairing a rent in a sheet. After one brief glance to see who had entered her private domain, she rose to her feet and came rushing forward, with quite amazing speed for someone of her advanced years, to clasp as much of Daniel as she could encompass in her arms.

There was clearly a bond of affection between them that put Katherine in mind of her own relationship with Bridie. It was not unusual for loyal, elderly retainers to be given far more licence, so it came as no surprise to hear the housekeeper administer a scold when Daniel lifted her quite off her feet a moment later in order to plant a smacking kiss on one lined cheek.

Katherine's only partially suppressed chuckle instantly alerted the housekeeper to her presence. She glanced enquiringly up at her master, before subjecting the stranger to a rather prolonged stare which grew increasingly disapproving.

Daniel immediately relinquished his hold, before reaching out one hand to remove the floppy, misshapen hat, and allow those gorgeous auburn locks to fall about slender shoulders. If anything his housekeeper's expression became even more dour and she sniffed quite pointedly.

'You can take that disapproving look off your face, Janet Browning!' he ordered sternly.

Her only response was to sniff again.

'It might interest you to know that it was none other than Miss O'Malley who was responsible for my recent absence from home.'

'Ha!' Grey eyes subjected the figure indecently clad in masculine attire to a further reproachful glare. 'I don't doubt it!'

'I do not think your position is improving, Daniel,' Katherine remarked, *sotto voce*, disposed to be more amused than anything else by the servant's quite evident misconceptions.

He was inclined to agree, although he wasn't slow to note his housekeeper's faintly puzzled expression at the unmistakable refinement in Katherine's voice. 'Yes, Janet. Miss O'Malley is unquestionably a lady of virtue. And it is for this very reason that you are to take very good care of her. I shall explain everything more fully to you presently. In the meantime, I want you to find her something suitable to wear.'

'Well, that I don't object to doing,' she didn't hesitate to assure him, 'though why a lady should be parading round in breeches, I cannot imagine!'

'Because, you inquisitive old besom, for her own

safety she has been masquerading as my nephew for the last couple of days.'

Janet tutted. 'It appears to me, Master Daniel, that you've been indulging in mischief again. You always were one for getting into scrapes.'

Katherine couldn't help laughing softly at Daniel's look of exasperation. It seemed that they both suffered the same problems—servants who persisted in treating them as though they were still irresponsible, mischievous children who should be kept in leading-strings.

'Oh, that is nothing, Mrs Browning. I've figured as his wife and his sister,' she enlightened her. 'In fact, I've reached the point where I've forgotten just who I really am.'

'But I haven't, Katherine,' Daniel assured her gently, and with such a wealth of tenderness in his eyes that Janet hardly recognised the being whom she had known from the day of his birth. 'Tomorrow you must swiftly accustom yourself to yet another role—that of my cousin, Louise Durand, whom I have brought over from France, and to whom Janet shall act as chaperon.'

'In that case, sir,' his loyal servant announced, 'I'll begin my duties at once by ensuring the young lady is made comfortable in your grandmother's old room.'

Having her hand captured in a surprisingly firm grasp, Katherine had little choice but to accompany the house-keeper up a rather handsome wooden staircase to the upper floor. If the servant still retained doubts about her respectability she certainly kept these reservations to herself, and by the time Katherine had helped to put clean sheets on the bed, and had returned to the kitchen to fill a pitcher with hot water herself, the housekeeper was positively beaming with approval and evincing

every sign of being very pleased at having another female residing under the roof.

Once Katherine had returned to the bedchamber, she
took stock of her surroundings, while making herself appear more respectable by donning clothes which, she
suspected, had once belonged to Daniel's mother. The
furniture, elegant and well made, was undoubtedly
French in design, and had more than likely belonged to
the former occupant of the room. Although the primrose
bed-hangings and the drapes at the window were slightly
faded, as was the delicately patterned wallpaper, it was
a pleasant bedchamber, tastefully decorated and comfortable, and Katherine was more than happy to make
use of it for the duration of her stay.

Not that she had been given much choice in the matter, she reminded herself, as she began arranging her hair
in a simple style by making use of the combs, brushes
and pins which most likely had also belonged to the
room's former occupant. Daniel, in his usual high-
handed fashion, had insisted that she remain in his house
until such time as Sir Giles could be apprised of their
return. She didn't object in the least, but she was determined, for the duration of her stay, not to be idle. That
part of her life was now well and truly over. She was
resolved not to spend the years ahead living an unpro-
ductive existence where she had nothing better to do
with her time than indulge in fruitless socialising with
that large circle of people in Bath with whom she had
very little in common.

Once satisfied with the arrangement of her hair, Katherine did not delay in returning to the large kitchen,
where she discovered both Janet and McGann compan-
ionably seated at the table. She would dearly have loved
to see over the whole house, but decided that that could

wait until later, and that it was more important for her
to become better acquainted with the two people whom
she strongly suspected had come to mean far more to
Daniel than mere servants.

'No, please do not get up,' she adjured them as they
both made to rise. 'Would you mind very much if I
joined you?'

Her polite manner instantly won her a further warm
look of approval from the housekeeper, though the glint
easily discernible in masculine eyes stemmed, Katherine
strongly suspected, from something quite different. It
was no difficult matter to induce them both to talk about
the master of the house who, she quickly discovered,
was upstairs in his bedchamber, changing his attire.

It swiftly became apparent that both held him in the
highest esteem. Janet, who had come to work in the
house shortly after Daniel's father, Edwin Ross, had purchased the property some forty years before, had been
present at Daniel's birth. She had been present too on
that sad day, two years later, when his lovely mother
had died after giving birth to a stillborn child, and had
remained throughout those years when his grandmother,
a woman of immense character, who had escaped from
France with her daughter at the time of the Terror, had
taken charge of the house and Daniel's upbringing.

'I have to say that the house has never been the same
these past ten years, not since his grandmother passed
away,' Janet admitted solemnly. 'It's been a sad and
lonely place, nothing like the happy home it once was.'

'But surely you didn't remain here alone whilst Major
Ross was away in Spain?' Katherine, somewhat surprised, was prompted to ask. The house might not be on
the scale of even a small mansion, but it was far too
large for just one servant to maintain, and one who,

moreover, was definitely not in her first flush of youth. 'Surely there are other servants here to help you?'

'Well, there's McGann here now, and a stable lad who does the heavy lifting. Then there's Mr Prentiss, who's been the land manager for many years. He always sends men over to the house to see to repairs and chop logs for the fires.'

'But isn't there any other female employed here to help you with the general household chores?' Katherine persisted, and was appalled when Janet shook her head. 'That really is too bad of Daniel! This house is too big for only one person to manage.'

'Now, there's a considerate soul!' Janet beamed. 'It would take a female to appreciate the work a woman has to do. And I cannot deny I could do with some help about the place now that Master Daniel has returned. I do have one of the village girls come up once a week to help clean the place. But when the master was away fighting in Spain, and most of the rooms in holland covers, there weren't really any need for extra permanent help. I did intend to mention the matter at the beginning of the year, but then the master upped and spent some time in London, and was back only a few days before he went off again.'

'Well, don't you worry, Janet. I shall ensure the matter is brought to his attention before I leave here,' Katherine promised. 'It's unthinkable that you should be expected to manage the house by yourself. I wonder that your master didn't see to matters long before now.'

'He's had other things to think about in recent years,' McGann put in, not hesitating to come to the Major's defence. 'I don't think his thoughts dwelled too often on his home back here when he were out in Spain.'

'Understandably not,' Katherine responded, striving to be fair. 'Have you known the Major long?'

'Six year, or thereabouts. I were his batman and sergeant, Miss Katherine. He were a Captain when we first met. Won his majority after Badajoz. And no one deserved it more!'

'I'm sure you're right,' Katherine agreed softly, her mind's eye having no difficulty in conjuring up an image of those telltale scars. 'You were no doubt involved in many battles together.'

'That we were, Miss Katherine, and all of them hard-fought,' McGann confirmed, needing little encouragement to reminisce. 'The ''grasshoppers'' were always the ones picked to go out on skirmishes.'

'Grasshoppers?' Katherine echoed, bemused.

'Ahh, bless you, miss! That's what the Frogs called us on account of our green uniforms, but they had a grudging respect for us too, I reckon. The 95th had some of the best shots in the army. And there were none better with a Baker rifle than the Major. To be sure we've been in some tough spots, me and the Major. Talavera was one of the worst. I thought at one point we'd be singing with the angels before that battle was over.'

Katherine's eyes glinted with unholy amusement. 'Or in the Major's case possibly crying, ''Hell, it's hot!'''

'I heard that, young woman!'

Whilst her companions dissolved into laughter, Katherine swung round in the chair to discover Daniel framed in the open doorway. 'Oh, are you here?' she remarked, totally unmoved by his unexpected appearance. 'Well, you know what they say about eavesdroppers, don't you, Daniel?'

'I'll give you eavesdroppers, you impertinent baggage!' he threatened, though the unmistakable flicker of affection in his eyes didn't go unnoticed by any one of those seated at the table.

Janet exchanged a swift glance with McGann before hurriedly rising to her feet. 'Well, I haven't time to sit about gossiping all day. I've the dinner to prepare.'

'And I shall help,' Katherine informed her, rising also and catching a look of distinct disapproval taking possession of Daniel's features.

'I cannot imagine why you're glowering at me in that objectionable way,' she told him, instantly proving to one and all that she wasn't in the least in awe of the master of the house. 'Janet cannot possibly be expected to manage everything, especially not with a guest staying here. And as I'm not completely useless in a kitchen, I see no earthly reason why I shouldn't lend a hand. So if you'll kindly remove yourself from under our feet, and take McGann with you, Janet and I shall make a start on dinner.'

Although muttering under his breath, Daniel departed as requested, and went into the large sitting-room, McGann, chuckling wickedly, at his heels. 'It's all very well for you to laugh,' Daniel remonstrated, once he had the door firmly closed behind them, 'but I'd sooner be asked to manage a company of raw recruits than be responsible for that unruly little madam!'

'She's a spirited little filly, and no mistake. But nothing you can't handle, I'm thinking.'

Daniel refrained from comment, and merely invited his companion to take a seat before explaining precisely why Katherine was a guest in his house. 'So you can now appreciate why I need you to make contact with Sir Giles Osborne without delay,' he went on to say, once he had regaled his ex-sergeant with a reasonably detailed account of his recent exploits on the other side of the

Channel. 'With any luck you'll find him at his country home in Hampshire. Unfortunately, with the very real possibility of renewed conflict with France, he might well be in the capital. In which case you must go on to London with the letter I'm about to write. You are to hand it to Sir Giles personally, McGann, and await further instructions. In no circumstances are you to leave it with a servant or a secretary.'

'Understood, sir.'

By the time McGann was on the point of departure, Katherine had taken Janet into her confidence. Her explanation had taken somewhat longer, for she had found herself having to disclose the reason why a gently bred young woman should wish to embark on such a hazardous venture in the first place.

'But do you not enjoy living in Bath, miss?' Janet asked in some surprise, when Katherine had quite openly admitted that she had become increasingly dissatisfied with the life she had been leading in recent months. 'I've never been there myself, but I've been told it's an elegant place.'

'It isn't as fashionable as it once was,' Katherine responded, raising her head in time to see Daniel's trusted henchman riding out of the yard. 'There's no denying, though, that it's a pleasant place to live, and one is never short of company.' She shrugged. 'I suppose though, Janet, I'm a country girl at heart. I spent the first sixteen years of my life in Ireland, living in a house not unlike this one. Then, after both my parents died, I came here to Dorsetshire to live with my grandfather, Colonel Fairchild.'

Janet only just succeeded retaining her grasp on the bowl she was holding. 'You're Colonel Fairchild's granddaughter…? Then your mother must have been Miss Charlotte Fairchild.'

Fixing her short-sighted eyes on the figure busily working at the table, Janet scrutinised the delicate features. 'Yes…yes, I can see the resemblance now. I remember your dear mother well, Miss Katherine. She were a lovely-looking young woman, with a nature to match.'

'Yes.' Katherine sighed. 'I sometimes wish I were more like her in some ways. She was always so placid, so controlled, whereas I—'

'Tend to be a little volatile on occasions, and act without thinking,' Daniel finished for her, having entered the kitchen in time to catch the last fragments of conversation. 'I'm pleased to see that you two are becoming better acquainted,' he remarked, blithely ignoring the lethal darts emanating from a pair of turquoise-coloured eyes.

'Yes, I've been hearing an account of your recent doings.' Janet tutted, a clear indication that she did not wholeheartedly approve. 'When are you going to stop all this gallivanting about, Master Daniel, and settle down? You ain't a boy no longer. It's high time you began to think about the future and take responsibility for this fine place of yours.'

'I have every intention of doing precisely that,' he assured her before turning to Katherine who was unable to judge whether he was truly in earnest. 'Your explaining the situation to Janet has saved me the trouble of doing so. Much of what will happen next depends upon Sir Giles's response to my letter. I've sent McGann off to Hampshire to apprise him of your arrival in England.'

Katherine nodded. 'It's highly likely that he will want me to travel to London. In the meantime, Janet,' she

added, turning to her, 'it would seem that you will be
forced to put up with my presence here.'

'That'll be no hardship at all, miss,' she answered,
and this time there was no doubting the sincerity of the
assurance. 'What bothers me is what I'm to call you.'

'No need for you to trouble yourself unduly over that,'
Daniel put in, seating himself on the edge of the table,
where Katherine was busily engaged in making pastry.
'We shall put our heads together over dinner and work
out some tale which will satisfy the curious. Until word
gets about that I'm home, I doubt we'll be plagued with
many callers at the house. In the meantime, I would
suggest you continue to call our guest Miss Katherine.'
His lips twitched very slightly. 'But under no circumstances call her Kate. She only allows me to address her
in such a fashion.'

Katherine's look of exasperation only succeeded in
making him chuckle. 'Just because I became fagged to
death requesting you not to do so, does not necessarily
mean I now approve. My father always maintained that
you could lead a mule to water, but you could never
force it to drink.'

'Horse,' Daniel corrected.

'Mule is more appropriate in this instance,' she countered, which resulted in the kitchen resounding with the
housekeeper's appreciative chuckles.

'Oh, I think I'm going to enjoy having you here, Miss
Katherine!' Janet declared, much to her master's intense
relief, for he knew better than most that his housekeeper
did not take an immediate liking to everyone.

'That might well be so, but I am going to deprive you
of her company for the next half an hour or so by taking
her on a guided tour of the house and gardens—if she
would care to accompany me, that is?'

Seemingly Katherine didn't need asking twice, and Janet, watching them leave, caught sight of them a moment later, walking side by side across the yard.

Moving across to the window, she continued to study their progress as they headed towards the gate leading to the garden in which her master's grandmother had loved to work, and which was now sadly overgrown. But it could so easily be put to rights, she mused, a spark of hope igniting. The next few days would give her a clearer indication if her young master had been in earnest, and had made up his mind to settle down at last. Yet already she was forced to own that there had been a change in him. He seemed very relaxed and happy, something which he had not been for such a very long time. And there was that in his eyes when they rested upon that auburn-haired girl…

'We'll trust, Master Daniel, that word of your return doesn't get about too quickly,' she muttered, a worried frown dimming the hopeful glimmer in her eyes, 'otherwise you might receive a visitor to the house I for one would certainly prefer not to see.'

Chapter Thirteen

Katherine found it no difficult matter to settle down to country life at Rosslair. In fact, she loved it, and within a very short time had established a routine whereby she would help Janet in the kitchen for part of the day and spend the afternoons, weather permitting, in the garden. Daniel might frown dourly whenever he saw her down on her knees, doing battle with a particularly troublesome weed, but even he was forced to concede, before his first week back home had drawn to a close, that there was a noticeable improvement to the look of the rose garden.

The master of the house always made a point of returning home to bear her company during mealtimes. Breakfast and luncheon were always eaten in the kitchen, where Janet would join them to make the occasions very enjoyable. Nevertheless Katherine always looked forward to the evening meal when she and Daniel ate alone together in the privacy of the large front parlour, which also functioned as a dining-room.

Undoubtedly the parlour was Katherine's favourite room in the house. There was always a welcoming fire burning in the huge grate by which she and Daniel would sit together in the evenings, sometimes talking; sometimes in companionable silence: Daniel reading a book while she continued to make the new parlour curtains Daniel's grandmother had begun more than a decade before, and which she and Janet had come upon quite by chance in one of the trunks in the attic, whilst they had been searching for garments suitable for Katherine to wear.

Having been forced to don the late Mrs Ross's clothes was the one slight blot in what for Katherine had been a rewarding and very happy first week at Rosslair. The novelty of parading round in garments worn by ladies a quarter of a century before having swiftly dwindled, she longed to dress in her own fashionable clothes again. Unfortunately there had been no word from Sir Giles Osborne, and she had seen no sign of McGann either.

'You don't appear in the best of spirits this morning, sweetheart,' Daniel remarked, after consuming a substantial pile of ham and eggs, and glancing up to catch Katherine's pensive expression.'

'Oh, I'm all right,' she assured him, having no intention of burdening him with her rather insignificant concerns.

He had been very busy since their arrival at his home. Every day he had ridden out with his land manager, discussing ways to improve the yield from the vast acreage of farmland that Mr Prentiss had maintained well during his master's long absence from home.

'No, you're not,' Daniel countered, betraying that keen perception which Katherine sometimes found faintly unnerving. Increasingly she was beginning to suspect that she would never be able to keep anything secret from him, at least not for long.

'Oh, very well,' she relented. 'If you must know, I'm

not quite happy that we've received no word from Sir Giles.'

'Ah! But we have,' he surprised her by announcing. 'McGann arrived back late last night, after you'd gone to bed. I'm to receive further instructions in due course. In the meantime, Sir Giles wants you to stay here and not attempt to journey to London.'

Katherine didn't object to remaining at Rosslair in the least. If the truth were known, she was beginning to dread the thought of having to leave the place. There remained the problem, however, of her attire. 'I do not suppose Sir Giles mentioned anything about forwarding my clothes, did he? I left a trunk full of them in his care for when I should arrive in the capital.'

'Afraid not. And McGann certainly didn't bring anything back with him, except Sir Giles's letter.'

'Oh, confound it!'

Daniel appeared mildly surprised by the unexpected show of annoyance, but Janet perfectly understood, and suggested that a trip to the local market town was all that was required.

'You're sure to find something suitable,' Janet added. 'At the very least you can purchase some lengths of material which we can make up into dresses.'

'What's wrong with what she's wearing now?' Daniel asked, displaying all the tact of the typical male who paid scant attention to fashionable female apparel. 'I rather like her in those clothes. It's a pleasure to see a female clad in garments that emphasise a trim waist. And in its proper place too!'

Katherine's pained expression drew a chortle of laughter from Janet, a sound frequently heard reverberating round the kitchen in recent days. 'You might like them, but I happen to prefer the prevailing mode,' she countered. 'How can I possibly continue to go about looking like a leftover from the last century?'

Daniel's winning smile swiftly crushed her slight feeling of pique. 'All right, sweetheart. I'll take you into town in the gig. We can stop on the way at Lord Kilbride's residence. Prentiss told me yesterday that Kilbride's eldest son is being forced to sell his light travelling carriage and a pair of horses in order to pay gaming debts. We've not had a decent carriage here since I parted with Grandmother's aged landau some years ago. You pop upstairs and put on a cloak and bonnet, whilst I hitch up the horse to the gig.'

Katherine didn't need telling twice. Hurriedly finishing off the last mouthful of buttered roll, she hurried up the stairs to don the wide-brimmed straw bonnet that she had worn during the afternoons when working in the garden, and collect the rough woollen cloak that Daniel had purchased for her in France. Then she returned speedily to the kitchen to discover only Janet there, busily clearing away the breakfast dishes.

'I'll give you a hand until Daniel is ready to leave,' Katherine offered, and was a little surprised not to receive one of the housekeeper's grateful smiles in response.

'No need for you to be troubling yourself, Miss Katherine,' she eventually managed to squeeze past tightly compressed lips, clearly betraying disapproval. 'He'll be some time yet, I expect. He has a visitor.'

'Oh?' Katherine was mildly surprised. 'I didn't hear the door-knocker.'

'You wouldn't have. She arrived when the master was about to cross the yard to harness old Jonas to the gig. He took her into the front parlour. You'd best go through, miss, and let him know you're ready to leave.'

'Oh, no. I couldn't do that, Janet. It will not hurt to wait until his visitor has left.'

'You'd best go through in any case, miss, and make yourself known,' Janet persisted, determined, it seemed, to have her way. 'You can't go hiding yourself away every time someone calls at the house. And it's my belief this one will not be a rare visitor now that the master's returned.' She gave vent to an unladylike snort. 'Though how in the world she found out beats me. The master ain't ridden off his land since he's been back, as far as I'm aware.'

Clearly the housekeeper, for whatever reason, wished to have the kitchen to herself. And perhaps Janet was right, Katherine mused, for unless she wished to skulk away in corners for the duration of her stay in this house, she was bound to come into contact with Daniel's friends and neighbours sooner or later.

She hovered for a moment, uncertain, then made her way towards the parlour to discover the door slightly ajar. Once again she found herself hesitating, debating whether to knock or merely enter, and decided to compromise by pushing open the door and remaining on the threshold.

The pang of envy Katherine experienced at first sight of the female clad in a very stylish, dark blue riding habit was quickly swept aside by the sudden eruption of a far stronger emotion that left her feeling slightly numbed and reluctant to believe the evidence of her own eyes, as she gazed upon the intimate little tableau: the woman with her hands pressed lightly against Daniel's chest; he with his long fingers clasped about slender wrists. So locked was their gaze that they seemed oblivious to the sights and sounds about them, having eyes only for each other.

Then, as though sensing they were no longer alone, Daniel turned his head towards the door and Katherine wasn't certain whether it was a flicker of relief or embarrassment she detected in those dark eyes of his, or perhaps a mixture of both. He certainly didn't seem totally displeased to see her, for he immediately released his hold on his visitor and came smilingly forward.

'Your arrival is most opportune, Cousin Louise,' he told her, his eyes now clearly darting a warning, which Katherine perfectly understood. 'I should like to make you known to one of my oldest friends,' he added, taking such a firm grasp of one wrist that she had little choice but to accompany him into the room to make the visitor's acquaintance.

Katherine guessed, even before Daniel made her known to the woman regarding her with keen interest, that the visitor was none other than the female he had once hoped to marry. It was not at all difficult to understand why he had wished to wed her either, for Julia Ross was undoubtedly one of the most beautiful women Katherine had ever set eyes on. From the perfect arrangement of soft blonde curls to daintily shod feet, she was the epitome of lovely femininity. If there was a slight fault then perhaps it was a mouth that was fractionally too wide. Even so, it was difficult to imagine that the most hardened male could have withstood the allure of the thickly lashed, cornflower-blue eyes.

Beneath the crop of lustrous curls, fine brows rose in surprise. 'Your cousin, Daniel?' She did not attempt to hide her astonishment. 'I didn't realise you had any cousins.'

'Several in France, Julia,' he confirmed. 'Have you forgotten my mother was a Frenchwoman?'

Full lips curled into an easy smile. 'Of course, how
very foolish of me!'

Katherine then found her outstretched fingers clasped
briefly, while her own features were scrutinised. 'I quite
fail to perceive any resemblance between you and your
cousin, though, Daniel.'

'There wasn't a great deal between Simon and me,'
he reminded her, quick as a flash, before inviting her to
sit down. 'Besides which, Louise and I are only distantly
related.'

He then recaptured Katherine's wrist, once again giving her little option but to sit beside him on the sofa.
Not that she objected in the least to this cavalier treatment. She was quite prepared, for the time being at least,
to play the part of his docile little cousin, and more than
happy to follow his lead.

'I went over to France to bring my cousin to England,'
Daniel enlightened his visitor, after watching the cornflower-blue eyes flicker momentarily over Katherine's
attire. 'You must be aware by now of the unfortunate
events taking place across the Channel. It was utter
chaos at the ports. Unfortunately, all Louise's baggage
went missing, and she is having to wear some of my
mother's old clothes.'

There was undeniably a flicker of sympathy in the
blue eyes now, but Daniel was not slow to note that it
didn't quite disguise the suspicion which continued to
lurk there. 'Louise's elder sister married an Englishman,
a soldier, shortly after our troops entered Paris last year.
Once they had settled in England, it had been their intention to send for Louise. Unfortunately she hasn't
heard from them for several months. I called upon her
when I was in Paris, and assured her that she could always contact me if she were ever in need of my help.'

Katherine was quite amazed at the wonderful tale Daniel was concocting, but decided, having already wearied of her docile role, that it was high time she added something to the conversation. 'My brother-in-law, he has a house in Der—Derb— Bah! What is the place called, Daniel? My English, *madame*, it is not good, you understand,' she added, turning to Mrs Ross and raising both hands in a helpless little gesture. 'My big cousin I find is a boar, and orders me always to speak the English now.'

A soft gurgle of laughter rose in the air. 'I believe you mean bear, my dear,' Julia offered helpfully.

'Do I?' Katherine turned her head on one side, as though considering this, while masterfully suppressing a chuckle of her own at the darkling look she received from the man beside her. 'Perhaps you are right, *madame*.'

'As you have probably gathered by now, Julia, my young cousin has a somewhat perverse, Gallic sense of humour. Which,' he added, smiling sardonically, 'I'm inclined to believe she'll moderate before too long, especially if she knows what's good for her.'

'You see what I mean, *madame*?' Katherine was beginning to enjoy herself hugely, safe in the knowledge that Daniel could do little in retaliation whilst his guest remained. 'He is a brute, no? Ever since the day he came over to collect me from Paris he has bullied me unmercifully. I yearn to be with my own people again!'

'I'm certain you do,' the visitor agreed, sounding genuinely sympathetic. 'Have you had any success in locating their whereabouts, Daniel?'

'No, not yet, and possibly shan't for some considerable time,' he answered with a certain grim satisfaction. 'So my cousin must reconcile herself to remaining with me. In the meantime, Julia, I must see what I can do about replenishing at least part of her wardrobe. I have promised to take her into town this morning. In fact, I was on the point of hitching up the gig when you arrived.'

If she was offended by Daniel's obvious wish to bring her visit to an end, she betrayed no sign of it, and rose at once to her feet. 'What a pity I have called at such an inconvenient time!' She paused for a moment to slide her slender fingers into a pair of leather gloves. 'I was hoping to persuade you to escort me back to the Hall. Your uncle unfortunately suffered a further mild bout of gout recently, and is feeling a little depressed. But no matter. Perhaps you might ride over to pay us a visit some other time?'

Although uncertain whether it was the promise he had made to escort her into the local town that held Daniel mute, or there was some other reason why he seemed faintly reluctant to escort the lady he had once hoped to marry back to her home, Katherine didn't hesitate to assure him that she was quite willing to await his return, if he did wish to pay a visit to his uncle.

Mrs Ross was quite obviously delighted by the generosity of this unselfish gesture. Daniel's reaction was not so easy to judge, for he betrayed neither enthusiasm nor disappointment before he escorted his visitor out of the room, merely saying that he would return as soon as he could.

There was no mistaking Janet's feeling on the matter when Katherine rejoined her in the kitchen a few minutes later in time to see Daniel riding out of the stable-yard with his beautiful companion beside him.

'Now why on earth is he going off with her? I thought he was supposed to be taking you in to town?'

'I assured him I didn't object to delaying my shopping trip if he wished to escort Mrs Ross back to her home.'

'Well, I could have wished you hadn't, miss.'

'But why, Janet?' Katherine was at a loss to understand the housekeeper's obvious displeasure. 'After all, an hour or two makes no difference. Besides which, Mrs Ross informed Daniel that his uncle is wishful to see him.'

'Ha!' Janet scoffed. 'A likely story!'

More than just mildly curious, Katherine joined the housekeeper at the table. 'What are you saying, Janet? Is there some bad feeling between Daniel and his uncle?'

'Oh, no, miss. I weren't meaning that. They're fond of each other, right enough. Both Sir Joshua and Mr Edwin were very close and their sons were destined to be the same, more like brothers than cousins.'

Setting aside her sewing, Janet relapsed into a reminiscent mood. 'I have to say I was very fond of Master Simon myself. He were a good-natured boy. I have to say too, it was always Master Daniel who was responsible for getting them into a scrape. Forever into mischief he was. Still…' she sighed '…if his father had spent more time with him when he was a boy, he might have been more settled.'

'Were they not close?' Katherine asked gently.

'Oh, the old master loved him right enough. But after the mistress died there's no denying he withdrew into himself and concentrated all his efforts on improving his house and lands. It was a blessing Master Daniel's grandmother was here. She doted on him.'

'Whenever he has spoken of her it has always been with deep affection,' Katherine remarked.

'Oh, yes, miss, there was a real bond between them. But it's small wonder the young master grew restless, and showed little interest in the place. Perhaps if his father had spent more time with him, it might have been different.'

Katherine frowned at this. 'He seems contented here now, Janet. He was talking only the other evening of his plans to improve the land, and his intention of extending the house by adding a separate dining room and a library, and two extra bedchambers.'

'Oh, the love of the place has come to him, miss,' Janet agreed. 'But there was a time when I thought it might never do so. Years ago, when it was suggested that the young master should see something of the world and go out to India to work for the company Mr Edwin had a small share in, I thought it were no bad thing. His grandmother had passed away the year before, and he seemed more unsettled than ever.' She shook her head sadly. 'When I waved him off in the carriage, I never imagined the poor boy would be returning to an empty house...and everything.'

'You mean to discover the girl he loved had married his cousin during his absence,' Katherine remarked, not in the least reticent to reveal that she knew something of Daniel's history to Janet. 'My aunt Lavinia told me a little of his past.'

It seemed so strange, Katherine mused, clearly recalling that cold morning in early February, when she had sat with her aunt and cousin in the parlour, that her aunt's disclosures had had little effect upon her then, save a moderate feeling of sympathy towards the man whom she had so foolishly maligned. How differently she felt now! Daniel had come to mean so much to her... Perhaps more than she cared to admit.

Swiftly thrusting this disturbing reflection aside, she said, 'If my memory serves me correctly, my aunt seemed to suppose that pressure might have been brought to bear upon Julia to marry Daniel's cousin?'

'Pshaw!' Janet dismissed this with a wave of one hand. 'I heard that tale myself, and never believed a word of it! The Melroses doted on their daughter. They may have wished her to wait a year or two before becoming engaged to Master Daniel, and I cannot say I ever blamed them for that. She were only seventeen and he only just turned twenty when he set sail for India. But I don't believe for a moment they forced her into marriage with Master Simon. No, I reckon she just fancied becoming Lady Julia Ross when the old man died and Master Simon came into the title. There's no denying that some say that Sir Joshua served his nephew a bad turn by blessing the match, and that at least he ought to have insisted the wedding be delayed until after his nephew had returned.'

But not you, Katherine thought, but said, 'I imagine that Simon must have been very much in love with Julia.'

'Oh, yes, miss. He loved her right enough. And although Master Daniel might have bore him and his uncle some ill will when he came home from India, that's no longer the case, and he was genuinely sorry to hear of his cousin's death in that riding accident two years back.'

'Am I right in thinking that Julia has a son?' Katherine asked, as a further fleeting memory returned.

'Yes, and he's a nice little boy. Just like his father used to be!' Her smile was replaced by a look of concern. 'And like his father before him, he's proving to be a weak and sickly child, so I've heard. The good Lord knows, miss, I wouldn't want misfortune to befall the boy. Because if he died, then you know who would eventually inherit the title. Not that he has any desire to do so, mind you.'

Before that moment Katherine had given the matter no thought. 'Of course, Daniel would then come into the title!'

'Aye, miss. And if I'm right and it were the wish to become Lady Julia Ross that prompted her to marry Simon, if something does happen to her son, there's only one way she's ever going to achieve her ambition.'

'And you're very much afraid that Daniel might fall prey to the beautiful Julia's charms again, aren't you, Janet?'

'He'd be a fool if he did, miss. And Master Daniel's no fool.'

'Yet, the fact must be faced that in all these years he hasn't met anyone else he wished to marry,' Katherine responded, and then found herself the recipient of a prolonged and contemplative stare which was more than just faintly unnerving. 'What is it, Janet? Have I said something to upset you?'

'Oh, no, miss. I were merely wool-gathering, as you might say.'

'In that case, I shall leave you to do so in peace,' Katherine announced, rising from the table. 'I think I shall occupy my time until Daniel returns by continuing the weeding in the rose garden.'

As she made her way round to the side of the house, Katherine was glad of the protection she obtained from the old fashioned, wide-brimmed straw bonnet, for the day was bright and for early spring the sun's rays were remarkably strong. She swiftly found it necessary to discard her cloak, tossing it down on the grass close by, but surprisingly enough she soon grew tired of the task she normally attained great enjoyment from performing, and found her mind all too frequently returning to the conversation she had had with Janet.

Rising up from her knees, she went through the wicket-gate that granted access to a large meadow and, without paying too much attention to which direction she took, made her way across the wide area of grassland to yet another large field that Daniel had mentioned he had every intention of putting to the plough. After skirting several more fields, which also formed part of Daniel's land, she found herself entering a very familiar woodland area.

Suddenly realising she had walked much further than she had intended, Katherine decided it might prove beneficial to rest for a while before attempting the homeward trek, and promptly discovered a conveniently fallen tree, ideal for the purpose.

How odd that she should have come this way, she mused, gazing about the woodland which she and Helen Rushton had frequently explored during those few short months when she had resided with her grandfather. She had been contented then, living with her grandfather. But nowhere near as contented as she had been during these past few days living at Rosslair.

The thought, unbidden, came so naturally, so effortlessly that any attempt to persuade herself that it was quite otherwise, that it was merely living in the country again which had made her so blissfully happy, would have been fruitless. She might succeed in fooling others but not herself. She loved Rosslair…. But nowhere near as much as she had by imperceptible degrees come to love its master. There was little point in not facing the simple truth that it was Daniel's reappearance in her life which had resulted in her present wholly satisfied state of mind. But it was a situation that could not...must not continue for very much longer.

Oh, dear God! Why had it taken so long to realise that she had fallen desperately in love with the infuriatingly overbearing, adorable man? She had known right from that very first moment, when they had collided in the inn doorway, and the touch of his hands had left her with such a feeling of well-being, that there was something very singular about him. There was some excuse, she supposed, for not having appreciated just how strong the spark of attraction had been back then, on that bitterly cold day in January. But she ought to have realised long before leaving France that her feelings towards him had gone far beyond that of deep respect and friendship. At the very least she ought to have recognised that first uncomfortable pang of jealousy, when she had witnessed him receiving Josephine Carré's welcoming embrace. And she had experienced it yet again earlier, when she had caught him holding the great love of his life.

Oh, but what could she do? Even if Janet was right, and Julia was totally unworthy of him, there was nothing she could do to prevent a marriage taking place between Daniel and his old love. Shackled by fears that refused to leave her, she couldn't fight to win him...dared not. At least with Julia he might be blessed to live a long and contented life; whereas...

Burying her face in her hands, Katherine refused to give way to tears that might help to relieve the heartache for a while but which could never hope to bring lasting relief to a mind that would be forever tortured with what might have been possible if she had not been such a curse. There would be time enough to weep when she returned to Bath. She would have years to dwell on the happiness she would undoubtedly have attained had it been possible for her to become Mrs Daniel Ross. Life without him would be desolate, have little meaning, but better that than be forced to live with the knowledge that she had been responsible for any mishap befalling him.

The sooner she left Rosslair the better, she reflected, hating the mere thought but accepting there was no alternative. In the meantime she must take great care to behave towards him as she had always done. It could only spell complete disaster if he ever suspected that her feelings for him went any deeper than those of mere…of mere sisterly affection, she told herself, before she suddenly contemplated the dreadful possibility that Daniel, discerning demon that he was, had perhaps already guessed the true state of her heart long before she had herself.

The sound of high-pitched squeals succeeded in penetrating the heart-rending reflections, and a moment later Katherine removed her hands to see something rolling along the ground towards her. She bent to retrieve the object at her feet, and then clearly heard a breathless little voice announce, 'It went this way, Papa.'

A moment later a boy of about seven came scampering through the undergrowth, stopping dead in his tracks when he glimpsed her standing there, blocking the path. 'Would this be what you're looking for?' she asked, holding out the ball, which, after a moment's hesitation, he removed from her outstretched hand.

'Yes, thank you, ma'am,' he answered, before turning his head at the sound of his father's voice. 'I'm over here, Papa!'

A fair-haired gentleman, whom Katherine judged to be five or six years older than Daniel, came striding along the woodland track towards them. He betrayed

surprise at first catching sight of her, then his gaze as he
drew steadily closer grew very much more intense, his
clear grey eyes finally coming to rest on the fiery curls
clearly showing beneath her bonnet.

'This lady found my ball, Papa.'

The gentleman glanced down to cast a reassuring
smile at his son before his gaze returned to Katherine,
once again studying her intently before remarking, 'You
are a stranger in these parts, ma'am?'

Only just in time did Katherine remember her role.
'*Oui, monsieur.* I am staying for a short time with my
cousin, Major Ross.'

The boy's eyes, so very like his father's in both colour
and shape, stared up at her, puzzlement clearly discernible in their depths. 'Why are you speaking in that funny
way?'

Katherine could quite cheerfully have boxed his ears
for noticing that she had not spoken with a marked
French accent when she had first addressed him. Fortunately his father did the next best thing by reminding
him of his manners. 'James, that is not at all polite. This
young lady, unless I much mistake the matter, has recently come from France and is a—er—native of that
country.' He reached for Katherine's hand. 'Permit me
to introduce myself, *mademoiselle*. My name is Cranford…Charles Cranford. And this young imp is my son
James.'

'I am pleased to make your acquaintance, *monsieur*.
And you too, James. My name is Louise Durand.'

Katherine had by now guessed that the gentleman
with the piercing gaze was none other than the present
owner of the house in which her grandfather had once
resided, and thought it behoved her to apologise for tres-
passing on his land.

'Do not give it another thought, *mademoiselle*. The middle of the wood forms the boundary between your cousin's property and mine, but we do not quibble, and are both quite happy to permit the other to walk freely across the entire area.'

His reassuring smile went some way to soften his probing gaze. 'You have walked a goodly distance, *mademoiselle*. Can I not persuade you to come up to the house and partake of some refreshments? My wife would be delighted to make your acquaintance.'

Katherine hesitated. She knew she ought to return to Rosslair without delay, but the invitation to set foot inside her grandfather's old house to see how much it had changed since she had resided there was just too tempting to refuse. Besides which, it would grant her the opportunity to marshal all her resources before coming face to face with Daniel again, for the days ahead would undoubtedly prove the greatest challenge she had ever faced in her life.

Chapter Fourteen

Daniel arrived back at his home shortly before noon. He had remained at the Hall far longer than he had intended, mainly because Julia had seemed reluctant to allow him to take his leave, and had insisted on taking him up to the nursery to see her son. That part of the visit had unquestionably proved to be the most enjoyable. Young Geoffrey was the image of his father in both looks and nature. He was a charming boy, and it had been a pleasure to pass half an hour or so sitting on the nursery floor, keeping him entertained by playing with his toy soldiers.

If only the rest of his visit had passed so agreeably! he mused, dismounting and leaving his horse in the care of the stable-lad. He was forced to admit that by the time he had ridden over to the Hall he had surprisingly wearied of Julia's company. He had found her stilted conversation tiresome in the extreme and her evident curiosity about Katherine, quite frankly, distasteful.

Trying to converse with his uncle, whose hearing had become increasingly impaired since attaining middle age, had not proved particularly satisfying either. Yet he would far rather have preferred to remain in the library, forced to shout his every utterance, than be dragged into the parlour to spend a further half-hour with Julia and her mother who, since becoming a widow four years before, had taken up residence with her daughter at the Hall.

He had not set eyes on Eleanor Melrose since before he had embarked for India, and he had been shocked at the changes he had perceived in her. Although she had never been what one might describe as a vivacious, outgoing female, she had seemed a mere shadow of her former self, painfully lachrymose and decidedly jaded.

He well remembered that she was a woman who had always set great store by good manners and correct behaviour at all times; strict codes of conduct that she had instilled in her sole offspring from an early age. Daniel could well imagine that when Julia's looks began to fade, which undoubtedly they would in time, she would turn into a mirror image of her woebegone mother.

Dear Lord! What a lucky escape he had had when Julia decided to marry his cousin, Daniel reflected, shaking his head in wonder as he strode across the yard towards the house. Looking back, it was hard to imagine that he had been so set on marrying her himself once, and had been utterly heartbroken when he had discovered that she had chosen Simon instead.

One must put it down to the folly of youth, he supposed. Thank heavens he had acquired some sound common sense during the intervening years! He and Julia simply wouldn't have suited. He was far too outspoken and brusque for her delicate sensibilities. He needed a female who would not dissolve into floods of tears each time he raised his voice above a whisper and one who, moreover, was not afraid to stand up to him. And thank the Lord he'd found the very little virago for him!

Entering his home by way of the rear entrance, Daniel went striding into the kitchen to discover, much to his surprise, only his housekeeper present, for Katherine had made a point, since her arrival at Rosslair, of always helping Janet prepare both luncheon and dinner.

'Where's Kate?'

'She went out into the garden shortly after you left with Mrs Ross,' she answered, giving the broth a stir. 'I must say, sir, she has worked hard on those rose-beds since she's been here. She's green fingers like your dear grandmother, and no mistake! You can see the difference she's made already.'

'Mmm,' Daniel murmured, running impatient fingers through his thick, slightly waving brown hair, as he experienced a pang of conscience. 'I suppose I ought to be thinking of employing a full-time gardener and general handyman. I can't expect McGann to cope with everything.'

'Now there's a considerate soul for you, Janet!' McGann announced, entering the kitchen, with a pile of logs for the stove, in time to catch his master's final remark.

'If the truth be known, I was thinking more of Katherine than you,' Daniel enlightened him. 'I don't want her working her fingers to the bone attempting to get the garden in order.'

'She enjoys herself out there, sir,' Janet assured him. 'Besides, she ain't one to be idle. If she didn't work in the garden, she'd be doing something else.'

Janet smiled to herself as she detected her master's low growl of disapproval before he went stalking out. She turned in time to see him pass the window, heading in the direction of the garden, and was a little startled when he returned a minute or so later, carrying Katherine's cloak, and looking decidedly grim.

'She isn't there. Are you certain she didn't come back into the house?'

'She might have done,' Janet conceded. 'I'll go and check.'

'No, I'll do it!' Daniel responded curtly, leaving Janet now in little doubt as to his frame of mind.

She exchanged a concerned glance with McGann as she heard her master's raised voice calling Katherine's name filtering through from the hall. 'Dear Lord, I hope nothing has happened. The master did say to keep an eye on her.'

'Yes, damn it!' Daniel snarled, returning to the kitchen. 'So why the hell didn't you?'

'Easy, sir. Easy,' McGann soothed. He had seen the Major rant and rage at raw recruits who had done something foolhardy, but he had never heard him speak so sharply to Janet before. 'There's no saying that Miss Katherine didn't just take it into her head to go off for a wee walk, the day being so nice an' all. You can't expect Janet to watch her every moment.'

'It's all right, McGann.' Although touched by this staunch show of support, Janet was not in the least offended by her master's harsh reprimand. In fact, if it had not been for the qualms she was now experiencing herself over Katherine's well-being, she would have given vent to a whoop of pure joy, for she was more than willing to make allowances for the understandable concern of a man very much in love. 'The master is right. I ought to have kept a better watch over her. I'm sorry, sir.'

Daniel's anger instantly ebbed. 'No, Janet, it is I who ought to apologise.' He placed his arm briefly about her thin shoulders, almost bringing tears to her eyes with the smile he cast down at her. 'I'll leave you to make a thorough search of the house and gardens. McGann, you come with me. We'll search the surrounding country-side. There's no saying that what you suspect is true— the damnable little idiot might well have taken it into her head to go off by herself. I'll skin her alive when I find her!'

Janet was more successful in suppressing a chuckle than McGann who, shoulders shaking, followed the Major out to the yard. But an hour later, when all three reassembled in the kitchen, there wasn't so much as a semblance of a smile on anyone's face, least of all on Daniel's.

He paused in his worried pacing. 'Where the deuce could she have gone? She doesn't know anyone here-abouts now, so she wouldn't have taken it into her head to go visiting the neighbours.'

'Well, I've been thinking about that, sir.' Janet raised troubled eyes to his. 'You don't suppose she had a fancy to visit her grandfather's old place, do you?'

'But that's four miles away, Janet.'

'Not if you cut across the fields, it isn't,' she countered. 'It'd be no more than an hour's stroll.'

After silently conceding that it might be worthwhile checking this out, Daniel asked, 'Do you happen to know if the Cranfords are in residence, Janet?'

'I'm certain Mrs Cranford is there. Her husband has been away in London for the past few weeks, so I understand. He might be back now, though. It's the party next week... Or had you forgotten?'

'I've better things to think about than parties, Janet,' he responded testily, just as a carriage, which seemed vaguely familiar, entered the yard, and a moment later none other than the person whose absence was causing him no little concern alighted from it.

The immense relief Daniel experienced at seeing her completely unharmed was swiftly tempered by a surge of irritation as he watched her trip lightly towards the house, swinging her bonnet to and fro by its ribbons and smiling brightly, just as though she hadn't a care in the world. Her cheerful greeting as she entered the kitchen, swiftly followed by the laughingly uttered hope that she hadn't kept them all waiting for luncheon, only resulted in fuelling his rapidly mounting wrath.

'Where the hell have you been?'

The bellowed demand, humiliatingly clear and belittling, echoed round the large room, leaving no one in any doubt, least of all Katherine, as to his mood. Hands on hips, and now glowering like some ferocious creature about to pounce on its hapless prey, Daniel betrayed no signs of the anguish he had been experiencing only minutes before.

'Kindly do not adopt that dictatorial tone with me, sir,' Katherine told him, chin lifting as she turned to face him squarely. 'When you have managed to regain control of your temper, I shall be only too happy to enlighten you. In the meantime, I shall be in the parlour.' And so saying, she turned on her heels and headed for the door, leaving Daniel almost gaping at her retreating form in astonishment.

He recovered soon enough. 'Did you hear that?' he demanded of neither of his remaining listeners in particular, both of whom were having the utmost difficulty in suppressing smiles at his expression of outrage. 'You come back here at once, you damnable little shrew!' he yelled, striding purposefully across to the door himself.

'I haven't finished with you yet...no, not by a long chalk!'

His threat fell on deaf ears, even though his firm, stalking footsteps did not. Katherine, well aware that he was right behind her, continued to walk calmly into the parlour, and across to the chest in the corner of the large room in order to collect the curtain that she had been sewing the evening before.

She experienced a strange mixture of annoyance and relief. Although she refused to be addressed in such a fashion, and had no intention of tamely kowtowing to such dictatorial behaviour, his intolerable outburst had, she was forced silently to own, made it so very much easier to face him again; had made it a simple matter not to reveal those feelings which she must now strive to keep well hidden from those all too perceptive brown eyes.

'If you have followed me in here to continue bellowing like a bull, I think it best you leave,' she told him, determined to maintain her self-control.

'Damn it, woman!' His knuckles clearly showed white as he grasped the door. 'Who's master here?'

'No one is disputing your authority, Daniel,' Katherine responded, before calmly settling herself in one of the chairs by the hearth. 'My position under this roof, however, evidently is in need of some clarification. I am not your chattel, sir, and I shall not tolerate being spoken to in such a fashion, most especially in front of servants. If you envisage that this will put an undue strain upon you, then I think it best I remove forthwith to the local inn.'

For answer he slammed the door closed, and went stalking over to the decanters. Katherine heard the chink of glass, and could almost feel those brown orbs firing angry darts into the back of her head.

Swiftly suppressing a smile, she concentrated for a moment on threading her needle. 'I can appreciate that we all give vent to our emotions from time to time. And I am no exception.'

'Ha! An understatement if ever there was one!'

She ignored the muttered interruption. 'Even so, unlike you, I do attempt to maintain some control, whereas the rein you hold over your temper possesses no more strength than this sewing yarn.'

A sigh of pure exasperation floated across to the hearth. 'If my outburst…my very understandable outburst, I might add, offended your delicate sensibilities, then you must appreciate that I have not spent the past few years making polite conversation in fashionable drawing-rooms.'

'That is patently obvious,' she swiftly returned, attaining a deal of wicked satisfaction in pointing this out. 'If, however, you have any desire to be included in polite society, you must swiftly acquire at least a few basic manners. Which reminds me, Mrs Cranford hasn't received a reply yet to the invitation she sent you, and particularly requested me to remind you of the party being held at her house next week.'

The hand raising the glass to Daniel's lips checked for a moment. 'So you did go over to your grandfather's old house.'

'Yes,' she admitted. 'I didn't intend to walk so far. I had hoped to be back before you returned.' Out of the corner of her eye, she saw him lower his tall frame into a nearby chair. His expression betrayed clearly enough that he remained in no good humour, but at least he was no longer looking as black as thunder. 'Did you enjoy your visit to your uncle?'

The heavy frown descended once more. 'No, damn it, I did not! My uncle's as deaf as a post. And I cannot abide insipid female conversation.' He paused to sample the contents of his glass. Which evidently had a soothing effect on his temper, for he sounded far more composed as he added, 'I quite enjoyed the time I spent with the boy, though.'

Katherine raised her head at this. 'Your late cousin's son?' Receiving only a nod in response she added, 'Janet seems to think he's something of a sickly child.'

'Rubbish! Julia fusses too much.' Disapproval was clearly back in his voice. 'There's nothing wrong with little Geoffrey. He's a stout little fellow who'll no doubt live to a ripe old age… At least, I sincerely hope he does. I have no desire to step into his shoes.'

Katherine did not doubt the truth of this. She knew Daniel well enough to be sure that possessing a title would mean little to him. She also realised now that whatever feelings he still retained for Julia Ross love did not number among them, and could not help feeling that it might have been better, at least for her sake, if it had, for he couldn't have made it clearer by his attitude over her recent absence that he was not indifferent to her.

'Well, if it's any consolation,' she remarked, swiftly channelling her thoughts in a new direction, 'I came away from my visit with mixed feelings too. I thought Mrs Cranford most charming. She insisted I return here in their carriage, and she also invited me to the party next week.' She frowned slightly. 'I'm not too sure about her husband, though. I found his regard faintly unnerving.'

Daniel studied her for a moment over the rim of his glass. 'In what way?'

'Oh, I don't know. He just kept staring at me. It made me feel a little uncomfortable,' she admitted, just as the door opened, and Janet entered to inform them that a Mr Ashcroft had arrived and was wishful to see them.

'Ashcroft…?' Daniel's brows snapped together again. 'Never heard of the fellow! Probably here trying to sell me something. Tell him to take himself off!'

'No, wait!' Katherine, placing her sewing to one side, didn't hesitate to countermand the order. 'If it's the person I think it is, I most certainly wish to see him. Ask him to come in, Janet.'

When Daniel watched the slight, middle-aged man, who bore all the appearance of a downtrodden and over-worked lawyer's clerk, enter a few moments later, he thought his suspicions were correct, until Katherine darted forward to clasp the man's bony fingers.

'Oh, it is you, Mr Ashcroft! How happy I am to see that you arrived back safely.'

'And I you, Miss O'Malley,' he assured her, before darting a wary glance at the tall figure who now stood staring frowningly down at him from a position in front of the hearth.

'Are you acquainted with Major Ross, sir?' Katherine enquired, drawing the diffident, middle-aged man forward.

'No, I've not had the pleasure,' he admitted, extending a nervous hand in the direction of the tall man who continued to regard him with faintly hostile eyes. 'But I've heard a great deal about you, sir, from Sir Giles.'

'Ha! Have you, by gad!'

Mr Ashcroft not surprisingly appeared faintly unnerved by the gruff response, and so Katherine hurriedly intervened. 'Do not pay Major Ross any mind, dear sir. He's in a bad humour, but will recover presently, I assure you.'

Ignoring Daniel's muttered oath, Katherine invited their visitor to take a seat. 'Can I offer you some refreshment? A glass of wine, perhaps?'

'No, thank you, dear young lady. And I must not stay. I came here only to pass on a message from Sir Giles.' Mr Ashcroft risked a fleeting look up at Daniel once again, before fixing his gaze on Katherine's far more amiable countenance. 'You are to stay here with Major Ross, and attend the party Mr and Mrs Cranford are holding on Friday next. I am to pay a brief visit to Mr Cranford as soon as I leave here to apprise him of the situation. Unfortunately he had left London before news of your safe arrival reached us.'

'Ah!' Katherine exclaimed, enlightenment dawning. 'So Sir Giles and Mr Cranford are engaged in the same work, are they?'

'Er—in a manner of speaking, yes, miss,' he admitted, casting yet a further tentative glance in the general direction of the hearth. 'Sir Giles has every intention of making your presence known in the—er—right quarter, as you might say, at the appropriate time, and has taken the precaution of sending two of his best men down here to look after you.'

Betraying great fortitude, he then turned his attention to Daniel. 'Sir Giles wishes me to assure you, sir, that the young lady will be in no danger. You are to make use of the two men who travelled with me from the capital in any capacity you think fit. There will be others arriving soon in the locale, and my sister and I shall ourselves be putting up at the local inn. Needless to say, there must be no contact between us once I leave here.'

'Evidently Sir Giles expects the traitor to act as soon as he knows of Katherine's safe arrival,' Daniel remarked, after tossing the remaining contents of his glass down his throat.

'Sir Giles knows how to play the game, sir. He's refining every detail at this very moment. The men he's sent down are merely a precaution, sir, nothing more,' Mr Ashcroft didn't hesitate to assure him. 'Sir Giles knew you'd expect nothing less. The traitor will be given insufficient time to act before next Friday. He'll need to make contact with his associates. But Sir Giles is convinced that if an attempt to…to abduct Miss O'Malley will be made, it will occur on the day of the party, perhaps even at the event itself. Time is not on the traitor's side, sir. He must prevent Sir Giles from escorting Miss O'Malley to London.'

Daniel appeared decidedly grim, and Katherine was experiencing certain misgivings now that all the scheming and planning were showing signs of achieving a result, but steadfastly refused to betray her feelings of unease. 'Then we must all be patient and wait for events to unfold.'

'Believe me when I tell you, Miss O'Malley, that your safety is Sir Giles's main concern,' he reiterated. 'Try as best you can to continue as normal.' Mr Ashcroft made to leave, but then bethought himself of something else. 'By the by, I've brought your trunk of clothes from London, miss. I'll instruct the two men I'm leaving here to carry it into the house for you.'

'Oh, you darling man!' Katherine darted forward to place a kiss on Mr Ashcroft's thin cheek, which had the effect of sending him quite pink with pleasure before he took his leave.

Daniel, unable to suppress a smile, went over to the

decanters to replenish his glass. 'How typical of a woman! At a time like this the only thing that concerns you is clothes.'

'But of course! It will be sheer bliss to don my own garments again. Besides which, Daniel, you know yourself we've nothing to worry about for the next few days.'

'Possibly not,' he conceded. 'At least now I've no qualms about sending a note to my uncle accepting his invitation to accompany him to the local market town to view some livestock next Friday morning. And those two men will certainly come in handy about the place. For a start, I shall set one to work in the garden to keep a permanent eye on you and make sure you don't take it into your head to go wandering off again.'

'Do so, by all means. I shall enjoy the company,' she assured him, refusing to become nettled. 'It's just a pity Sir Giles didn't think to send us a female.'

Daniel raised his brows in surprise. 'Not necessary. Janet can keep an eye on you whilst you're indoors.'

'And how typical of a man!' Katherine parried, casting him a look of exasperation before reaching for the door-handle. 'Janet has far too much to do to watch me all day. It's high time, Daniel Ross, that you sorted out your domestic situation. Janet is in desperate need of help about the place. The sooner this house has a mistress to take charge the better!'

Smiling tenderly, Daniel gazed down into his glass. 'It has already acquired the only one it will ever have whilst I remain master here,' he murmured, the instant Katherine had departed, closing the door quietly behind her.

Chapter Fifteen

'Can I not persuade you to step into the house for a glass of burgundy before you set off home, my boy?' Sir Joshua's invitation was heard even by the footman who emerged from the house in order to assist his master to alight from the carriage.

Daniel hesitated. The visit to the market town had proved surprisingly enjoyable. Not only had he been impressed by the high standard of farm stock offered for sale, but he had come upon a number of neighbours whom he had not seen in a very long time, and had received several invitations to dine. He was eager to return to Rosslair and tell Katherine about the trip, but decided that that could wait a while longer. Sir Joshua didn't socialise to any great extent these days, his hearing having become an increasing handicap, and Daniel had gained the distinct impression that his uncle pined for a little masculine company from time to time.

'That sounds a fine idea,' he responded, accompanying him into the house. 'But I can't stay for too long. There are matters I must attend to back home. And there's the party at the Cranfords' place this evening, remember?'

'Going to be a large affair, by all accounts,' Sir Joshua remarked, before his attention was claimed by his butler who informed him that he had a visitor awaiting him in the parlour.

Although his hearing might be sadly impaired, there was absolutely nothing amiss with his mental faculties, as he proved when he entered the comfortable room, and recognised at once the fashionably attired young gentleman whom his daughter-in-law had been entertaining during his absence.

'Why, it's young George Gifford, ain't it?' he announced loudly, as his unexpected visitor rose from the chair to shake his outstretched hand. 'Some relation of Lord Waverley's, if my memory serves me correctly.'

'Y-yes, that's r-right, sir,' he responded, casting a penetrating glance beyond his host's left shoulder at the spot where Daniel stood.

'Are you acquainted with my nephew, Major Ross?'

'N-no, I've not had the p-pleasure, Sir Joshua.'

Daniel's eyes narrowed as the dandified sprig took his outstretched hand in a surprisingly firm clasp. 'We have never been introduced, Mr Gifford, but I feel certain that I've seen you somewhere before.'

'Quite p-possibly, sir. I've been s-staying in London with Lord Waverley for the p-past few weeks. Perhaps it was there.'

'No, I do not think so,' Daniel countered, accepting the glass of wine Julia held out to him. 'I haven't been in the capital for several weeks.'

'No, been gadding about across the Channel, would you believe?' Sir Joshua put in, seating himself in his favourite chair and staring owlishly up at his nephew, who had positioned himself by the hearth. 'And what's this Julia has been telling me about you bringing back a young female relation of yours?'

Daniel saw Julia's eyes turn swiftly in his direction, but it was the sudden arresting look he perceived in Mr Gifford's dark orbs as the young man resumed his seat which momentarily captured his attention. 'Yes, dear Louise is still with me, I'm delighted to say. I'm escorting her to the party tonight, as it happens.'

'Look forward to meeting the gel,' Sir Joshua declared, before sampling his wine. 'Can't recall your ever mentioning her before, though.'

'No?' Daniel shrugged. 'Well, as I believe I explained to Julia, Louise and I are only distantly related. My grandmother did have a few relations who, like herself, managed to escape the Terror.'

'Damned fine woman, your grandmother,' Sir Joshua announced. 'I was fond of her.'

Daniel's expression softened noticeably. 'I'm certain you will like Louise Durand when you meet her, sir. She is very like my grandmother in many ways.'

'But not in looks. That you must own,' Julia, much to Daniel's annoyance, was not reticent to point out. 'Why, she has flaming red hair!'

Plainly she remained sceptical about the kinship, and Daniel, although continuing to gaze across at his uncle, was conscious of her staring fixedly in his direction, as though expecting him to explain the precise relationship. He found himself experiencing a resurgence of the irritation he had felt when he had accompanied her back to the Hall earlier in the week. Even had he wished to do so he could not at this juncture reveal Katherine's true identity, but he experienced no reluctance whatsoever in revealing the depths of his feelings towards her.

'Her similarity to my grandmother is in character, not

looks. She is quite simply a breath of fresh air. Her mere presence under the roof has turned my house into a home. I could never be content if she remained away from Rosslair for any length of time.'

Unlike his daughter-in-law, who looked as though she had just received a sharp slap across the face, Sir Joshua positively beamed with delight. 'Well, if that's the way of it, my boy, I sincerely do look forward to meeting the girl!' He then returned his attention to his unexpected guest, who was staring thoughtfully down into the contents of his glass, and asked him where he was putting up.

'W-with the C-cranfords, sir,' he answered with a start, as though he had been locked in a world of his own. 'Set out y-yesterday evening. I-I've never been in this part of the world b-before, and wished to see s-something of the countryside. My c-cousin should be arriving any time now.'

'Is Waverley coming down?' Sir Joshua appeared mildly surprised. 'I would have thought, with all this business flaring up again across the Channel, he would have remained in the capital.' He frowned as he continued to stare across at his young visitor. 'Isn't your cousin connected in some way with the War Office? Or am I thinking of someone else?'

'He w-was once, sir, I believe. So too was Viscount Davenham. And he intends to be at the party tonight. Sir Giles Osborne also means to attend, so I've heard.'

'Good gad!' Sir Joshua's bushy, greying brows rose this time. 'If that's the case they can't be taking recent events very seriously.'

'That I c-couldn't say.' Quickly finishing off his wine, Mr Gifford rose to his feet. 'I'd b-better be getting back now, sir. Thought I'd just call to see you as I was in the area, and I l-look forward to seeing you again at the p-party tonight.'

'Are you well acquainted with him, Uncle?' Daniel asked, after Julia, still appearing rather shaken, accompanied Mr Gifford from the room.

Sir Joshua shook his head. 'Met him only once before, when I travelled up to town with Cranford last month and we dined together at our club. Waverley was there. He introduced us.'

Daniel could not rid himself of the suspicion that he had seen the young man somewhere before, and began to experience a decidedly uneasy feeling. There was just something artificial about him. His stuttering speech made him appear nervy, and his fashionable attire slightly dandified, but there was no timidity about the directness of his gaze. 'Was Sir Giles Osborne at the club that night, by any chance?'

'Why, I do believe he was, yes! And Lord Davenham too. We all sat at the same table, playing cards. Are you acquainted with him?'

Daniel's eyes narrowed speculatively. His uncle had travelled to London with Cranford round about the time he himself had set forth on his journey to France. Could it possibly have been that night at the club that Sir Giles had told his totally fabricated tale about Justine leaving certain documents in the hands of a lawyer? It was certainly a possibility, and if he had, then it was reasonable to assume that he suspected someone seated at that table of being the traitor.

Cranford and Sir Joshua were certainly out of the reckoning. Sir Joshua had never had any connection with the War Office. Furthermore, Sir Giles would never have selected Daniel himself to aid him if he had suspected for a moment that Sir Joshua was a traitor. Their rela-

tionship was just too close. Gifford at twenty-three, or
four at most, was too young to be the traitor, although
he could well be in league now with the man Sir Giles
was determined to unearth. So that just left Davenham
and Waverley, both of whom had had some connection
with the War Office, and both of whom had been at
White's on that particular night. More disturbing still
was that both men were to be among the guests at the
Cranfords' party that evening.

'I'm not acquainted with either Davenham or Waverley,' Daniel admitted. 'But I do know Sir Giles.'

'Ah, yes. Now you mention it, I do believe Osborne
remarked upon the fact,' Sir Joshua disclosed, before his
frown returned. 'Deuced odd that young Gifford should
put himself to the trouble of paying me a visit on so
brief an acquaintance, especially as he didn't seem inclined to remain very long after we'd returned, don't you
agree?'

'Perhaps he didn't wish to outstay his welcome,' Daniel responded, staring intently at an imaginary spot on
the carpet. Or maybe he discovered what he came here
to find out, he added silently to himself.

That evening, while she busied herself getting ready
for the party, Katherine succeeded in maintaining a flow
of light-hearted conversation with Janet who, showing
no little expertise, was arranging those striking auburn
locks in a more elaborate style for the occasion. Yet
beneath the carefree exterior Katherine felt as if she were
being ripped in two. She knew her stay at Rosslair was
rapidly drawing to an end, and she found the mere
thought of leaving excruciating, while at the same time
she knew it was for the best, for she was not made of
iron, and sooner or later she would buckle under the

strain of striving to keep her feelings towards the master of the house well hidden.

She was under no illusions that this evening would prove to be the greatest trial of all, for not only must she continue behaving like some fond sister towards Daniel, she must also adopt the role which Sir Giles expected her to play: a double burden, but one she refused to attempt to postpone. So, after taking one last look at her overall appearance in the full length mirror, she picked up her shawl, and left the room.

She discovered Daniel awaiting her in the hall. Although he possessed some fine clothes, he hadn't taken the trouble to acquire any fashionable evening apparel since his return to England the previous year. Consequently he had chosen to don, of all things, the Rifleman-green dress uniform he had worn on the occasion of her cousin's engagement party, which she found a faintly poignant coincidence, for she had chosen to wear none other than the gown she had worn on that particular occasion.

Daniel turned as he detected her light footfall on the stairs, and smiled wryly as he cast appreciative eyes over her faultless appearance. 'I have seen you wearing some charming dresses during these past days, Kate, but I think that particular gown will always retain a very special place in my memory long after it has been consigned to the rag box.'

She didn't pretend to misunderstand. 'Yes, it is somewhat ironic, is it not, that we should have chosen to dress in these particular garments this evening?' She came to stand before him, her eyes gently teasing as she stared up at those ruggedly attractive features. 'I hope it isn't an omen and we end the evening by being at outs with each other.'

She had intended the remark as a joke, but it was clear that he wasn't amused. 'You do not have to go through with this, Kate. It isn't too late to change your mind. No one would think any less of you if you did cry off.'

One would have needed to be deaf not to have detected the note of deep concern in his voice, and blind not to see the worry etched in each rugged contour of that beloved face, which would remain imprinted in her memory until her last breath.

He had been in a strangely subdued mood since he arrived home early in the afternoon, after his visit to the market town. He had openly admitted to enjoying the visit, and yet something had occurred to trouble him during his absence from home. 'I should,' she countered softly. 'I would be a liar if I said I wasn't a little apprehensive. But you know that Mr Ashcroft assured us both that I will be guarded throughout the entire evening.'

The troubled expression remained. Clearly he was unconvinced, but Katherine had more faith. 'Sir Giles has done everything humanly possible to ensure my safety thus far, Daniel,' she reminded him. 'He could not have provided me with a better protector than you. If our roles were reversed, I know that you would see this thing through to the end.'

He didn't attempt to deny it, and yet she sensed that he was suppressing the strong desire to sweep her up in his arms, carry her back up the stairs and lock her in her room. He was more than capable of doing it, too! Surprisingly, though, all he did was merely raise his hands and take a gentle hold of her upper arms. 'Then I would ask only one thing. At the risk of receiving a second rebuff, my precious virago, will you dance with me this evening?'

For several moments Katherine was obliged to grasp

her bottom lip between her teeth to stop it from trembling, as a surge of conflicting emotions, not least of which was a searing sense of shame, came perilously close to crushing the praiseworthy self-control she had managed to exert over herself during these past days. Only the tenuous thread of determination she still managed to retain enabled her to meet the tender gaze of the man she had once so naïvely held in such foolish contempt.

Raising her own hands, she placed them on the shoulders of the black-braided dark green jacket that suited him so well. 'I would be so very honoured to stand up with you tonight…my grasshopper.'

For one heart-stopping moment she thought he might kiss her, and feared she could never summon up enough will to resist if he tried. Fortunately her reserves of resolve were not further depleted, for McGann, forcing them to part, came striding into the hall to inform them that the carriage was ready and waiting at the door.

'I wish you'd let me come with you, sir,' he remarked with a hopeful glance in his master's direction.

'No, McGann.' Daniel's voice brooked no argument. 'Those two bodyguards Sir Giles sent have proved reliable. They will provide sufficient protection for the journey. Besides, I want you to keep watch here, to look after Janet, just in case we should receive an unwanted visitor.'

Mention of the housekeeper thankfully enabled Katherine to turn her thoughts in a new direction, as it brought forcibly to mind a conversation she had had with Janet earlier in the day, and prevented her from dwelling on the fact, as she went outside to the waiting carriage, that in all probability she would never again set foot in the house which she had come perilously close to treating as her very own home.

'Janet wishes to retire, Daniel,' she enlightened him, as the carriage began to move out of the yard. 'Apparently your father promised her one of the cottages he had constructed on his land,' she went on when he made no comment.

'If she said my father promised her that, then I for one do not doubt it,' he eventually remarked, appearing more subdued than ever.

'I can appreciate your reluctance in parting with her,' she responded softly, understanding his feelings perfectly. 'Good housekeepers are hard to find, and Janet is a treasure. But you must take her wishes into consideration. She's no longer young and the work is too much for her.'

'Yes, you're right, of course,' he agreed. 'Do you happen to know of anyone suitable who could fill her shoes?'

Oh, yes—she knew of someone, sure enough. She knew of the ideal replacement. But not for the world would she ever part with her dear Bridie, not even for him. Besides, she had the feeling that she was going to need that unfailingly loyal Irish woman's loving support during the weeks, months, maybe even years ahead.

'You must be aware by now, Kate, that I value your opinion,' Daniel prompted, when the view from the window appeared to have captured her interest. 'I wouldn't have dreamt of purchasing this comfortable carriage and team of fine horses if I hadn't received your full approval.'

'Liar,' she said softly, while praying her resolve, which was weakening with every passing second, did not crumple completely. 'You had made up your mind to purchase this fine turnout the instant you set your eyes upon it. And you'll manage to acquire a housekeeper without any help from me, too.' You are going to have to do so, she added silently.

Blessedly the journey to her grandfather's old house was soon accomplished, and Katherine was able, with a reasonable degree of success, to concentrate her thoughts on the vital role she had been entrusted to play that night.

No sooner had they been greeted by their host and hostess than Sir Giles Osborne approached them, appearing remarkably composed. 'Well, *mes enfants*, all goes well, I think,' he purred silkily.

'And it had better continue to do so,' Daniel muttered at his most grim, the effect of which was to bring one of those rare smiles to the taciturn baronet's thin-lipped mouth.

'I do not doubt that my days on this earth would be well and truly numbered if, indeed, it does not prove to be the case,' Sir Giles parried before instructing Daniel to go away and mix with his friends and neighbours. 'You may safely leave your so charming cousin in my care.

'Well, how goes it with you, Mademoiselle Durand?' he enquired, when Daniel, much to Katherine's surprise, did as bidden. 'I trust you didn't find the journey from France too—er—fatiguing, child?'

'It was certainly memorable,' she answered, refusing to divulge more of what for her would undoubtedly prove to be the happiest period in her life.

Sir Giles's eyes glinted with a flicker of amusement. 'Knowing the good Major as I do, I do not doubt it,' he murmured. 'Your ordeal, however, will not last for much

longer. I have every expectation that an attempt to abduct you will take place this evening. Have no fear,
child. Even as we speak, your every movement is being
closely monitored by my people. We have not much
time,' he went on hurriedly, 'for unless I much mistake
the matter there is a certain young gentleman about to
request you to dance with him. Do so. Refuse the company of no one. You may safely even promenade in the
garden, for I have several men stationed outside. When
the attempt comes, do not put up the least resistance. Be
assured you will not be in unfriendly hands for long.'

Although Sir Giles had sounded supremely confident,
Katherine experienced a moment's disquiet as she
stepped out on to the dance floor. Undoubtedly the traitor was here in the room, watching her every move,
studying her features to see if indeed she did bear some
resemblance to the young Frenchwoman whose life he
had not hesitated to extinguish four years before. It went
without saying that he would as readily put a period to
hers also.

Resisting the temptation to gaze about her at the fashionably attired gentlemen lining the walls, Katherine did
her best to maintain her role by speaking in a marked
French accent to the diffident young man who had asked
her to dance. So determined was she to adhere to Sir
Giles's instructions that she refused none of the gallants
who subsequently requested her as a partner and, when
the evening was almost half over, even went so far as
to step outside with a dashing young cavalry officer in
a scarlet coat to take an exploratory stroll about that
section of the garden which had been illuminated for the
occasion by brightly coloured lanterns.

Thankfully nothing untoward occurred even then. Unfortunately the relief she experienced was short-lived, for

the first person she glimpsed on returning to the salon was Daniel, heading purposefully towards her to claim her hand for the supper-dance.

All at once she felt as if all eyes instantly turned in their direction as they took to the floor. She was being incredibly foolish, of course, she told herself, and even if it was true, it was possibly owing to the fact that they made a striking couple in their corresponding dark green attire. Sadly she was not so successful in thrusting from her mind the realisation that this was the first and possibly the last time she would ever stand up with the man who would always possess her heart.

Forced yet again to call upon those rapidly depleting reserves of resolve, she somehow managed a semblance of a smile as Daniel began to swirl her about the dance-floor with remarkable grace for a man of his size.

'You never cease to amaze me, my big cousin,' she announced, maintaining quite beautifully the false accent. 'Where on earth did you learn to dance so well? On the battlefields out in the Peninsula, I suppose?'

Clearly he noticed nothing false in the teasing manner, for he did not hesitate to respond in kind. 'Naturally. One needs to be nimble of foot to dodge bullets.'

Although the foolish response was spoken lightly enough, she could not fail to detect the underlying tension in him. 'Have you received further instructions from Sir Giles?'

'Yes, damn his eyes! I've been told to keep away from you as much as possible.'

'Then perhaps we ought not to be dancing now.'

'Yes, we should,' he countered, his tone becoming increasingly clipped. 'And I've told the old rogue that I've every intention of escorting you in to supper.'

Knowing him as she did, Katherine didn't suppose for

a moment that he had been unduly polite when he had made his intentions perfectly plain. 'Sir Giles knows what he's about, Daniel. You cannot deny that he's shrewd. He did not say as much, but I gained the distinct impression that the man he's after is indeed among the guests this evening.'

'Oh, yes, he's here right enough, my angel,' Daniel confirmed, after neatly avoiding a collision with the dashing young officer who had escorted Katherine outside a short time before, and who was now twirling his partner about the room with far more zest than grace. 'And, unless I much mistake the matter, that devil Osborne now knows precisely who he is too. He's certainly not been idle during these past weeks.'

'Admit it, Daniel!' she prompted. 'You've a grudging respect for the man.'

'Ha!' he scoffed. 'I'd sooner trust a snake!' He saw the hint of scepticism in the turquoise eyes gazing up at him, and relented. 'He knows his business—I'll give him that. And he's taken every precaution to ensure your safety. If I wasn't firmly convinced of it, you wouldn't be here now.'

Daniel cast a brief glance over at one corner of the room, where their host stood conversing with several of his guests. 'Cranford, as we both know, is in the old demon's confidence. It wouldn't surprise me to discover that he's being groomed to step into Osborne's shoes when the time comes for Sir Giles to retire. And Cranford, I noticed, has engaged extra staff for this occasion.'

Until that moment Katherine had not paid too much attention to the three footmen moving about the room, bearing trays of champagne. 'Then I've truly nothing to worry about. But I'd dearly love to know who the traitor is.'

'I'm afraid I cannot help you there,' Daniel admitted. 'Cranford may know, but I doubt too many others are in Sir Giles's confidence. I'm certainly not. But you can bet your sweet life our traitor is among the pot-bellied peerage here tonight, high up on the social ladder. That, I suspect, is why Osborne is so keen to catch him here, in this quiet backwater, where there will be few witnesses to the event. It goes without saying that if Osborne is successful, the whole business will be hushed up. That is how these people work. The traitor's identity will never become generally known.'

Katherine considered that, for someone who belonged to the landed gentry, Daniel betrayed precious little respect for his own class. 'If what you surmise is true, then perhaps it behoves me to attempt to encourage those middle-aged roués present to partner me in a dance.'

'Don't be so naïve, girl!' he scolded, clearly annoyed that she would even contemplate doing such a thing. 'It will avail you nothing if you tried,' he went on in a milder tone. 'You don't suppose for a moment the villain would risk exposure by attempting anything himself, do you? No, he'll have others here who will do his dirty work for him if he suspects you do indeed pose a threat, and that you might well prove to be none other than Justine Baron's sister.'

As no attempt had been made to abduct her thus far Katherine could not help thinking that the traitor had not been duped, and didn't know whether to feel relieved or disappointed to think that all Sir Giles's planning and that eventful flight from the French capital had been in vain. All the same, she could never feel sorry she had been involved in the venture, even though she very much feared that to her dying day she would be tortured by bittersweet memories of the man who was now swirling her so expertly round the room.

As the dance drew to an end Katherine, desperately striving not to dwell on what undoubtedly would be her barren future, allowed Daniel to lead her across the hall into the dining-room, where a large number of guests had already gathered to enjoy the delicious supper.

She might have wished that he had not chosen to join his uncle's party, whom she had noticed were the last guests to arrive, for although she did take an instant liking to Sir Joshua, she was under sufficient strain already to maintain the pretence of light-heartedness, without having to cope with his probing questions into the exact relationship between his nephew and herself. Like Daniel, she found Mrs Melrose's polite utterances rather insipid. Worse still was Julia's faintly cool reception. Having experienced the noxious emotion herself, Katherine could now recognise jealousy without difficulty when she saw it. Evidently Daniel's former love now viewed her as a rival. How little the woman knew!

Fortunately Katherine was not forced to endure the ordeal for too long, for no sooner had several couples begun to drift back to the large salon than the gentleman who had first claimed her for his partner appeared at her side again, with a stuttered reminder that she had promised him a second dance.

She couldn't recall doing any such thing; nor could she even remember the young gentleman's name. Nevertheless she did not think twice about returning with him to the salon, where couples were already taking up positions for a set of country dances.

'You must forgive me, *monsieur*, but I have been introduced to so many people this evening that I am having a little difficulty in recalling your name.'

'G-Gifford, ma'am…George G-Gifford. I-I'm here with the gentleman who is to s-sponsor me during the f-forthcoming Season.'

Katherine couldn't imagine that the event would turn out to be an overwhelming success, given the young man's evident shyness and painful stutter. It wasn't that he was ill-looking. In fact, some women might consider him quite handsome, and yet she couldn't help thinking that the hard, dark eyes seemed oddly at variance with the boyish good looks and diffident manner.

Just as the musicians struck up a chord, Katherine noticed Daniel enter the room, with Julia clinging possessively to his arm. She noticed him staring fixedly in her direction, with an almost frozen look on his face, as though he had just received a severe shock. She did her utmost to thrust his odd expression from her mind and concentrate on her own partner, managing with a reasonable amount of success to converse with him whenever they came together in the set. At least Mr Gifford proved to be a graceful dancer, so it came as something of a surprise when he managed to step on the hem of her gown, just as the dance was drawing to a close.

'Oh, I am so s-sorry, *mademoiselle*. I have torn y-your gown. W-will you permit me to escort you to the ladies' withdrawing-room? S-so clumsy of me.'

Katherine assured him that there was no need to put himself to the trouble, and that she could find her own way without assistance to the bedchamber their hostess had set aside for the purpose. She discovered him at her side all the same, when she slipped out into the deserted hall. It was then that she sensed the unassuming young gentleman was not quite what he seemed, the split second before his fingers grasped her arm just above the elbow, and she was propelled with considerable force towards the room which had once functioned as her grandfather's library.

Although her every instinct urged her in those first heart-stopping moments to reach out for the vase on a nearby table and bring it down hard on Mr Gifford's head, or at the very least let out a scream for help, she paid heed to Sir Giles's warning and didn't attempt to put up even a token resistance. Naturally it came as no surprise, after Mr Gifford had flung wide the door, and had almost thrust her into the darkened room, to discover a burly figure lurking in the shadows, ready with lengths of rope and a gag which he proceeded to put to immediate use.

'You know what to do.' There was no hint of a stutter in Mr Gifford's voice now, and his features were hardened by a look of pure malice, a look Katherine felt certain she had seen on someone's face in the not too distant past.

That was it! she suddenly realised. That was precisely what Daniel had been attempting to convey a few minutes before. He had, she felt certain, suddenly recognised Gifford. But from where? Where had they run across him? She turned her head, but before she had a chance to study his malevolent expression more closely, a hood was thrust over her head.

Tossed over a brawny shoulder, she was then carried from the house by way of the glass-panelled door which her grandfather had had installed to allow more light into the room and to grant swift access to the garden. Unfortunately this section of garden was quite separate from that part which had been lit so prettily for the occasion, and was not visible from the windows of the salon where the party was taking place. It was only a matter of a few yards, she clearly remembered, before one reached the shrubbery, beyond which ran a narrow lane, wide enough for a carriage.

Her perilous situation suddenly hit her with frightening clarity. Throughout her flight from France she had never experienced real fear, simply because Daniel had been with her. But he wasn't with her now. Bound and gagged, she was as helpless as a new-born babe and couldn't possibly escape without help. If Sir Giles's well laid plans went wrong, and her captor succeeded in getting her away unseen, then her situation was dire indeed.

She was not unduly surprised when her abductor made directly for the shrubbery. Nor was she astonished to detect the chinking of a harness a minute or two later before she was bundled none too gently on to the floor of a carriage. She felt it sway slightly, as though he was attempting to enter. Sounds of a scuffle quickly followed, a sickening thud and a groan. Then the vehicle swayed again as someone succeeded in entering this time.

Her companion did not attempt to move or speak until the equipage had turned on to the main road, then hands slid beneath her arms, lifting her on to the seat, and the bonds securing her wrists and ankles were swiftly removed. The gentleness of her companion's actions was enough to convince her that she was now perfectly safe, undoubtedly under the protection of one of Sir Giles's own people, and yet with the best will in the world she could not stop her hand from trembling as she pulled off the hood and removed the gag. Then she found herself gaping like a half-wit, for her rescuer was none other than Mr Ashcroft.

'Are you all right, my dear?' he enquired. 'I trust the blackguard wasn't too rough with you.'

'I was urged by Sir Giles not to put up a struggle,

which was possibly why I came through the ordeal relatively unscathed,' she admitted, rubbing the circulation back into her sore wrists. 'Though if I'm honest, I'd be forced to admit that it went against the grain somewhat for me not to attempt to put up at least a token resistance.'

'I'm glad you did not. You're in no danger now,' Mr Ashcroft assured her gently. 'We've had men scouting the area for days. Earlier in the evening, when this carriage was spotted drawing up in the lane, we felt certain that an attempt would be made tonight to abduct you by way of the side entrance. You were never in any real danger. Needless to say one of our own people is now tooling this vehicle. The original driver and the scoundrel who carried you from the house have been taken into custody. The rest we can safely leave to Sir Giles.'

A hundred questions sprang into Katherine's mind, but she found herself asking only one. 'Where are you taking me—back to Rosslair?'

'We are to make a brief stop at the inn in order to collect my sister. Until Sir Giles has located the whereabouts of every member of the spy network, you are to remain safely hidden,' Mr Ashcroft responded. 'It is better that you do not return to Major Ross's home.'

'Yes,' Katherine agreed hollowly, 'it would be much safer…for all concerned…if I did not return there.'

Chapter Sixteen

'This is utterly insupportable!' Daniel declared, after examining the several letters McGann had collected that morning from the receiving office, and discovering no word yet again from either Katherine or Sir Giles. 'I would far rather face a French column on the field of battle than endure this intolerable waiting a moment longer!'

'Oh, dear. The Major's blood's up,' McGann whispered, joining Janet at the table. 'Very bad sign, that. You mark my words, there'll be trouble afore long.'

'Shush,' she hissed, before turning her attention back to her master, who had begun to pace up and down, which he was inclined to do whenever angry or upset. 'But, sir, you know what Sir Giles said, when he came here on the morning after the party to collect Miss Katherine's belongings,' she reminded him in an attempt to soothe his evidently mounting ire.

Although she had never perfectly understood the precise nature of the work in which Katherine and her master had been engaged, Janet did know that they had been involved in something very secret on behalf of the government. 'The good gentleman did say that Miss Kath-

erine was in safe hands and would remain so until the
business be cleared up completely.'

'But it's been over a month, Janet,' Daniel pointed
out, not in the least mollified. 'I should have heard something by now.' He resumed his restless pacing. 'That old
fox is hiding something. I sense it. And if I discover one
hair of my darling girl's beautiful head has been harmed,
I'll take the greatest pleasure in breaking every bone in
Osborne's body!'

'Oh, dear. He means it an' all,' McGann confirmed,
sotto voce.

'It's all my fault, of course,' Daniel continued, ignoring the interruption. 'I should never have agreed to Osborne taking her away from here.' He paused yet again
in his perambulations to run impatient fingers through
his hair. 'Furthermore I should have declared myself
when we were in France. But no, I foolishly decided to
do the gentlemanly thing and not put more pressure on
her by making her feel uncomfortable.'

Janet cast McGann a secretive little smile. 'We know
well enough how fond you are of her, sir.'

'Fond…? Ha! A most inappropriate word, Janet! I'm
damnably sure I cannot live without her… At least I'll
never be wholly content unless she's by my side.'

Daniel joined them at the table, his expression softening marginally. 'She's a brave little soul. She saved
my life, you know?'

It was plain that they did not know. McGann recovered from the shock first. 'Well, to be sure, 'tis no more
than you'd expect. The girl's got good Irish blood flow-
ing through her veins, so she has.'

'She's Anglo-Irish, McGann,' Daniel reminded him
softly. 'And what's more, she's mine.'

He rose again abruptly, resolve etched in each rugged

contour of his face. 'And by God, she's coming home, back here where she belongs!'

Although Katherine clearly heard the click of the door and then the familiar footfall on the carpet, she continued to stare through the bedchamber window at the view upon which she had absently gazed too often during these past few weeks, and one which she would have had the utmost difficulty in describing if asked to do so.

Daily she was becoming increasingly uninterested in the sights and sounds about her, and although she remained powerless to fight off the debilitating lethargy that continued to hold her firmly in its grasp, at least she retained innate good manners enough to accept the fact that she could not remain as a guest in Sir Giles Osborne's house for very much longer.

'Bridie, I believe it's time we were thinking of returning to Bath,' she announced, in a voice which distinctly lacked any vestige of enthusiasm. 'Perhaps Sir Giles will be kind enough to put his travelling carriage at our disposal. If not, we must make arrangements to hire a post-chaise.'

Bridie regarded her young mistress in silence, at a complete loss to know what to do for the best. She had helped Katherine through many heartbreaking periods, but she had never seen her young mistress more desolate than this.

Contracting influenza from Sir Giles's sister had naturally not helped the situation. Nevertheless, Bridie had known the instant she had set foot inside the house that Katherine was not herself. Her young mistress might have succeeded in concealing her bouts of weeping from Sir Giles and Miss Mary Osborne, but she herself had easily detected the telltale signs and had guessed the truth even before she had heard Katherine call out that certain someone's name in her sleep.

She knew, perhaps better than anyone else, just how steadfastly determined Katherine had been during the past years not to become too attached to another living soul in an attempt to protect herself from further searing hurt. She also knew that a very special gentleman had succeeded in breaking down those defences, and that at some point during their six-week separation her young mistress had fallen deeply in love.

She regarded the slender figure staring resolutely out of the window in some concern. If this show of total apathy was the result of her young mistress's love not being returned, then Bridie did not doubt that Katherine would eventually begin to mend. She very much feared, though, that the opposite was true, and that Major Daniel Ross was every bit as much in love with Katherine as she was with him.

Placing the jug of lemonade down on the table, she noticed the contents of the breakfast tray, which she had brought up earlier, were virtually untouched. 'Would you be looking at that now! You've hardly eaten a mouthful,' she scolded gently. 'How you suppose you'll have strength enough to make the journey back to Bath, the good Lord only knows! Why, there's more fat in Cook's dripping-tray than there is on you now, Miss Kate.'

'I wasn't hungry. I'll no doubt eat a bite for luncheon. Do not fuss so, Bridie.'

'You'll need to eat more than a bite to put the weight back on,' she returned sharply, but knew that it would avail her nothing to pursue the matter, and in her young mistress's present state badgering her was likely to do more harm than good. 'Well, at least when you do return to Bath you won't be plagued with Miss Mountjoy's company for too long. She said she'd remain in the house until you'd returned. But it's my belief she's made up her mind to live with her sister.'

Even this piece of encouraging news failed to elicit a reaction, so Bridie didn't waste her breath in further conversation. Instead, she picked up the tray and was about to leave, when the sound of a thunderous hammering filtered into the room. 'Now, who do you suppose that might be, pounding on a gentleman's front door in such an ill-bred fashion?'

Once again receiving no response, Bridie went out in time to see a tall figure, dressed in riding garb, step into the hall. The butler evidently recognised him, for the high-ranking servant went immediately into the library. Before she had descended the staircase, the visitor was being shown into the book-lined room, and the butler was closing the door, but not before Bridie heard a deep, attractive voice, both clear and carrying, demand, 'Where is she, Osborne? What have you done with my darling girl?'

Sir Giles, who had immediately risen from his favourite chair by the hearth, certainly didn't appear in the least discomposed by his visitor's blunt manner and decidedly hostile expression. 'My dear Ross! What a pleasure it is to see you! Just a passing visit, I imagine. Can I offer you some refreshment…? A glass of burgundy, perhaps?'

'Be careful, Osborne,' Daniel warned with dangerous restraint. 'My patience is by no stretch of the imagination limitless.'

'No, forbearance was never your strong suit, was it, my dear boy?' Sir Giles swiftly raised one bony, long-fingered hand in a gesture of surrender. 'All right….all right! Miss O'Malley is here.'

'Then why the devil didn't you let me know?' Daniel demanded, relieved but not one iota appeased. 'You promised you would once the business was completely cleared up. And you cannot tell me you haven't caught every last one of 'em by now.' The curl to his lip betrayed his contempt. 'I saw that damned piece in the newspaper: *It is with the deepest regret that we announce the deaths of The Right Hon. Lord W——y and his cousin Mr George G——d. Their bodies were discovered after an intensive search*, et cetera et cetera— Ha!' Daniel scoffed. 'By the time you'd finished prising information out of them, there's no way on God's earth you could have let them stand trial!'

'That, my dear boy, as you well know, is never an option,' Sir Giles reminded him. 'Believe it or not, it is a part of my work that I do not enjoy. But it is better for all concerned, most especially the innocent members of their immediate families, that the misdeeds of certain high-ranking gentlemen never become common knowledge. And the Government would be hard pressed to withstand further scandal at the present time.

'But you did not come here to discuss the unsavoury aspects of my work,' Sir Giles continued, after refreshing himself from the contents of his glass. 'Miss O'Malley is indeed here, and in no danger now that we have every member of the spy ring safely under lock and key—at least those few who still remain alive,' he amended, as he noted the sceptical arch of one dark brow. 'Unfortunately she has not been well. She was kind enough, whilst I was away in London, to help nurse my sister through a bout of influenza, and for her pains contracted the illness herself.'

Grey eyes never wavered from Daniel's face. 'The poor child has been quite poorly, and has been keeping to her bedchamber. I shall, however, enquire whether it is possible for you to see her.'

Sir Giles then summoned his butler and requested him to locate the whereabouts of Katherine's maid. 'What think you of the events taking place across the Channel?' he asked, the instant his servant had withdrawn to carry out his instructions. 'The allied armies, as you are undoubtedly aware, are amassing in Belgium. Will you be joining them, I wonder?'

He received no response and smiled grimly. 'No, I thought not. You, no doubt, will have far more important matters of a personal nature to attend to. Dear me.' His shoulders shook in silent laughter. 'I never thought to play Cupid. Please do not hesitate to call upon me if you think I can be of further assistance. My brother-in-law is, I might remind you, a bishop and, as it happens, is paying us a visit at the end of the week. It would be no difficult matter to obtain a special licence. And it goes without saying that you are most welcome to put up here and await his arrival.'

Before Daniel was offered the opportunity to respond to this piece of rank impertinence, the door behind him opened and he turned to see a plump, middle-aged woman enter. He watched her cast an enquiring glance in Sir Giles's direction before fixing her dark eyes on his physiognomy.

'It's Bridie, isn't it? I've heard much about you.'

'Holy Mary, Mother of God!' she exclaimed, reaching out and surprising him somewhat by capturing one of his hands in both of hers. 'So 'tis yourself, Major Ross! May heaven be praised! If you hadn't come for her, sir, I think I'd have fetched you myself.'

Daniel was suddenly filled with foreboding. 'Good gad! Is she so ill, then?'

''Tis not the influenza,' Bridie hurriedly assured him, tears moistening her eyes now. 'But she's suffering, sir…suffering something cruel.'

Daniel was not slow to understand what the devoted Irishwoman was trying to tell him, and cursed himself silently for every kind of a fool for remaining away from Katherine for so long.

He had been certain for some little time that she was not indifferent to him; and even though she had done her level best to keep her feelings well hidden whilst she had remained at his home, he had been granted the dearest wish of his heart on the evening of the Cranfords' party, when she had just for one unguarded moment betrayed the true state of her own by addressing him as 'my grasshopper'. Since then, of course, she had been granted ample time to fret herself unnecessarily over those old foolish fears, which he most definitely would never have permitted her to do if she had remained with him at Rosslair.

He suddenly found himself experiencing more anger than sympathy. 'Is she, by gad!' There was no mistaking the determined set to his square, powerful jaw. 'Well, we'll soon put a stop to that!'

'One may always rely on Major Ross,' Sir Giles remarked, not quite steadily, as he watched Daniel stride purposefully across the room to the table on which several fine wines were kept in sparkling crystal decanters. 'I have done so on several occasions. And have always found him equal to any task.'

Daniel, choosing not to comment on this tribute from a man whose respect was not easily won, selected the decanter containing the claret and picked up two glasses, before remarking, 'I might consider holding you to one or two of your former impertinent suggestions, Osborne. But first, I shall accept your offer of refreshment and will relieve you of this fine wine. I dare swear my darling girl has had nothing fit to drink for some appreciable time.'

'There's freshly made lemonade on the bedside table, sir,' Bridie did not hesitate to assure him. 'I placed it there myself this very morn.'

'I need say no more,' was Daniel's response before he went out, leaving the library resounding with Sir Giles's appreciative masculine laughter.

'Which is her room, Bridie?' he asked, as the maid scurried after him across the hall, looking if possible both hopeful and worried.

'Second on the right at the top of the stairs, sir. But I think I ought to go up and inform Miss Katherine that you wish to see her.'

'And I had made up my mind that you were a sensible woman.' Daniel paused as he reached the bottom of the stairs to cast the loyal maid a mild look of reproach. 'Don't disappoint me, Bridie. One never reveals one's plan of campaign to the enemy. A swift, unexpected attack more often than not brings victory.'

His smile, both warm and reassuring, swept away the last of her doubts. 'Have no fear, Bridie. She'll come about. I'll see to that.'

Assuming it to be Bridie who had entered the room without knocking, Katherine continued to stare out of the window. It was only after it had occurred to her as odd that her normally loquacious maid was unusually quiet that she abandoned her idle contemplation of the

Hampshire countryside and turned her head to look across the room.

For several moments she refused to believe the evidence of her own eyes. Firmly convinced that, tormented by bittersweet memories, her tortured mind had successfully conjured up his image, she blinked several times in an attempt to dispel the vision, but it stubbornly refused to disappear and, worse, it was now moving slowly towards her.

If the truth were known, Daniel was as much shocked by her appearance as she evidently was by his own. Clearly she had lost weight and looked so pale and drawn that it came as no surprise that she swayed slightly when she attempted to rise, and was obliged to grasp the back of the *chaise-longue* for support.

He was beside her in an instant, depositing decanter and glasses on a low table, before cradling her protectively against him. 'Oh, my darling girl. Whatever have they done to you?' he murmured, placing his lips gently to one corner of her mouth.

It was several moments before Katherine could regain sufficient wits about her to put up even a token struggle, but it was enough. Daniel released her immediately and, after seating himself, drew her gently down beside him.

Determined not to give way this time to the tears which nowadays were never far from the surface, Katherine delved into the pocket of her dressing gown and drew out her handkerchief. 'This really is too bad of you,' she managed in a shaky whisper, before using the lace-edged piece of fine lawn to good effect. 'What do they mean by allowing you to enter my bedchamber quite unannounced?'

'I'd like to know what they mean by allowing you to get into this state!' he countered, at his most grim. 'Osborne promised faithfully to take every care of you. And yet here you are looking fagged to death!'

For all that her thoughts were in turmoil, Katherine couldn't help smiling at this. He was nothing if not brutally frank. Furthermore, he was speaking no less than the truth. Her mirror had told her earlier that morning that she was definitely not looking her best, though whether it was the loss of weight or the lace cap that neatly confined her hair of which he thoroughly disapproved was difficult to judge.

'You mustn't blame Sir Giles, Daniel,' she told him, speedily coming to the baronet's defence. 'He instructed that I be brought here for my own safety. He wasn't to know his sister Mary had succumbed to a bout of influenza during his absence. I helped nurse her, with the result that I unfortunately contracted the malady myself, which has left me feeling very low.'

One dark brow rose in a sceptical arch, evidence enough that he was not convinced that her recent illness was wholly responsible for her present rather haggard appearance. So Katherine decided it might be wise to turn his thoughts in a new direction by asking if he'd seen the report in the newspaper about the death of a certain peer of the realm and his distant cousin.

'Ha!' he scoffed. 'Yes, I read it, right enough. Fatally attacked by a lawless gang, my eye!'

He was plainly disgusted by the whole unsavoury business, and Katherine could easily appreciate why. Daniel was a soldier, and an honourable man. He would not consider killing someone on the field of battle as murder. However he would certainly look upon what had happened to the traitor and his accomplices as precisely that.

On the few occasions Sir Giles had visited her since

his return to the house the week before, he had not once attempted to enlighten her on what had taken place after she had been whisked away on the night of the Cranfords' party. As his work was secret, she had refrained from asking questions, but experienced no such qualms where Daniel was concerned.

'Nothing very spectacular,' he responded, and she thought for a moment she was destined to remain in ignorance, but then he added, 'I saw you go off with Gifford, of course, and guessed at once.'

Katherine frowned as memory stirred. 'When you returned to the salon that night with Julia, you were looking across at me most strangely,' she reminded him. 'Am I right in thinking that you recognised Gifford from somewhere?'

'Clever girl! Yes, I did. I saw him earlier in the day at my uncle's house, and was firmly convinced I'd seen him somewhere before, but it wasn't until I saw him standing behind you, about to take up his position in the dance, that I realised just where I'd seen him. Evidently Waverley chose him as his envoy and Gifford went over to France. With their contacts, Gifford had no difficulty in reaching Paris, and arrived there before me. Undoubtedly he was just one of many scouring the inns for a red-haired female. He was the man seated behind you at the table in the coffee room on the morning we were forced to flee the city. His grey wig and beard proved a reasonable disguise, but it was those hard, dark eyes of his that gave him away.'

'He was the one who followed Marie and myself that morning. I remember thinking at the time that there was something odd about him,' she divulged, before asking what happened after she failed to return to the salon on the night of the party.

'Your continued absence quite naturally was remarked upon. Several of the guests had already begun to take their leave, and when you couldn't be located anywhere in the house, Gifford casually divulged that you had complained of a headache. Cranford then suggested that you had in all probability not wished to cause a fuss and had begged a ride back to Rosslair in a neighbour's carriage. I quite naturally left shortly afterwards, but not before I had received Cranford's assurance that you were unharmed and were being taken to a place of safety.

'I was forced to be content with that until the following morning, when Sir Giles paid me a visit. Although he flatly refused to disclose where you were being housed, he did reveal that the traitor and his young accomplice, Gifford, both of whom had been invited to stay overnight with the Cranfords, had been taken into custody. Seemingly, the following morning, the other guests were led to believe that the two men had made an early start in order to be back in London by nightfall. And no one was any the wiser, until the deaths were reported in the newspapers. By which time Sir Giles had extracted all the information he required from the traitor and his cousin.'

He did not need to go into details, for Katherine could guess that the means adopted to attain such information was nothing short of torture. She sighed. 'It is indeed an unsavoury business, Daniel. All the same, I cannot regret my involvement. Besides which, I have learned a salutary lesson—one should never accept people at face value.'

She watched one dark brow rise questioningly, and smiled. 'I do not know what your opinion might be of Sir Giles's sister, but I suspect Miss Mary Osborne is far from the dithering creature she appears to be. I should have realised that at my cousin's engagement party, when I discovered how intelligently she played the game of whist. When I arrived here she was indeed feeling poorly, but she betrayed no surprise at all at my unexpected arrival, and I have since learned from Bridie that Miss Osborne has been putting it about that I came to Hampshire to stay with my aunt and uncle, completely forgetting they had taken Caroline to the capital in order to purchase her bride clothes, and that Miss Osborne was happily putting me up here until my relations returned. Yes, I strongly suspect she knows precisely the nature of the work her brother undertakes on behalf of the government, and is of immense help to him on occasions.'

'Yes, you may be right, my little love,' he responded, as he reached for the decanter. 'But I could have wished the confounded woman had not passed her ailment on to you. Here, drink this. It will put some colour back into your cheeks. It's high time I took you in hand once more.'

Casting him a decidedly wary glance, Katherine accepted the glass of wine, and obediently took a sip, before announcing, 'I have decided to return to Bath at the end of the week.'

'Oh, you have, have you...? Well, you're not!' He was at his most dictatorial. 'You are returning to Rosslair with me when I consider you fit enough to travel. We'll take Bridie with us. She'll make an ideal replacement for Janet, don't you agree?'

After taking a further fortifying sip of the fine wine, Katherine placed the glass down on the table and rose to her feet. 'No, Daniel, I shall not be returning to Rosslair,' she told him in a voice that was remarkably controlled considering she could quite easily have burst into tears.

Surprisingly receiving no response, though acutely aware those dark eyes never wavered from her direction, she walked slowly over to the window, and once again fixed her gaze on that all too familiar view. 'It is better that I return to Bath.'

'Better for whom?' he parried. 'Certainly not for me. I want the woman I love by my side.'

Katherine closed her eyes. Would that she could obliterate the pain which never left her as easily as she could blot out that vista! Had his declaration of love come as a complete surprise, it might have been easier to bear, but in her heart of hearts she had known for quite some time the depths of his feelings for her.

She had been offered ample opportunity during these past wretched weeks to think about their short but eventful association. Once she had set aside her infantile dislike, her feelings towards him had swiftly deepened. His had too, she realised that now. On those few occasions when he had kissed her, he might so easily have taken advantage of her innocence and taken his lovemaking so very much further. Perhaps if he had, the heartbreaking stance she was being forced to take now would not have been necessary.

'I love you too, Daniel,' she forced herself to admit, even though each word rasped painfully against the sides of her throat. 'And that is precisely why I cannot marry and live with you at Rosslair. I just couldn't bear it if anything ever happened to you because of me.'

Tossing the contents of his glass down his throat, Daniel rose to his feet. The catch in her voice had been hard to withstand, and he was torn between the desire to take her in his arms and soothe away those foolish fears and the violent urge to shake her until her teeth rattled for forcing herself to believe such errant nonsense in the first place. He remained, however, resolutely standing those few feet away, knowing that whatever he said now could well determine his future happiness.

'It is hard to imagine that a woman who could endure so much hardship without a word of complaint, a woman who goes headlong into a fray in order to help a fellow human being without a thought for her own safety, could be such a spineless, snivelling little coward.'

This brought her head round as he knew it would, and for a moment he thought he detected just a glimmer of that determined spirit flicker in those gorgeous turquoise eyes. Then she appeared merely bemused, uncertain.

'I-I don't know what you mean, Daniel.'

'Oh, yes, you do,' he countered, resolved not to spare her. 'You may have succeeded in convincing yourself you're some kind of nemesis, but you'll not succeed in fooling me. It's nonsense and you know it. What you are, though, Katherine, is a damnable little coward! What you're so desperately afraid of is losing someone else you love. But it hasn't stopped you falling in love, has it?' he continued, determined to make her face the truth. 'I can understand your wishing to protect yourself from possible future grief, and make allowances for it. But what I find totally unforgivable is that not only are you prepared to throw away your own future happiness, you are heartlessly prepared to sacrifice mine.'

'No, Daniel, that isn't true!' she cried. 'Nothing in this world means more to me than you do. You'll meet someone else...I know you will.'

'Perhaps,' he conceded, turning and thereby concealing his expression of delight. He knew that fear of suffering again the pain of loss had brought her to this pretty pass, but he believed that her love for him would succeed in setting her free. Victory was at hand. It was time to play his trump card! 'But I'm not prepared to wait around for her to cross my path.'

Katherine, watching him through a haze of barely suppressed tears walk slowly towards the door, suddenly experienced blind panic. There was just something too decisive in that elegant stride of his. 'Daniel, where are you going? Back…back to Rosslair?'

Schooling his features, he checked and turned back to look at her. 'Oh, no, my dear. When you were there the house felt—for the first time since my grandmother died—like a home. It's cheerless without you.'

Katherine swallowed in an attempt to ease the painful ache in her throat enough to ask, 'Then-then, where are you going?'

'Unless I much mistake the matter a battle will take place in Belgium in the not too distant future, which will settle these past years of conflict one way or the other. I no longer have my commission, but I'm certain Wellington will find something for me to do.'

'No!' she screamed, and for all that she was far from well, she succeeded in reaching the door before him, and pressed her back firmly against it, barring his exit. 'It's madness! No one would expect it of you. You've done more than enough for our country.' The determined sparkle was back in her eyes in full measure as she curled her slender fingers into fists and began to pummel his chest. 'I won't let you go…I won't!…I won't!'

Reaching out, Daniel swiftly put a stop to the assault upon him by lifting her effortlessly high in the air, his fingers easily spanning the slender waist. 'Understand this, Miss Katherine Fairchild O'Malley, there is only one way you are going to succeed in stopping me.'

Although he was smiling almost triumphantly now, there could be no mistaking the hard determination in his eyes, and Katherine found her own resolution swiftly crumbling.

'Then may God forgive me,' she said softly, wrapping her arms about his neck. 'But I can't...I won't let you go.'

Marie Dubois sat outside the farmhouse, enjoying the pleasant September sun. On her knee Louise's youngest child was sleeping soundly, and she too could quite happily have dozed if the peace and quiet had not been rudely interrupted by the sudden arrival of a boisterous three-year-old boy and a very pretty lady with red-gold hair.

'Did we disturb you, Marie?'

'Not at all, Louise,' she lied. 'You have not been long in town.'

'No, we accomplished all the marketing very quickly.'

'And we even have a letter here for you,' a deep voice behind her remarked, and Marie turned to see Louise's handsome husband framed in the doorway, his expression betraying faint disapproval as he handed her the missive. 'Three letters from England in less than a year. I'm beginning to think we have a collaborator in our midst.'

'Do not tease her, Pierre,' his wife scolded gently. 'You know the last letter was from an acquaintance in England who wrote to inform her that Justine's murderer had been apprehended and had at last paid for his crime.'

Marie merely smiled as she broke the seal to find a second letter neatly folded inside the first. Both Pierre and Louise knew that she had played a part in attempting to bring Justine's murderer to justice, but they knew none of the details. Nor did they know that her previous letters had been written by Sir Giles Osborne. There were certain facts which Marie was sensible enough never to reveal. She could not, however, hide her joy when she read the signature on this most recent correspondence, and uttered a tiny exclamation, after reading the second letter written in a neat, stylish hand.

'Not bad news, I trust?' Louise ventured, when she saw tears spring to her faithful Marie's grey eyes.

'No, you may read them,' Marie answered, handing over both sheets, and then watching as her former charge's forehead puckered.

'But who is this Major Daniel Ross, Marie? And how come you to know him? He is a soldier, is he not?'

'There, what did I tell you!' her husband put in. 'A traitor in our midst!'

Marie cast him an impatient glance. 'You know that is not true. Besides, the war between our two countries is finally over. England is no longer our enemy.'

'Maybe not,' Pierre agreed, no longer smiling. 'But the wounds have yet to heal. I lost two brothers in Spain, remember?'

'And many Englishmen were killed too,' Marie reminded him, before turning to Louise. 'Major Daniel Ross is none other than the gentleman who rescued you from that evil place, Louise, and brought us here.'

'But-but he was a Frenchman. I shall never forget Antoine Durand. I shall never be able to thank him enough for what he did.'

'Nor I,' Pierre put in. 'I shall be forever in his debt.'

'Then you shall both be forever in the debt of an Englishman,' Marie informed them, experiencing a degree of wicked satisfaction at their astonished expressions. 'His mother, I understand, was French. That is why he is able to speak our language so well. But Major Ross is an Englishman, a brave man who fought in Wellington's Army in the Peninsula. He writes to tell me that he is now married, and living happily in Dorsetshire.'

'This second letter, Marie, it is written in English,' Louise reminded her. 'My English is not so good, and I do not understand it too well. But is it not from Major Ross's wife? How came you to know her?'

'Yes.' Marie's smile was gentle as she took back the letter. 'It is indeed from Katherine. I shall translate for you.

'*My dearest Marie*, she writes. *We parted so swiftly that I hardly had time to say goodbye to you. I do not intend to do so now, because it is my dearest wish that you, Louise, and her family will visit us here in England next year. At the moment we are in disorder at Rosslair, with the builders invading the house, but the extension should be completed within a very few weeks, so there will be plenty of room to put you all up, hopefully in the spring.*

I am very much enjoying married life, Marie. My devoted Bridie is now housekeeper here, and very content with her new status, and her predecessor is happily enjoying retirement in one of the cottages Daniel's father had built many years ago.

Earlier this month we travelled to Hampshire to attend my cousin's wedding. Like so many, her husband, Captain Charlesworth, was injured at Waterloo, but thankfully not badly. Daniel was not involved in that carnage. I stopped him from going by marrying him last May, and he, in turn, has freed me from the shackles of my foolish fears.

I shall explain all when I see you, dear Marie. Please do say that you will visit us. The English countryside is so very pretty in the spring. I should dearly love you to see it. Affectionately yours, Katherine.'

Louise cast her husband a puzzled glance. 'But who is this Katherine, Marie? Did you meet her in Paris when you were there earlier this year?'

'Yes. And it is largely thanks to Katherine that your sister's murderer was finally called to account for his crime. I shall tell you all about her presently. But first, I wish to know whether you will accompany me to England, for I have every intention of paying Major and Mrs Ross a visit next year.'

Louise cast a hopeful glance in her husband's direction. 'We cannot allow her to undertake the journey alone, Pierre. And I should very much like to embrace the woman who avenged the death of my dear sister.'

He was silent for a moment, then he said, 'And I should very much like to shake the hand of the man who made it possible for me to marry Justine Baron's sister.'

Consequently they set out on their visit to Dorsetshire in the spring of the following year, and could not have planned their trip better, for they arrived at Rosslair in time to celebrate the birth of Liam Edwin Ross.

*　*　*　*　*

LIVE THE EMOTION

Modern Romance™
...seduction and
passion guaranteed

Tender Romance™
...love affairs that
last a lifetime

Medical Romance™
...medical drama
on the pulse

Historical Romance™
...rich, vivid and
passionate

Sensual Romance™
...sassy, sexy and
seductive

Blaze Romance™
...the temperature's
rising

27 new titles every month.

Live the emotion

MILLS & BOON®

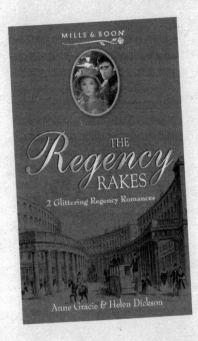

MILLS & BOON®

STEPHANIE LAURENS

A Season for Marriage

Available from 18th July 2003

Available at most branches of WH Smith,
Tesco, Martins, Borders, Eason, Sainsbury's
and all good paperback bookshops.

0703/135/MB67

FREE!

2 Books
and a surprise gift!

We would like to take this opportunity to thank you for reading this Mills & Boon® book by offering you the chance to take TWO more specially selected titles from the Historical Romance™ series absolutely FREE! We're also making this offer to introduce you to the benefits of the Reader Service™—

- ★ FREE home delivery
- ★ FREE gifts and competitions
- ★ FREE monthly Newsletter
- ★ Books available before they're in the shops
- ★ Exclusive Reader Service discount

Accepting these FREE books and gift places you under no obligation to buy; you may cancel at any time, even after receiving your free shipment. Simply complete your details below and return the entire page to the address below. *You don't even need a stamp!*

YES! Please send me 2 free Historical Romance books and a surprise gift. I understand that unless you hear from me, I will receive 4 superb new titles every month for just £3.49 each, postage and packing free. I am under no obligation to purchase any books and may cancel my subscription at any time. The free books and gift will be mine to keep in any case.

H3ZEB

Ms/Mrs/Miss/Mr ....Initials...............................
BLOCK CAPITALS PLEASE

Surname...

Address...

....

....Postcode ....

Send this whole page to:
UK: The Reader Service, FREEPOST CN81, Croydon, CR9 3WZ
EIRE: The Reader Service, PO Box 4546, Kilcock, County Kildare (stamp required)